MW00773534

Nothing Serious

Nothing Serious

A NOVEL

Emily J. Smith

wm

WILLIAM MORROW
An Imprint of HarperCollins*Publishers*

HarperCollins books may be purchased for educational, business, or sales promotional use. For information, please email the Special Markets Department at SPsales@harpercollins.com.

FIRST EDITION

Designed by Kyle O'Brien

Library of Congress Cataloging-in-Publication Data

Names: Smith, Emily J, author.
Title: Nothing serious : a novel / Emily J. Smith.
Description: First edition. | New York, NY : William Morrow, 2025. |
Identifiers: LCCN 2024004215 (print) | LCCN 2024004216 (ebook) | ISBN
    9780063385832 (hardcover) | ISBN 9780063385849 (trade paperback) | ISBN
    9780063385856 (ebook)
Subjects: LCGFT: Thrillers (Fiction) | Novels.
Classification: LCC PS3619.M5839 N68 2025 (print) | LCC PS3619.M5839
    (ebook) | DDC 813/.6–dc23/eng/20240610
LC record available at https://lccn.loc.gov/2024004215
LC ebook record available at https://lccn.loc.gov/2024004216

ISBN 978-0-06-338583-2

24 25 26 27 28 LBC 5 4 3 2 1

For my sister

Content Warning

THIS BOOK MENTIONS eating disorders, alcoholism, abuse, sexual assault, murder, suicide, and drugs.

Chapter One

NEITHER OF THEM knew how to dance—only jump. The other people in the crammed Lower Haight basement gave them space, more as a precautionary measure than any kind of courtesy. But Edie and Peter were a decade older than everyone else on the floor and hardly noticed. They were like two kids bouncing on a bed, so wild was their joy, so tiresome was their energy.

The song changed.

Edie bent her knees, attempting to "get low," moving closer to the floor with each beat. Peter followed her with ease. They were as far down as their respective thirty-five-year-old knees could take them when their eyes met, thighs on the verge of collapse.

Edie fell first.

"Shit," she shouted between breaths of laughter, reaching for his hand to pull herself up from the sticky wooden floor. Peter lifted her toward him. She was tall but he was taller, and she let her head rest against his chest, just below his neck. She could tell by the moisture in the air and the sweat on her brow that her thin, fraying curls had expanded into a cloud of frizz above her head, but she was too drunk to attempt a remedy.

To Edie's delight, Peter's girlfriend, Nicole, had recently stopped coming to parties where she knew there would be dancing. It wasn't that Nicole hated dancing; it was just that she hated dancing with Peter. Not because he was a terrible dancer, but because he was enthusiastically bad.

But Edie and Peter had been jumping together since college. Back then they'd stomp on Peter's torn sofa after a long day of engineering labs, screaming along to Pearl Jam or Red Hot Chili Peppers or whatever angsty male pop CD was in rotation until they crashed, then drifting into debate about capitalism or sexism or whether cups should really be round when squares stacked so efficiently, until their eyes closed.

Fifteen years later, they still reverted to this youthful version of themselves when they were together, like siblings settling into their roles, drawing out in each other something the rest of the world could not. Sure, Nicole knew the details of Peter's current life better than Edie—which underwear he preferred, the sounds he made when he slept, whether his smooth, straight hair still curled in the morning— but Edie knew the seed of his very being, a seed inevitably buried by the gnawing pull of adulthood. Nicole would never know this part of him because he was no longer capable of showing it. And though Edie couldn't quite prove it, she knew that Peter liked this earlier, foundational version of himself best, and would always love Edie for being the only one who could see it.

Edie wanted to live and die in the old version of herself. At thirty-five, Peter could have anything he wanted because in the past ten years Peter had become very, very rich. But whereas Peter had grown more confident with time, Edie had grown more insecure. As a teenager, she'd flip through the J.Crew catalog at night, picturing herself as a grown woman in the sleek, angular suits, running a company and bossing men around, returning to a tastefully designed home, which she surely owned, where her husband and child were waiting with love and dinner. But adulthood was no longer a fantasy to shape, it was a reality to deal with. Her uniform was old Reebok sneakers and whatever hoodie was clean, she could barely tolerate the men around her enough to wake up each morning, let alone run her own company, and she had nothing but streaming services in her one-room home, if you could call a rented studio apartment a home, to return to. There was no single thing to blame, just a continuous string of dreams that hadn't worked out. Being with Peter made her feel like the ambitious know-it-all she was in college because he expected nothing less. She was allowed to be her old self with him. He reminded her who she was.

She placed her hands on his shoulders, like softballs in her palms. It still surprised her, how round and firm they'd become, how different he was from the skinny nerd she used to know. She had stopped dreaming that something might happen between them when Nicole had moved in. Instead, she took solace in the fact that he would never really be wholly happy with her, that part of him would always need Edie.

"How's your cult going?" she shouted into his ear, Rihanna blaring in the background.

"Some cults are good, E." He loved the chance to defend himself, and she loved making him try. "Just because you had one bad Cross-Fit experience."

"After ten minutes of exercise, you can't move for a week. How is that good?"

"If you tried it more than once, maybe you'd know." His hands were tight on her hips.

"Sorry I don't want to align myself with a bunch of libertarians who pride themselves on competition and aggression. But I'm glad it works for you!"

"And yet you work in tech?"

She had to laugh (or cry).

He looked down at her with his big olive eyes, shining with pleasure at their usual push and pull.

When the song ended, Peter leaned closer, his mouth to her ear. "I have to tell you something." She braced herself. They had reached the age when this phrase was a predictable prelude: marriage or children, one then the other. Surely, he hadn't proposed to Nicole without consulting with Edie, but she'd assumed the topic was on the horizon.

"Nicole and I broke up."

The music faded and she jumped back to look at him, desperate for more than these small, impossible words, life-changing words, which he was somehow dropping like an afterthought on the dance floor. He had to be fucking with her. He and Nicole had considered "taking a break" in the past, but a full-on breakup, and without discussing it with Edie first? Her heart raced beneath her damp V-neck T-shirt. "What the fuck, Peter?"

"It's too loud in here," he shouted, Drake now unbearably pounding. She followed him through the sweaty basement crowd, up the stairs, and down the hall until they found an empty corner.

Although Edie considered Peter a gem, a sparkling pearl in the middle of the foul, murky ocean otherwise known as Dating at Thirty-Five in San Francisco, he was still a man. And what had happened, she realized, as he began to describe the previous evening, was that he had stopped "feeling" his girlfriend of seven years.

"I feel terrible about it." He shook his head, staring down at his gray New Balances. "I really thought we could make it work."

The thing about Peter was that he really did want to make it work. He wanted to be an average guy who could fall in love with an average woman and have a kid and buy a house, and be a good dad with a good dog who was very good at playing fetch. But Peter had become a multimillionaire at twenty-nine when his adtech company, PrimalSearch, went public, a year after he'd gotten together with Nicole. Back then, the tech scene was still emergent and the city was full of nerdy, insecure men. Which is to say, it was a woman's market. When Nicole expressed interest, Peter thought he'd won the lottery. Edie hated the idea of "love at first sight," a phenomenon reserved for the beautiful, but Peter refused to admit it was anything but.

Time passed and his million in stocks multiplied by five, then ten, then twenty, until the idea of working was nothing more than a cute distraction. He started sleeping in and spending most afternoons at CrossFit, going into the office just enough to feel like he had a place to be. He bought a multimillion-dollar Victorian on Dolores Park and hired a personal stylist. With each year that passed, his skinny boyish body became more muscular, and his graying hair hotter, merely by the fact that it stayed on his head.

Meanwhile, San Francisco was becoming an actual destination for everyday people, not just a haven for nerds—Edie included herself in this category—which meant that now, in 2017, attractive women were no longer a rare find. So, by the time Peter hit his midthirties he had power, power he had never had a chance to leverage. And he was curious.

Or at least that's how she interpreted his underwhelming, not-feeling-it line, which he couldn't stop repeating as if the simple repetition might give it shape, like kneading dough.

They had never been a good fit anyway, she reminded herself. Nicole looked like she'd been plucked from a Madewell campaign, with thick chestnut hair and well-behaved bangs. She was petite and somehow always seemed to be smiling. She was charming enough to float breezily along in conversation without adding much of herself, like a perfectly suitable side dish.

"I know you didn't mean to hurt her." It was second nature to affirm him. To Edie, Peter was still the lanky boy in college who was there for her when her life had depended on it.

"Exactly." He nodded. "That's the last thing I wanted." He kept his head down, the way he must have looked as a boy, Edie thought, getting gently scolded by the nanny. "But she said if I didn't propose, we were over."

Well, then. That explained the suddenness of the news. Edie couldn't help but feel proud of Nicole for forcing him to confront what must have felt inevitable.

"I should have ended it years ago. She's almost forty. She wants to have kids."

Edie had forgotten Nicole was four years older than them. She panicked at the thought that a woman could put *seven years* into a man and have it end in an instant. Meanwhile, here she was, unable to even get started.

"Don't blame yourself," she got out, despite her own mounting discomfort. "She could have left at any time." He had loved Nicole. Edie was shocked when he'd agreed to go to couples therapy years ago, and read books with names like *Attached* and *How Can I Get Through to You?* "You were doing your best. She wasn't, like, held hostage."

"That's right." More nodding. "Thanks, E." He looked up, concern on his face. "I totally forgot to ask—how was your doctor's appointment?"

She assumed he'd forgotten about her fertility check-in, especially given his news, and was touched by his interest. "It was fine. We don't have to talk about it now."

"Please, I want to take my mind off the breakup. And I know you've been worried about the appointment." He angled his body toward her, blocking her from the newly formed crowd.

The doctor had been kind when he broke the news, or at least not overly sentimental. Like any other diagnosis, it was simply fact. Her follicle count was below average for her age, which was already above average for pregnancy. If she decided to have a child in the future, hers would be a geriatric pregnancy, he'd added (rather cruelly, Edie couldn't help but think).

"Do you want children?" the doctor had asked. When she opened her mouth to explain that she wasn't sure, she was shocked to realize that she was on the verge of tears. She managed to get out a curt "Don't know," before retreating back to silence. To no longer have the option was to confront her own mortality, like when a small child sees their own blood for the first time. It was terrifying. "I want to have the option," she added. After all, she had scheduled this checkup.

"I'm going to freeze my eggs," she declared to Peter, as if this were an empowering choice, not a dire recommendation from a concerned gynecologist.

"That's great!" He looked so happy for her. "Now you can take your time."

"Right." It was all so depressing.

"Hey." He took her arm in his hand. "I'm really proud of you. If I can help at all—bring you groceries, help with the shots—tell me."

His eyes lingered on hers and she considered saying it right there. Her love for him had grown, from a platonic gratitude for the kind boy in her dorms, to a deep admiration and awe at the way he seemed to make life work for him, to now—the first time in their lives that they were both single—an overwhelming need to finally formalize their closeness. There was no one in the world who knew her better than he did, and she knew the same was true for him. They *understood* one another. They had *fun* together. He was finally free. They could finally try.

He touched his nose with his index finger, before her words could form. "Want any?"

She shook her head. Peter never went to a party without drugs but she never let herself take them, sure that if she did, she wouldn't be able to stop. He never pushed. "How about you get us drinks while I run to the bathroom? I'll meet you in the kitchen."

HER PHONE BUZZED as she refilled their glasses with whatever was left on the foldout table—Smirnoff and tonic. The alert barely hit her consciousness. She mindlessly swiped it open.

"New match?" Peter said, back from the bathroom, his coke eyes peeking over her shoulder at her Tinder prospect. He grabbed her phone before she had a chance to see the face on her screen, but his laughter told her everything she needed to know.

"You can do better than that," he said, and began to swipe for her, as always. His standards for her were higher than her own, and he proceeded to reject each new face.

She took a long sip of her drink and considered this new world, a world in which Peter Masterson was now single. A world where Peter was now single and telling her that she, a thirty-five-year-old woman in San Francisco, should still be picky.

"Let's go back to the dance floor. I can't think about any of this right now." He looked up and held out her phone. "None of these guys are good enough for you anyway."

Chapter Two

THE NEXT MORNING, huddled under the fluorescent lights of her office bathroom, Edie tapped open Tinder. Nothing had happened between her and Peter last night, and she knew she'd have to be patient. Even if he had technically left Nicole, it was a sudden, major change in his life. He'd barely wanted to talk about it before running off to get high. He needed time to process. And she needed a distraction.

The man wore a robot mask, but Edie swiped right anyway. According to the one line of text on his profile, he was a professor and didn't want his students recognizing him. She liked the professor part, and in the split second she gave herself to form a judgment, she failed to register that this forty-five-year-old man was swiping on women young enough to be his students. They didn't match anyway.

She flushed the toilet. No one was ever in the women's bathroom at Tixster. She let her hands rest under the automated faucet, staring at her reflection. She didn't love what she saw but by now she was tired of trying to change it. Her scalp was too easy to spot through her thin, frizzy curls, and the smile lines from her nose to the tips of her mouth seemed cavernous. More and more frequently, she couldn't seem to catch her own eyes, as if she were in a trance, and maybe she was. In the hours from ten to seven, she floated from one meeting to the next, playing the part of a woman in charge. It was easier to play if she wasn't all there.

She walked from one end of the bright yellow office to the other, offering how's-it-goings without pausing for answers. The room was loud, from the voices of the open-office setup, but also visually— oversize photos of concerts and crowds lined Tixster's walls. The company gave everyone a budget for desk decor, so each day she passed succulents in pots shaped like cats, a life-size Han Solo cut-out, a family of stuffed teddy bears, and too many crystals. Her desk was bare except for a photo of her and her mother in a simple black frame. It was taken when Edie graduated from Stanford Business School, the only time her mother ever visited California—her dad had stayed home to work—before her fall. She'd pocketed the deco-ration money, instead.

Elizabeth approached Edie's desk as she took her seat. Elizabeth insisted everyone call her Elizabeth. Not Liz, not Beth, even Lizzy wouldn't do—Edie had tried them all. Elizabeth demanded people give her every syllable of their time.

"Morning, Edie!" Elizabeth chirped. "How was your weekend?"

Mondays and Fridays were the only days people at Tixster had anything to say to one another. Edie knew Elizabeth was only talking to her because Edie was her boss, but, despite herself, Edie appre-ciated the attention. The rest of her team were men and couldn't be bothered. "Good," Edie lied, unable to remember a single thing about it other than Peter's news.

Elizabeth's neatly shaped eyebrows popped up, waiting for more.

"How was *your* weekend?" Edie asked in turn.

"So good! We went to the new exhibit at the MOMA."

She didn't specify the composition of her "we." Elizabeth had moved in with her college boyfriend last year once he'd finished law school, granting her access to a one-bedroom apartment, while Edie, almost a decade her senior, had not yet graduated from her studio.

Elizabeth would probably be married by twenty-seven, the age that, so many years ago, Edie had planned to be, back when she believed she could plan those sorts of things.

"How was that?"

Elizabeth jumped into a description of an exhibit and, like the steady, mumbled buzz of NPR, her voice gently nudged Edie's brain awake. All her co-workers ever did was brag about consuming art. Their weekends were a visual résumé of cultural experiences: a way to show the world that they were artsy without ever creating actual art.

In the last five years Tixster had become an international platform of self-congratulation. People posted the cultural events they had attended on their Page—concerts, exhibits, DJ sets, the occasional poetry reading for the obscure—while friends and strangers applauded with "Claps." It'd started as a discovery platform, for users to meet other people attending the same events. But it quickly became clear that people's need for validation far surpassed their desire for connection, so "Claps" were born. The app was very popular.

Edie had joined Tixster two years ago for the money when she finally admitted that she needed a tech salary to survive in San Francisco. The salary from her previous job at a nonprofit—the best she'd ever had, a family of sorts—was hardly enough to cover her rent and pay off her student loans, let alone support her mother, who could no longer work after she'd fallen and needed in-home care. It wasn't hard for Edie to get the job at Tixster; she'd studied computer engineering at Cornell when "tech" was mostly microprocessors and defense companies—she'd chosen the highest paying major, knowing her loans would be large—so there were few women in her field at her level. The problem was that Edie hated tech companies.

"I posted some shots on my Tixster page if you're interested." Elizabeth seemed to have concluded her story.

Edie squeezed out a smile. She had done nothing interesting with her weekend. Other than dance with Peter, all she'd done was go on dates. But those felt like more of a life sentence than a choice. She felt as if her time to find a partner and start a family was narrowing like a real-life game of "escape-the-room." Despite the fact that Edie didn't have an active desire for children, she did feel an aching urge to move forward, to establish the *real life* that her colleagues were (apparently quite easily) settling into.

"Great to see Pages getting good use," she said as Elizabeth's freshly painted fingers held out her phone, displaying attempts at artful compositions of the exhibit.

Really the posts made Edie want to die. It was the slow dilution of actual beauty through the exploitative performance of its consumption. But that was what Pages were for—the key performance indicator was number of posts, followed by number of Claps—and Edie was the director of Pages at Tixster.

"Very cool," Edie said, handing Elizabeth's phone back to her after pretending to admire a self-consciously framed photo of a painting depicting what looked like a perfectly ordinary square. "Okay, time for work," Edie said, pulling a mock sad face before turning to her screen. She took out her Nutri-Grain bar, the same strawberry treat she allotted herself each morning, and opened her calendar.

Edie's first meeting of the day was in Burning Man. All conference rooms were named after events and Burning Man was the biggest room in the building. She was one of four women in the twenty-person meeting, one of whom was taking notes. A group of guys from the mobile team presented their "process," which was mostly photos of them surrounded by sticky notes for reasons that were unclear. When her phone buzzed it felt like a gift from the gods.

What do you think? It was a text from Peter, with an image attached—of a woman.

She opened the text cautiously, like a Tupperware that's been sitting in the fridge for months. Her hair was long and thick and wavy in that flawlessly messy way that either took hours in front of a mirror or incredible genetic luck. Her features were bold and unforgiving but also proportional. She was tall and thin but not in a sickly way. She had a Julia Roberts smile, wider than Edie's entire face and full of Chiclet-white teeth. Her skin was smooth and olive, which made her enormous dewy eyes pop. In short, she was stunning. Edie's heart sank as she realized what she was looking at.

Next screen: Her smile was tempered as if she were hiding a secret, there were deep lines around her mouth and eyes, marking a face that had let itself live, like a good, worn hoodie. Her eyes were bright and telling. Next screen: all text. She had a PhD from Princeton and a reference to Cardi B in her profile.

This was a dating profile. Peter was already on the apps.

"So, in conclusion, we want to maximize the value of our user base," the VP said, as if it weren't the most obvious fact in the world. The meeting seemed to be ending.

Going out with her tonight! Meet up after?

Was he absolutely insane?

P, she seems great. But online dating is a lot. I think you should take it slow. She sent the text before she had a chance to read it over. Then added, **I don't want you to get hurt.**

He had not only found the perfect woman in under twenty-four hours, he had matched and scheduled a date with her. Edie knew how impossible it was to find an attractive man capable of love at her age. What she tried to forget, though, was its harrowing flip side—the city was crawling with brilliant, competent women ready to jump at the possibility of potential.

PEOPLE SHUFFLED OUT of the room and Edie followed. Her boss, Derek, zoomed by on a scooter toward his standing desk. No one wanted to walk at Tixster, but everyone wanted to stand. Edie always wanted to sit. She ran five miles every night and couldn't be bothered with the quasi-exercise of the standing desk, which she had a feeling burned about as many calories as chewing a stick of gum, while coating the entire day with slight discomfort. Instead, she sat in her cushy chair, looking up at her co-workers like trees in a forest.

"Lunch?" Derek called from his perch a few feet away. "Tom and I are hitting up that new organic burrito bowl place."

"No thanks." She smiled. "I'm good." She needed to concentrate.

"We should catch up at some point." His look signaled disapproval.

Derek regularly canceled their weekly one-on-ones and she refused to give him the satisfaction of feeling like he'd spent time with her without actually doing it on the clock.

"Definitely," she said, and headed toward the bathroom.

Elizabeth was washing her hands when she entered. They smiled at one another. Edie raised her eyebrows for no reason, then jumped into a stall. She played with the toilet paper roller, trying to make some noise in the face of the devastating silence that endured while Elizabeth looked at herself in the mirror for what seemed like an embarrassing length of time, until she had the place to herself.

The woman's profile was from Bumble, her least favorite of the apps. Thinking of an opening message was the worst part of online dating; ignoring creeps was far easier than coming up with a witty first line.

It didn't take long to find his profile. She swiped frequently enough that any new prospects surfaced quickly. Of course, it was perfect. Its slight imperfections added just the right amount of charm, like how earnestly he smiled in his first photo, looking straight at the camera like a small child on picture day. There were no gym selfies or beach shots, but a photo of him at the grill gave a clear sense of his body.

She didn't want to love Peter. They had never dated or even kissed so she had no reason to believe they should be together. Yet seeing him in the pool of icons, available for any woman in the greater Bay Area to swipe, felt wrong, like a knife twisting in her back. She deserved him.

She took screenshots to study, to reference, to understand what he was looking for. And to send to Alex. Then she closed the app and restarted her entire phone so she could open it again without having to see his face.

Your dude is the cheesiest motherfucker alive, Alex had replied by the time her phone restarted.

I think I love him? Edie texted back.

Alex was her best friend. Peter was the only one who knew the core of Edie, but Alex knew everything else. They'd worked together at Safe Home Society—a seven-person domestic violence nonprofit in the Mission—before Edie had joined Tixster. Alex was an illustrator for Safe Home and hosted fundraisers in her loft. She'd lived in San Francisco for ten years, which was the only reason she could afford to stay; her loft was, in a sense, her currency. The first time Alex invited Edie over, she'd declined. Alex was an artist, which felt like another species to Edie, and one she couldn't imagine imposing her blandness on. But then Alex's long-term girlfriend had suddenly ended things, and heartbreak was a language Edie knew well. They hadn't stopped talking since.

He loves himself, too, Alex replied with three vomiting emoji faces. She was not a fan.

Edie was flipping through the screenshots, staring at the photo of Peter sipping a tall glass of IPA in the beer garden where they met nearly every Saturday, a photo she had taken only months ago, when his name flashed on her screen.

Don't worry, I'm ready! Nicole and I should have broken up years ago. Text you later!

She kept her head down as she walked to her desk. A calendar reminder to book her first egg freezing consultation was waiting with a note to herself, **Do not put this off!!!** And so she didn't.

Chapter Three

HER DATE'S PONYTAIL was longer than she'd anticipated. Not that she could blame everything on the ponytail. Surely some men with ponytails were perfectly hygienic. But she had learned to assess a person's character by the small hints available.

Sadly, the ponytail wasn't the worst of it. Her date, Dave, was obsessed with Muppets and spent all of dinner explaining their history. This, too, was her own fault, agreeing to dinner on a first date.

As Dave went on about Jim Henson the way other people might talk about Gandhi or God, she imagined what she would be doing if she were a wiser woman. Most likely eating Chinese food with her usual shows, like the warm sensation of coming home to family.

But by the time the plates were cleared, she had put in enough time and had enough vodka that anything began to feel justifiable. He was passionate! Wasn't that what she'd always said—that she just wanted someone *passionate* about *something*. What was so wrong with puppets, after all? Maybe he was perfect for her, good enough, at least.

Though she couldn't quite convince herself to listen to the words, especially now that Peter was single, she had to admire the energy in his voice. "That's very cool," she said.

He looked pleased. "Thanks."

There was a long silence and she used every ounce of her will-power not to break it. She didn't enjoy tallying who-asked-who questions, but if she didn't force silence once in a while, she was often the only one asking. To pass the time, she let her mind wander to her research on Peter's date. Her name was Anaya, and as an adjunct professor of feminist studies at UCSF, she had written three books that had very few reviews on Amazon but, sadly, looked quite interesting. One was even about dating, though Edie doubted someone as beautiful as Anaya could ever be in the trenches. She had a Twitter account, but no Instagram, so Edie only had one headshot to go off of, aside from the photos Peter had shared, when picturing them together. Their conversation was probably flowing easily by now. Unlike *Dave*, Peter was always ready with a question.

After a few sips of wine, Dave seemed to realize that no one was speaking. "What are you into?" he asked.

The downside of being asked questions was that she had to think of an answer and on this particular topic she had little to offer. "I'm really into running," she said pathetically. For years her life had revolved around her job at Safe Home Society. As chief of staff, she had juggled a bit of everything—scholarships, retreats, donations, their partner hotline. She had no time for anything besides work and she preferred it that way. Her optimum state of being was one of obsession. If she did something she preferred to do it 200 percent or not at all. She often stayed at the SHS office till ten at night, sometimes later, drafting up new programs and measurement plans, taking calls with partner organizations on the other side of the world. The number of hours didn't faze her; to not be working was far worse.

"Okay," Dave replied, clearly hoping for more.

"I used to work at a nonprofit," she continued. "I was really obsessed with the work. It took up my life."

"Oh cool." His face lit up. "Why'd you leave your job if you loved it?" he asked and she could sense the judgment creeping into his voice. To not love your job was the greatest millennial offense.

She looked up, anticipating his reaction. "It didn't pay," she said flatly.

She knew he would flinch. If not liking what you did was bad, admitting you did something for money in San Francisco was nothing short of blasphemy.

"The nonprofit couldn't pay what I wanted and I needed the money." SHS's funding was draining and the city was changing. Her once fine salary hadn't budged since she'd started and within a few short years it suddenly felt like scraps, something for a college intern, not a Stanford Business School graduate carrying over a hundred grand in debt. She watched her friends and colleagues, people she once considered peers, become millionaires ten times over, while she still chased happy hour specials.

For a long time, she tried to remind herself that money wasn't an indicator of happiness, that the people she envied had their own emptiness and longing. At least she was doing something with her days that mattered. It worked, for a while.

Then she'd gotten the call on a Tuesday at 8 p.m., 11 p.m. East Coast time, she remembered because she had just canceled dinner plans to stay late in the office. Her mother had fallen down the stairs, her knees were failing but she usually managed. Edie flew out the next morning. Her mother needed surgery, which included a long bill of out-of-pocket costs. She needed a walker that wasn't covered by insurance. She needed someone to help her do simple tasks like cooking and bathing because she couldn't trust Edie's father to do anything.

Edie remembered the first night her dad came home drunk, her mom's shouting, a breathy shriek, her dad's voice, muffled but booming. She knew her father was an alcoholic. Her mom had told her he drank regularly before she was born. She didn't mean it maliciously, her mom was grateful, almost disbelieving that he'd stopped.

As a child, her father had been Edie's idol. They spent weekends together in the garage of their Upstate New York home, recording audio segments about the goings-on in their small town. Piles of cassette tapes covered his long desk—an old wooden door that Edie had helped sand and paint—with scribbled titles on masking tape labels. With her help, they would build worlds together, narrating the changing of the maple trees or the new sandwich specials at the town grocer. But his stories rarely got picked up, and when they did, they paid almost nothing. Eventually, he increased his hours at the bottling factory and stopped recording.

Edie didn't know what made him start drinking again. Her mom said it was his job at the factory, the long winters. But he had endured all that for years, and though Edie would never say this to her mother—she knew it sounded ridiculous—the only thing that had *really* changed, were the changes she was experiencing. Now he had to live with a teenage girl. She was no longer adventurous and playful and brimming with potential. She was awkward and self-conscious and clearly not turning into anything special. After that first night, there was always a twelve pack of Bud in the fridge.

When her mother was released from the hospital, Edie asked if she wanted to leave him.

"Where would I go? It's impossible."

Looking down at her mom on the couch, the woman who had sacrificed everything for her, in desperate need of financial support, she had never felt more useless. She had turned her life upside down to do something she cared about, moved across the country to attend business school, buried herself in a job that was like the work version of her soul mate. But confronted with the one thing that mattered to her more than anything, she was utterly helpless.

She gave her notice to SHS the day she returned. She would pay off her loans and save enough money to buy her mom a small apartment in the Bay Area, so Edie could take care of her and get her away from her father. She just needed a few years to save. A month later she had an offer from Tixster.

She didn't like Dave enough to get into it. "So you're a marketing analyst?" she asked, sensing he'd be happy to change the subject if it circled back to him. "You like it?"

He did, very much. He explained something about a love for succinct metrics and Edie had to hide her smile at the idea that this was a more acceptable answer than liking a job for money. When the bill came Edie reached for her wallet. Though she thoroughly believed that she should have been paid for her time, given she had interviewed this man like a reporter, she refused to give him the satisfaction of thinking he'd pleased her.

When Dave said he'd had a good time and asked if she wanted to go next door for a drink, she declined quickly, grateful she'd paid for the absence of guilt.

VALENCIA STREET WAS a strip mall of first dates. Somewhere nearby Peter was on his date with Anaya or, if Edie was lucky, just finishing up. She texted to ask if he was done yet like a child waiting for dinner. She couldn't risk standing still, for fear Dave might ask what she was doing. Instead, she walked with purpose to nowhere in particular. She relaxed into her podcast—a true crime drama that her Twitter feed wouldn't shut up about—then felt a slight vibration against her hand, which she had not realized was gripping her phone tightly in her pocket.

Nope, still going strong. Want to meet her?

She leaned against an empty bike rack. That Peter wanted to introduce her to his first ever online date felt momentous. He could have been bored; Peter had pulled that move with Nicole many times, inviting Edie to spice up their conversation. But that seemed improbable given the "going strong." The other, more likely option was that he wanted to show her off. To prove that Edie had been wrong and online dating wasn't that bad after all.

But his motivations were irrelevant. She had needs of her own. Meeting the women Peter fell for gave her the information she needed when he would inevitably ask for her advice. Though she'd always been frustrated with his choices in women, she was rarely jealous of them. She had never met someone who fit with Peter as well as she did. And she preferred to feel confident, to pepper her explanation with details, when she advised him to end it.

Wow, she texted with a surprise-face emoji. **Sure! Where?**

She had always had a high tolerance for pain.

THEY WERE SITTING at a booth when Edie entered the dark, smelly bar she was sure Peter had picked. He was facing the door and she spotted him immediately. She saw Anaya's thick, shining hair as she walked toward the booth.

Only when she reached their table did the ridiculousness of the situation flood over her. If a man she was out with had asked his best friend—let alone a female friend—to join them on their first date Edie would have walked out. But her adrenaline had been too high and her date too bad to consider how embarrassing the whole thing would feel for everyone, least of all herself. If she hadn't already reached the table she might have turned around.

She had anticipated a tempered smile, a cloak of contempt covering justifiable rage. But there was no anger hidden in Anaya's face. On the contrary, Edie felt the way she imagined a celebrity might feel upon being recognized. When Anaya stood up to greet her, her eyes warm and striking, her smile twisted in a knowing smirk, Edie's concerns melted. "You must be Edie."

APPARENTLY, PETER HAD told Anaya that Edie was a "high-up" at Tixster. He also introduced Anaya as a feminist professor while Edie did her best to pretend this was new information.

"Did you always want to be an engineer?" Anaya asked when Edie returned from the bar with a vodka soda. She noticed Anaya's drink was also clear and bubbly and decorated with a lime. She wore a paisley blouse—cornflower blue and bright yellow with little specks of pink—that Edie wouldn't have bought in a million years but looked stunning on this woman. It was buttoned up to the top, as if showing skin was for the desperate, under a thin leather jacket, and Edie felt terribly silly in what she had thought was her cool and simple deep-V T-shirt.

"Kind of. I didn't actually know what an engineer was when I started," Edie laughed. "Neither of my parents ever graduated from college, so none of us had a clue. But I always loved math and science."

"Edie wanted to be a spy when she was a kid," Peter added, kindly leaving out that her dorm room had been wallpapered with *Matrix* and *Mission Impossible* posters. He shot her a smile with his big green eyes that seemed to penetrate through her entire body. He knew every last inch of her. In a sense, he owned her.

Anaya laughed and looked to Edie for confirmation.

She took a sip of vodka. "It's true. I was obsessed with spy stuff. I thought computer engineering would inch me closer to the CIA. And also pay for college."

Anaya shook her head in sympathy. "I don't understand why we can't keep more women in tech. They're getting locked out of the highest paying jobs, it's awful."

Edie nodded. She thought about this more than nearly anything else, but wasn't in the mood to get into it. Most of the dialogue around *women in tech* was flat and boring and largely missed the point. Diversity planning was well and good but any real change had to happen outside of the office. It required a seismic shift in culture.

"So, you like Tixster?" Anaya continued.

Edie hated admitting how much she hated her job. She wanted to be a proud woman in tech, not a begrudging one who bolstered the very stereotypes she was trying to fight. "I love coding," she started. "But these tech companies all feel very useless. Like Tixster—you can't post original art or events that actually matter, like support groups or protests or anything like that. It's just an ego-stroking tool feeding on people's insecurities." She caught herself sounding rant-y but Anaya was nodding encouragingly.

"I've noticed that." She sipped her drink. "These tech companies design apps to exploit us, they cater to superficial cravings, not who we actually are and what we need. It's like they suppress what makes us human."

"Exactly." Edie could feel herself grinning. "I used to work for a nonprofit," she continued. "When I was doing that, I felt like I was doing something important, beyond just solving puzzles or whatever. I loved it."

Anaya's nods were thoughtful. "That seems to be very common for women."

Edie flinched. "For sure," she offered. "But I hate that it's a woman thing. Men are just as capable of caring about making a difference."

"Hey." Peter hunched into the table. "I care," he said, and Anaya offered a weak smile.

"No, you don't," Edie said. "You just like hard problems."

He laughed.

"My nonprofit was all women," Edie offered. "Women are raised to be helpers. We feel bad if we're doing something for ourselves and I hate that."

"I mean I care a little," Peter tried again.

"I think that's right," Anaya replied. Edie was perversely grateful that she was ignoring Peter. "And we're rewarded for caring. If a woman throws herself into something for no other reason than she loves it, or wants to make money, or anything selfish we're shamed for it. We're expected to have a purpose beyond ourselves. At the cost of ourselves, really. I think it all ties back to motherhood."

It was extreme and little too hand-waving feminist for Edie's taste but she didn't disagree.

"The environmental nonprofit I volunteer with is almost all men," Peter interjected. "Maybe men are just drawn to bigger issues."

Edie winced and pinched his leg. She'd told him not to say shit like that.

"'Cause we're insecure, we need to feel important," he added. "I'm not saying it's a good thing, men are terrible."

When Edie looked up, Anaya's head was tilted, her face painted with a patient smile. "Men love to call themselves terrible. It's funny because they really don't have to be." She took a sip of her drink. "What do you mean—men are drawn to *bigger* issues?"

"You know, whatever." He waved his hands. "Issues that affect more people."

"Peter." Edie put her hand on his shoulder, then turned to Anaya. "This is why he's a good engineer, very analytical, but"—turning back to Peter—"you oversimplify things."

"No, it's good," Anaya started, and Edie could hear the pinch of restraint in her voice, "that some people don't have problems affecting them every single day, so they have the luxury to invest in—not *bigger* by any means, please—but issues they want to spend time on, not just challenges they have to address to survive." Her tone was authoritative and teasing at once.

Edie watched Peter toss Anaya an apologetic smile, eyes shining. "You're right. I'm sorry for saying that." And she watched Anaya, with a faint smirk, receive the power of his approval.

Anaya shifted her large eyes back to Edie, who was grateful for the attention. "It must be tough sometimes, working in such a male-dominated field. What makes you stick with it?"

It occurred to Edie that this was the most enjoyable date she could remember being on. "Honestly, I *always* fantasized about becoming a gender studies major. To basically do what you do. But I was obsessed with not quitting. Almost every woman I'd started out with had changed majors. I decided, maybe unwisely, it was better to experience gender bias than read about it."

Anaya leaned into the table, grabbing Edie's hand before she'd even finished her sentence. Her skin felt soft, like a child. A chill rushed down Edie's back. "I thought the same thing. I'm not kidding. I considered dropping out of gender studies to be an engineer every single day. Like, why am I just *reading* about this when I could be *living* it?"

Anaya's smile was warm and intense. Edie had to look away. "Weird," she admitted.

"I feel like I should leave you two alone," Peter laughed, reminding them that he was still there.

This time they both ignored him.

"How do you like teaching?" Edie asked Anaya.

"I don't love it," she started.

Edie smiled. Everyone in San Francisco was so afraid of negativity, as if they'd be struck down for uttering a simple dislike.

"But I love the writing part. If I could just write all day, I would."

"You're a writer?" Edie feigned surprise.

Peter nodded as if needing to participate in some way.

"Yeah. I've written a few books on gender, on *dating*." She shot a glance at Peter, who raised his eyebrows playfully. From the looks of it, this was covered ground for them.

"What about it?" Edie asked, still skeptical she could possibly know the half of it.

Anaya didn't answer. Instead, she smiled, returning Edie's look back to her. *What about it?* Everything *about it*—her look said.

Edie smiled. "Online dating is so terrible. And I feel like it just keeps getting worse." She caught herself. "For women, that is."

"You could delete the apps," Anaya offered and Edie noticed Peter turn to her, waiting for a reaction.

"No I can't." She felt betrayed, as if Anaya should have understood. "I can't just, like, give up."

Anaya laughed. "Give up what? Misery? If you're not enjoying it, why not?"

Edie was on the verge of anger when Anaya jumped in again.

"I'm kidding. Of course, I get it—there's no other way to date these days. But it's something I ask myself all the time—why am I still putting up with this?"

Her use of the present tense thrilled Edie. To align herself with this struggle in the presence of Peter implied, at least in this conversation, she had more power than him.

"I stopped dating for years, and I was way happier." Her voice was slower, almost longing. "People think partnership is this ultimate goal, but most married people I know seem miserable." Edie couldn't disagree. "And the single people I know, at least the ones who understand there's nothing *wrong* with them, and just embrace the freedom of it, seem happy. I mean, lonely sometimes, sure, but I don't know, they seem more in touch."

It was the kind of thing Edie wanted to think, that she *did* think, intellectually at least. But she didn't believe it, not really. Not in her bones. Not in a way where she might actually stop swiping the stupid apps, where she could, as Anaya said, embrace the freedom of it.

"Yeah," Edie said, and the insufficiency of her response made her heart race. She tried to think of something else to say. "It's just . . ." She paused. "I wouldn't care that much if it weren't for the kid thing. I feel like I'm running out of time because . . ." She trailed off, trying to justify her need but there was nothing complicated about it. "Because I am."

Anaya's eyes, alert and probing, were so dark and beautiful it was impossible to look away. "So you want kids."

Edie laughed. The thought of her taking care of a child still felt absurd. "Yeah, I mean, I don't want them *now*. But I assume I will eventually."

Anaya laughed, too, but harder. "You can't live your life based on what you think you'll want in the future." She spread her hands out on the table, and Edie wished hers weren't clinging to her glass of vodka so that they might touch. "You have no idea who you'll be in a few years. You have no idea what you'll want."

Edie had never imagined a world in which what she wanted was not planned and prepared for. It felt absurd to think she might not be able to predict who she'd be a few years from now.

"She's freezing her eggs," Peter said, nudging his shoulder into hers.

"I just want more time to figure it out." Her voice was defensive.

Anaya nodded. "I get it. We need to do what makes us happy now, as much as we can, at least. If what you need is more time— great." She sat back in her seat. "It took a long time for me to realize I didn't want kids."

Edie felt like a record had stopped and it took everything she had not to look at Peter, who she knew definitely wanted kids, despite having taken no concrete steps toward that goal.

"That's what my new book is about. Well not kids, exactly, but how we figure out what it is we actually want as women when we're so cluttered with 'shoulds.' When we grow up being sold a very specific image of successful womanhood." She stopped herself quickly. "Something like that. I'm still figuring out the best way to describe it." For the first time all night, she looked uncertain of herself.

"That sounds fantastic." Edie nodded and wished Anaya would keep talking but she took a sip of her drink, instead.

When she started again, her voice had a new shakiness. "It's probably the most personal thing I've ever written. I think honesty is our only real chance at connection, it's why I write, but it's been really hard deciding what I want to include. It's like, do you really want to share the biggest trauma of your life with the general public?" She laughed, weakly.

Edie sat rapt. Talk of trauma on a first date solidified that she cared more about their conversation than Peter's appraisal. "I can't imagine. I can barely talk about my parents with my friends."

"She cries every time she mentions her dad," Peter added and she wished he would disappear.

Anaya's eyes locked with Edie's. She understood.

"I'd love to read it," Edie said. "Or any of your work."

Anaya smiled at her with what felt like sincere gratitude, her eyes desperately alive, and Edie knew, in that moment, that Peter would fall in love with her. The worst part was, she couldn't blame him.

"That's very kind of you," Anaya said. "That book is a work in progress, but I can send you the links to my other books if you're interested."

Edie appreciated that she didn't say that she would send Peter the links to send to her. "I would love that. When does the new book come out?"

Anaya laughed self-consciously. "Oh god, there's so much I still need to figure out. I've been working on it for fifteen years now."

Edie stared blankly, unable to comprehend that level of dedication to anything.

"Maybe next year? Maybe never?" She laughed a sad, shallow laugh.

"Don't say that," Edie nearly gasped. *Never* was not a word that entered the tech lexicon. *Now, yesterday, quick, iterate, always, constantly* were the words that made up her world. That someone could put so much into something and think it might *never* be done seemed like the most tragic thing in the world. "You'll finish it," she assured her. "You have to."

Chapter Four

TIXSTER'S COFFEEPOT WAS empty and Edie wanted to kill herself. The energy of the evening had worn off and the reality had sunk in. Peter would start dating Anaya seriously, he wouldn't be able to help himself. It was the same thing with Nicole, he just kind of fell into serious relationships. He hated being alone, thrived on the security of a beautiful face beside him. He considered himself independent, and in many ways, he was—he generally did whatever he wanted—he just liked having a woman with him to witness it.

When Edie didn't hear from him the next morning, she'd assumed they were still having sex. She imagined it was one of those dates that only happens in movies, or with people who looked like they could be in movies, where two people call in sick and pretend life doesn't exist beyond their lean, braided bodies.

Edie had slept in Peter's bed more times than she could count. He had always been proud that Nicole didn't care when Edie slept over, as if that meant she was "chill" or whatever. But Edie knew her indifference was the ultimate insult, that she wanted Edie to know that even when Peter lay beside her in bed, she had nothing to worry about.

The first time Peter and Edie shared a bed together was the

night they'd met, after Peter punched her boyfriend in the face. She had been trying to do it herself but Matt had pinned both her hands down with one of his and was using his other to push himself inside her. It wasn't that he'd never been inside her. They had been dating, and sleeping together, for months. But at least a few times every month Matt would knock on her dorm room door, drunk, and want sex.

The first time Matt did this, Edie was thrilled. They weren't dating then. He was just the hot son-of-a-senator in her Thermodynamics class. Edie's classes were almost all boys all the time but very few of them were hot. Most of them were skinny and smelly. She sat in the back row of most classes, to avoid the smell and the eyes that would inevitably follow her, which is where she met Matt. People knew Matt because his dad was in politics, and he sat smack in the center of the last row every class. The two of them would laugh at how incomprehensible the professor was, how nerdy their classmates were, how insufficient Febreze was as a replacement for actual detergent. It made Edie feel like she fit in—not with the class at large, but with what she considered the best part of it—to laugh with Matt, to have his attention, this boy-in-the-back who seemed so much better than everyone else.

She knew he would be at the party that night, which was why she wore her special dress, tight and covered in silver sequins. She still had it in her closet somewhere, but, fifteen years later, she'd be lucky if she could fit a thigh in it. She'd been on her fourth drink, trying to hold it steady while bouncing on the dance floor, clear liquid spilling all over her hand, when Matt came up from behind her. He put his arms around her starved waist and began grinding into her. Her body tingled as she put her free hand on his, resting on her stomach and inching lower with each beat. When the song ended, she turned around, his arms still holding her, and they kissed, long and sloppy. They didn't stop kissing until a friend grabbed her arm, pulled them off the dance floor, and plopped them in the corner of

the party, which they hid in for a minute before he swept her home
to his room.

It was her first time and she couldn't remember any of it. But
waking up next to Matt, his smell all over her body, his bare chest
free for her to rest her head on, was as good as any sex she could have
imagined. She had never had a boyfriend and his large, sweaty body
beside her felt like a prize, proof that she was a woman men like Matt
wanted. From there they began seeing each other regularly. The sex
didn't feel great but it was exciting, and afterward, she felt proud.
Like finishing a long, hard run.

He was rough with her, pounding for longer than she would have
liked, but it was nothing she couldn't handle. It was what he needed
to get off, he explained, and though it didn't make her orgasm (her
nerves actually went kind of numb), there was something about being used in this way, being the means to his end, that turned her on,
made her feel powerful. When he left, she'd lie alone in her bed and
pleasure herself with the thought of it.

Then she started to want more. On their three-month anniversary she made dinner reservations at the nice Italian restaurant in
Collegetown. Ten minutes before he was supposed to come get her,
he called her room and told her he was tied up in a basketball game,
he would come by later. That's when she stopped denying that he
only ever came by later.

By their fourth month together, Matt did not turn her on at all.
She dreaded him. But she couldn't bring herself to call it off. She
wasn't afraid he would be sad; she was pretty sure he didn't even like
her. She was afraid *she* would be sad, or, rather, devastated. She felt
sure that she would never be with someone as handsome and cool as
Matt again. And yet she was bound in anxiety: fear he might show up
at any moment, worrying what he was doing if he didn't, pretending
to welcome the kisses that shrouded her in shame. Every second she
was with him felt like wearing the wrong skin, as if her identity was
distorted by his presence.

So, when Matt came over later that night, she told him she wanted to break up and he told her to go fuck herself. She'd be crazy to break up with him, he said, and threw her down on the bed. She laughed at first. "Stop, I'm serious." She could smell the whiskey and Coke on his breath. She noticed a large stain on his gray T-shirt, mustard or vomit, she wasn't sure. The smell of his sweat made her sick. As he kissed her neck, she felt tears starting to well. She kept repeating that she was serious but her voice came out shaky and hearing the fragility of her own words broke her. Matt unbuttoned her shirt and pressed himself into her.

"Matt, stop!" she tried to scream but just like in a dream her voice refused to work.

He shoved his face into her neck. "That's hot," he whispered. His belt was open but his pants were still zipped. She could feel him through his jeans.

She closed her eyes and her whole body stiffened. But when she heard a knock on the door her eyes shot open. "Help!" she yelled without thinking and Matt leaned into her.

"Shut up," he whispered, smiling as if they were in on the same joke.

The door opened. He was abnormally tall and skinny, like a string bean or the guy from Scooby-Doo, she remembered thinking. She had seen him walking around the dorm building, but she'd had no idea that he lived a few doors down. Her first thought was that he should run away, that Matt would destroy him.

Peter told her later that he saw the tears streaming down her face, so when Matt turned to look at him, he didn't hesitate before punching him squarely in the face. And then again, and again, and again.

Edie slipped out from under him and off the bed. The tall guy threw his arm around her and took her out of the room before Matt had a chance to look up.

———

THE COFFEEPOT HAD finished dripping and a line had formed to reap its riches. Back at her desk she broke down and texted Peter. **She was pretty great. Have fun?**

Yeah she was great. I kinda wish it wasn't so good on my first try! He added a smiley face.

I'm so sorry for you. Perfect woman on your first try.

For all the things Peter had to offer, his ability to admit the ways in which he was kind of terrible was maybe what she loved about him most.

I'm just sayin

When will we see her again . . . ?

Don't steal her from me!

Edie laughed and sent a face with hearts for eyes.

Dinner later? she asked.

Sorry, date! ♥

ANAYA'S WRITING WAS easy to find. As Edie scrolled through the descriptions, they seemed so up her alley she thought she might have dreamt them into existence.

Most of the women Peter dated, like Nicole, were a different species of a woman, which made it easy. She knew he would ultimately be miserable with them, or if he wasn't then he wasn't who she thought he was, and then they weren't right for each other anyway. But Anaya felt of the same breed as Edie, only a far better version.

It was this idea that they were of the same ilk—emotionally at least, if not physically—that being like Anaya was somewhere within her reach, that drove Edie to buy every one of her books. She felt an obsessive need to learn every inch of her brain, to inhabit it, as if she might understand how far she could take her own. And it just so happened that much of her brain was available for sale on the internet.

She purchased all of her books, then confirmed plans with the data scientist from Tinder whom she'd been ignoring all week, before heading to her team meeting.

"Just a reminder," Elizabeth said as people took their seats, "tonight is the Tixster Ping-Pong tournament!" She looked around with a tight, bursting smile, holding eye contact with each team member before turning to Edie. "Edie, I hope you can make it?"

She had completely forgotten and didn't want to cancel her date. "Do you know if Derek is going?"

Elizabeth frowned. "He has to take care of the baby."

How nice to have a family, a perpetual excuse of import. "I'm sorry, I also have plans I can't break." She tried her best to sound disappointed.

THE DATA SCIENTIST looked much better than his pictures and seemed disturbingly normal. He made eye contact and spoke in full sentences and even attempted to fill the gaps in conversation when silence spread over the table.

These small fragments of competency thrilled Edie, and when he asked if she wanted a second drink, she realized she actually did.

"This is fun," she offered. "Like surprisingly fun," she laughed. She was intentional about her adjectives. *Fun* resonated with men. Men liked *fun*.

When he leaned over the table to kiss her after their second drink, it felt good—too good. Everything about him was smooth, and her red-flag radar shot up.

"How 'bout we go back to your place?" he asked.

She repeated her rule, practiced, now, at saying it out loud, knowing the temporary sting of embarrassment was worth it. "I don't have sex unless I'm in a committed relationship. Just so you know." No sex without monogamy was the rule she'd set for herself on her thirty-second birthday, three years ago, after one-too-many disappointments.

She hadn't had sex since.

The data scientist had been leaning toward her and now he sat back in his chair, smile faded, eyes lazy. "I respect that," he said with a tone of indifference.

"I'm really enjoying this, though. One more drink?" she offered.

"If we're being honest," he started, and Edie braced for what she knew was coming next, "I'm not really looking for anything serious."

Edie might as well have had this line tattooed on her eyelids. It had become a mantra of sorts, not one she repeated herself, but one repeated to her by others. She appreciated that he was upfront, but she'd kind of forced him into it—her rule was never a bad one in the end—so she couldn't give him too much credit. Better to feel this wave of disappointment in the bar where she was far less tempted to give in than in the bedroom, where the sadness would overwhelm her and she'd take what she could get, hoping, in a way that had grown embarrassing because she knew how hopeless it really was, that in doing so she would convince him of more.

AS WAS HER postdate ritual, she texted Peter a summary of the evening. But now it felt different. Before she knew he'd be on the couch, miserable with Nicole, eager to dissect the intricacies of the online dating world he could only observe from afar. A world that to Edie felt like a high security prison she couldn't escape. But now he was in that world with her, and her gut clenched at the possibility that he might actually like it.

She watched her phone sit idle for two hours as she finished a box of cereal and assured Netflix that yes, she *was* still watching. But just as her eyes began to close, an email came in. That name, bolded in her inbox, gave Edie butterflies like she hadn't felt in years.

Anaya had sent a list of her books, as promised.

Edie! It was so great to meet you the other night. I loved hearing about your complicated relationship with tech, and I'm excited for you to have more time to consider the kids decision. It's such a rare pleasure to meet someone you genuinely connect with, and right off the bat. At least in the world of online dating it's more or less unheard of. ☺ I was touched by your interest in my writing and think you might like my recent book best (the one I mentioned I'm working on). In the meantime, I'm sharing the others below.

x,

Anaya

Edie spent the next forty-five minutes drafting a reply. It soothed her, like her early days of coding, trying to convey a sentiment simply, shuffling words around until they fit just right. She didn't let on that she'd already bought every book. But she did assure Anaya, with great enthusiasm, that she felt that rare connection, too.

THE NEXT MORNING Peter apologized for not responding to her last text.

How was your date with Anaya? Edie asked with a smiley face.

The date wasn't with Anaya. But it was great! Let's meet up later!

PETER WRAPPED HIS long arms around her and squeezed. She breathed in the smell that felt like home, a mix of artificial pine and Ivory soap. That someone so rich could stay so committed to the same basic products was a constant wonder to her, who, though still digging herself out of debt, thought her whole life might be saved with each new curl cream.

"So, you're already going out with another woman?" she asked, cozying into the corner of his large leather sectional. She was being dramatic but Peter loved being the center of a drama.

He laughed and handed her a glass of wine. "Anaya was my first online date! I don't owe the girl anything."

"She's not a girl." She had assumed Anaya had emailed her after seeing Peter. Now, knowing they hadn't been together, Edie felt an even deeper commitment toward her.

"The *woman*." He smiled, taking a seat on the other side of the long couch.

"Her name is Anaya."

"Look, I agree! She's fantastic. I feel very lucky. But I'm just seeing what's out there."

"Does she know you're seeing other people?"

"Who?"

"Anaya!" Edie felt like a mother protecting a child. Admittedly, it wasn't great that she was now rooting for the woman who Peter would inevitably fall for when she, herself, was in love with Peter. But it was so rare for Peter to choose someone who was upfront with her needs and wants in a way that Peter had always respected in women but had never actually chosen in a partner, that she couldn't help but want him—at least on some level—to want her.

"You're being crazy," Peter said, twirling his glass.

Edie didn't argue.

"We went on one date. To already talk about seeing other people would be insane." When he looked up, a speck of doubt flashed across his face. "Right? I thought it was assumed that we see other people until we have 'the talk' or whatever?"

Edie laughed. "Mister dating expert over here." Anything he knew about online dating, he'd learned from her. But she'd been a good teacher; he wasn't wrong. "I just wish a guy could enjoy a woman and not feel like he needed to search far and wide in case there's someone slightly better. It's like men are constantly optimizing, it's gross."

"Is it possible—just throwing this out there—that someone might be projecting?"

"Of course I am." She was aware of her own tendency to always look for someone better, and that, unlike Peter, she couldn't afford to keep doing it.

"I really like her," Peter continued with a familiar softness to his voice. "But I literally just started online dating. I'm allowed to go out with more than one woman. Give me that."

His deftness at weaving between cocky and sensitive always cast a kind of spell on her.

"Just be honest," Edie offered. "If you're not looking for a relationship—tell her."

"We're going out tomorrow night." Peter looked proud. "I'll see how it goes."

She gave him a look to indicate that this was insufficient.

It was getting dark and she knew it'd be a cold bike ride home. "I gotta go."

"Stay for dinner?" he asked, pulling out his phone. "We can order in."

She hadn't budgeted for one of Peter's elaborate takeout bills and anyway, the books should have reached her doorstep by now. "Nah, I'm kind of tired." She grabbed her helmet and zipped up her hoodie. "I'll talk to you tomorrow."

Chapter Five

S HE KNEW IT was strange, bordering on stalker-ish, but she couldn't stop reading. She'd spent two days in bed, with the occasional trip to the loveseat. Dishes piled on her nightstand, on her small square counter, a few made it into the sink. Edie had almost finished all three of Anaya's books by the end of the weekend.

Her studio, the single room that held her entire life, was cold and drafty. It didn't get any sunlight, the two windows she had faced the building next door. But it was her first apartment without a room-mate and she had never loved a space more. When she shut her door, she didn't have to worry about whether her curls were frizzing or her jeans looked weird, if her comments were interesting, her questions engaging, her nods sympathetic. She could just be.

Everything was in its place. Her mom's *"Home is where the heart is"* keychain hung from a thumbtack over the light switch by the door. Her and her dad's cassette tapes lined the bottom of the bookshelf in chronological order. On the far wall was a photo Alex had taken of them on their lunch bench by the water when they worked at Safe Home together; she'd had it framed for Edie's thirtieth birthday. The picture was the only real decoration in the apartment, aside from her pillows. Not particularly nice pillows, certainly not expensive pillows, but you could get a pillowcase at Ikea for $4.99 and they were always coming out with new patterns. So pillows enveloped her as she pored through Anaya's pages.

Edie was not a *reader*. She'd never had space for classes that involved words. Every now and then a man she was dating or a guy at work would recommend a book and she would slog through it miserably before concluding that she just didn't like reading.

But she could not put Anaya's books down. Her writing layered the factual with the personal, leading with her own mistakes and making the whole enterprise feel more like a late-night conversation with a good friend than a women's self-help book, which, technically, they were. Not that Edie minded self-help, but she didn't like being lumped in with other women, who she viewed, despite herself, as needy and a bit weak.

BY SUNDAY NIGHT, she was so intimate with Anaya's voice it was absurdly, wonderfully, starting to infiltrate her own internal monologue, the way she sometimes used to dream in code. She noticed it in the rare moments she wasn't reading, like when she brushed her teeth, and her thoughts presented themselves with an articulation and clarity that felt foreign.

It wasn't until she'd reached the most recent book, which she had saved for last since she wanted to honor the text by working chronologically, that she noticed a change in tone. Even the cover was darker, a light gray compared to the bright yellow and baby blue of her previous two. It was not laced with optimism, like her first book about women and work, or humor like her second, about the rise of online dating, which Edie had highlighted in near entirety. While her other books were personal and honest, this new book—published a year ago—took on a somber earnestness that the others veiled.

The book was titled *Just Perfect*, and began with a viscerally descriptive chapter about her eating disorder. For the first time a sense of discomfort crept over Edie, as if she were reading something she shouldn't. She felt worried for Anaya that so much of herself was right there, on the page. She explained how her strict exercise routine and web of strange eating rules were less about weight, than the desire to feel like she was doing something right, that she was making some measurable progress. Edie barely noticed her eyes getting wet as she read. She had her own web of rules—she assumed all women did—which had been brutally strict, especially in her twenties. She had never really let herself consider, although somewhere beyond consciousness she knew, that it might be anything more than self-discipline, something to be proud of.

Edie put the book down and searched photos of Anaya. The first thing she did whenever she heard someone had an eating disorder was search for their image. She knew it was inappropriate; pathetic, too. Though her rules had been strict in college, she could barely consider herself a competitor anymore. Now she was a spectator, like a sports commentator who was once a star. But she still needed to see what other women with rules looked like, to compare her own discipline to theirs. Anaya's earlier photos were thin but not sickly; they were equals.

> My Chinese finger trap was purple and green and fraying from use. As a child, I was fascinated by the way it tightened its grip the harder I fought. I think about the toy often when I consider my relationships. The more attractive a woman becomes in the context of today's standards of perfection, the further she burrows into self-erasure.

At thirty-five she'd noticed a drastic drop in prospects—the "filter phenomenon," she called it. It seemed impossible for women her age—thirty-eight when the book was published (which put her at thirty-nine now, and made Edie feel proud of Peter for swiping right on an older woman)—to find an equal. The larger problem, she posited, was that women were drawn to men they admired, who pushed them to grow, while men often wanted partners who fit easily into their lives. She attributed this to men not needing to feel seen by a woman in order to validate their existence, the way women often needed men's approval to operate successfully in society.

When messy, ambitious women meet someone who understands their layers, who sees and hears them and appreciates each complex detail, logistics are a mere afterthought. We spend our whole lives dealing with the complicated logistics of womanhood, dating logistics can be dealt with—easily. But men's self-acceptance doesn't hinge on whether there is a woman in their day-to-day who fundamentally gets them. In fact, if they *are* truly seen by a woman, they may have to confront weaknesses that society rarely requires them to consider. The mutual understanding some women seek can be the very thing that makes some men hide.

Edie placed the book down on her bed. Reading had made her feel like she was filling in missing pieces of herself, identifying ideas lurking inside of her, but that she'd never been able to articulate, or maybe had just been afraid to.

Her apartment was dark save for her glowing screen. A box of cereal sat next to her and she grabbed a handful, pretending not to notice the crumbs that would join her in sleep.

She needed to give something back to Anaya after taking so much. She would not reveal that in just three days she had become an Anaya Thomas completist, but she could at least thank her again and let on that she loved her work. She tweaked the note until she could barely make sense of the sentences. She had two tight paragraphs that she couldn't help but think, with a bit of pride, sounded like Anaya's voice. As she pressed send her stomach dropped. She lay awake for a long time, envisioning Anaya's reply.

———

THAT WEEK, ON her regular run through the park, Edie imagined running by the university where Anaya worked. It sat on the southeast corner of Golden Gate, a short two-block detour from her usual route. She longed for contact, even just a smile, but it felt too creepy to go out of her way. She was too self-conscious to run through a campus full of young people anyway. Instead, she scanned faces along the Panhandle, looking up as bikes sped by, catching eyes then looking away, glancing beneath women's helmets for her thick, dark hair. But the only familiar face she spotted was a guy from Wisconsin who she'd spent the night with back in her twenties. She remembered his mattress was on the floor.

At home, she plated her steamed broccoli and tofu before grabbing the fuzzy faux fur throw her mom had sent when she'd finally moved into her own place—her mom had one in every color, her dog loved them; Edie's was pink—and plopped on the loveseat. It was a ridiculous piece of furniture—a pretend couch, too small to sleep on, even petite Alex's feet dangled over.

Social media caused nothing but envy but she checked it anyway lest her mind wander to Peter. Instagram was all babies. Most of her business school friends had at least one by now, although, could she even call them friends anymore? Once babies came into their lives they were too busy to reach out to her and she felt too derelict to impose herself on them. She searched for Anaya's name, but none of the results matched her face. She scanned Peter's followers for any new additions, but found nothing.

At a dead end, her mind began to wander to dangerous places, as it always did when left unattended. Nights alone, without Peter, without dates, without whatever dumb party was a bike ride away, reality crept in. She had nothing to live for, not really. She could impose goals on herself like she had in her twenties, but she could no longer trick herself into caring.

She closed Instagram and opened her real estate app. She'd get her mother out of that falling-down house, buy her a place where she could feel safe. Her mom was the only thing keeping her going.

Mom glowed on her screen. It wasn't a coincidence. She called every night. "Hi, Mom."

"How are you, sweetie?"

"Fine, good." There was never anything important to tell. They would get to the details, or not, downstream. "How are you?" She could hear the banging of what sounded like cabinets in the background.

"Hold on, I'm moving to the bedroom." A door shut, then silence. "Your father is mad about dinner. Always upset about something. God forbid I get anything right." Then, as if tying the tip of a balloon and flicking it into the air, "Enough about that."

Her dad rarely got angry in front of Edie, though she'd heard his shouts from bed as a kid. Edie's heart froze at the shift in his voice, from the cheerful, curious tone she recognized to a sharp, piercing ire at her mom. She imagined her mom reminded him, however unintentionally, of his failures, how he'd disappointed her as a husband and father, but with Edie he could still pretend. He had loved her and been nothing but proud of her. Edie would never acknowledge the bad parts. She couldn't even picture it—admitting to her father that she, too, was disappointed.

She didn't love what her dad had become, but she did love her dad. It wasn't logical, it was deep and visceral, she could barely even access it anymore, but she knew that her admiration for him, cemented in her first dozen years of life, shaped something central to her being.

Her parents never moved from the house she grew up in, though it barely stood up anymore. For a while she sent money when the toilet broke or the pipes were leaky, for a cleaner once a month. But her mom had lost most of her eyesight from diabetes and couldn't legally drive or use the computer to deposit checks, so Edie had been sending cash, and soon her father began to intercept it and use it for himself. She used this to justify moving her mother out of the house, which her dad wouldn't like, but at this point he didn't deserve to have a say.

"I'm only a few months from a down payment. I saw a small apartment in South San Francisco that could be perfect." Edie had a dozen alerts peppering her inbox; she was constantly calculating renting vs. buying, South Bay vs. East Bay, tracking market fluctuations so she knew exactly how much she needed to make an offer.

"You're sweet, sweetie. But this is not your responsibility." Her mom always insisted she was grateful for what she had. It was how she'd survived. "I have the candle you got me for Christmas burning on my dresser," she continued. "I love that candle. Where'd you get it?"

"I forget, Mom. Some shop in the Mission."

"The pine smell is just right, feels peaceful in here. I'm going to put on that CD I like, that young woman, what a voice." Edie let her run on. Her mom loved to describe the things that made her happy in excruciating detail, let her mind rest in it. "The birds are out. Isn't that funny, it's so late. Two are eating from the fountain. I put bread out. Up, one just flew away."

"That's nice, Mom. They love that fountain."

"And you know what day it is, don't you?"

It was a completely average day, as far as Edie could tell. "Oh." She smiled. "Pi Day."

"Pi Day!" her mom burst out. "And I'm eating a delicious slice of apple in your honor. I'll send you a picture after we talk."

Edie had thought Pi Day was the coolest holiday in the world as a child. Most of her friends weren't into math, so it felt like a secret only she was in on. The first computer program she ever wrote calculated pi—the longer it ran, the more decimal points it generated—and watching it run, she felt like a sort of god, the way all the men in Silicon Valley still seemed to feel. Her mother had driven her to the library every weekend to sit in the stacks on the dense gray carpet and read about quantum physics and relativity, reminding her that women can do anything men can, and making pies every year on Pi Day. Her dad had always believed in her, her success was nothing but obvious to him, but her mom did the work to make sure it was possible: shuttling her around to Mathletes, baking cookies during study sessions, and poring over FAFSA applications when college came around. "Sounds delicious." Edie smiled.

"Anything new?" Her tone was cautious and Edie knew she was asking about dating.

"Nope."

"Ever hear from Chris? Chris was a good guy, kind. Don't you think?"

Chris was the only man who had ever told Edie he loved her. "Yes, he was, Mom." She and Chris had met while she was living in Manhattan. He lived eighty blocks due north of her East Village apartment and was the nicest person she had ever been with. "And if I'd married Chris, I'd have died of boredom. We had nothing to say to one another. You know that."

"Talking is overrated. You need a man who loves you and treats you well. Oh, hello!" Her voice was bubbly, cooing. "You want to talk to your sister? Edie, someone wants to talk to you."

A smile spread across Edie's face. She couldn't help it; she loved that dog. "Hiii, Lolly."

Lolly groaned, an adorable guttural moan that shouldn't come from a twelve-pound dog, but Lolly Pop was fourteen years old. "Someone misses her sister. Don't you Ms. Loll-a-ball?"

"I miss her, too," Edie said, remembering for a second how good love felt.

She could hear more banging, fainter now. She wished she were closer, or that she had more space so her mom could come to her. Even just one more room would do.

"Your father is in a mood, otherwise I'd get him. I'm sure he wants to talk to you."

She was being kind. A conversation between Edie and her father, though often pleasant and even loving, took an energy that both of them rarely had. "That's okay."

"We're going to watch our shows," her mom said, referring to her and Lolly.

"Please not *SVU* again."

"It puts me to sleep! I love you." She said it almost as a question, needing an answer.

"Love you, too, Mom. You too, Lol."

SHE WAS SCROLLING mindlessly, admiring the thick, amber hair of the girlfriend of the brother of the wife of her ex-boyfriend Chris, when Anaya's name flashed across her screen.

Edie's "generous message" had meant the world to her, she said, with two exclamation points. Edie's heart raced at the words, the exclamation points, immortalized on her screen like a digital trophy—real, accessible proof of their shared excitement. She felt that this casual correspondence was her life's greatest achievement, as if she were emailing with royalty. The next paragraph was longer.

> I was curious, since you resonated so much with my recent book, if you wanted a peek at some pages of my new book? I think you might like what I've been working on lately (or, rather, struggling with ☺)— the fourth chapter. It's about navigating what we really want as women, beyond men's approval. I'm writing through a trauma that shaped who I am, so I'll admit up front—it's raw! But it's impossible to write honestly about self-discovery without getting into it. No worries at all if that's too much. I so appreciate all your kind words, Edie.

Edie, having abandoned all shame in the fury of her excitement, wrote back promptly. She would absolutely love to read an excerpt, it sounded amazing, she wrote, then spent many minutes trying to think of a more sophisticated word than *amazing*, to no avail. She thanked her with two exclamation marks, and, mirroring Anaya, also signed her name with an *x*.

Chapter Six

SHE DIDN'T LET herself touch dating apps before noon. It felt desperate, like drinking in the morning. Instead, she swiped through the day's headlines on her phone as she waited for the coffee to drip. It had been two days, and still no email from Anaya, she checked every few minutes, clinging to the news for distraction. The familiar motion, the flick of a thumb as she jumped from one article to the next, was soothing.

It was easier to keep her head down. The bright yellow walls of Tixster felt like sun in her eyes. The air was stale and industrial but familiar. A crowd of beautiful people with thick glasses and monochromatic colors crowded the breakfast area. Some waited in line for coffee, others carried compostable cups from the shop next door.

All the news was bad since last year's election. Headlines about climate change, dwindling health care, the decline of democracy as we knew it. She skimmed the words without processing how bad it really was, for fear her day would be ruined before it began. She was scrolling quickly through her feed when she saw the photo.

Her face, her smile, her hair, even when it was pulled back, were unmistakable. Edie clicked the image before she had time to read the headline. Anaya's brown eyes hooked her like the first time they'd met. Something about the photo—old, out of place, meant for a refrigerator door not a national newspaper—made her avoid the text on her screen, the way you force your eyes away from the inevitable last line of a book on the final page. But she could only stare at the image for so long before her eyes shot up to the headline.

Anaya Thomas, Feminist Writer and Professor, Found Dead in Her San Francisco Home

The phone dropped from her hands. Edie grabbed it quickly and steadied herself while the full text of the article loaded. She clicked on the screen to make it go faster but an ad popped up instead and her phone was a lagging piece of shit and now the coffee had finished and people were crowding her so she raced to the bathroom and locked herself in a stall.

Anaya Thomas, 39, was found dead early this morning. Her body was discovered in her Outer Sunset apartment when she didn't show up for work. It appears as if Thomas died of a drug overdose. The details are still being investigated.

She read the full article three times. It had maddeningly little detail. She had been teaching at UCSF for the past five years, published three books, and was admired by students and faculty alike. She was a competitive runner who frequently raised money for causes. *A feminist writer, documenting women's struggles for years, only to find she was hiding those very struggles herself,* was the ungenerous closing line. Edie stared at the metal flap door that protected her from the rest of the world. Tears pricked behind her eyes, the words not fully sinking in, and she held them in a knot in her throat, as she walked in a haze back to her desk.

She was rereading the article, now on a bigger screen, when her phone buzzed.

Hey. Can we get dinner later? Need to talk.

"WHAT HAPPENED?" THE words came out slow and shaky. Peter was already seated at their usual Mexican restaurant. The food was never good, so the place was never crowded.

He put his hands up as if she were physically attacking him. "Calm down. You're looking at me like I did something." He nodded at the seat across from him.

"Sorry, this is all just . . ." There were no words. "I can't believe it." She threw her hoodie, damp with sweat and tears from the bike ride over, across the back of her chair and took a seat. Crying on a bike was the San Francisco version of crying on the New York subway, tears flowing in the anonymity of the bustling public, no nagging urge to pull it together.

"I know." He stared down at the table, ran his hands through his hair.

"You were just with her this weekend. Did you talk to her yesterday? This is all so fucked-up, I don't understand." She couldn't keep her thoughts straight.

When he finally looked up, she felt a wave of panic, like a child seeing her father frightened for the first time. "E, I saw her last night," Peter said, his voice low and strained.

"What?" She thought—hoped—she'd misheard him.

His face looked as if it were tied in the tightest of knots, as if the intensity of his pain had been cranked up as high as it would go. "I was at her place last night."

Edie took a breath. It was hard to swallow.

He sat silently, head back in his hands. A man came by and re-filled their water.

"Were you there when it happened?" The man had left and there was barely anyone in the restaurant but she kept her voice low. Partly to stay inconspicuous and partly because she didn't have the energy for more.

"Of course not!" he said quickly, meeting her eyes. "Jesus."

"Did you give her the drugs?"

Eyes back down to the table, shaking his head. "I didn't plan on doing drugs."

"What did you give her?" She spoke slowly, steadying each word with a breath.

"We did some ketamine. She had been asking about it the week-end before. I didn't think she'd want to do it that night, but I told her I'd bring some."

"And you did it with her?"

"It was fine, we were totally fine."

She felt tears resurface behind her eyes but shut them off like a faucet. A couple entered the restaurant, a few years younger than she and Peter, giggling as they took each other's bike helmets off. She felt an urge to hug the waiter for seating them on the other side of the room. "How much did you do?" Edie knew very little about drugs, but didn't know what else to ask.

"Just a bump or two." His head was shaking. "She was drink-ing tequila, but not much. Honestly, it was nothing dangerous." He paused, staring at the table. Even across the room she could hear the couple laughing. "It was a rough conversation and I just thought it'd be easier." He glanced at Edie.

She considered walking out of the restaurant but she wasn't sure if her knees could manage standing. "You ended things with her last night?"

"I just told her what you told me to say."

Edie waited, breathless.

"That I wasn't ready for anything serious."

She shivered. That fucking line. "Do not put this on me, Peter."

"E, she was fine. She actually seemed happy when we said goodbye." He seemed to be talking to himself. "I remember thinking how weird that was."

She forced herself to inhale. "So, if you were surprised at how 'fine' she seemed"—she could barely get the words out—"then you expected her not to be fine. You knew this would hurt her, but you still got high and then left?" She held her stomach as if that might help the impossible tightness.

After college she and Peter weren't regularly in touch. She lived in New York and he was working sixty-hour weeks at Primals. Even when she moved out to the Bay Area, she rarely saw him those first few years while she was in business school. There were sides of him—a selfish, almost willful ignorance that prioritized pleasure—she knew she didn't know well, a layer she'd noticed grow thicker as his life improved without interruption. The side of him Alex loved to point out and the side Edie loved to ignore.

He looked up, a new urgency in his face. "I didn't do this. You can't OD on the amount of K we took." His voice was steady but his eyes were tired. He really did look sad. "She was fine when I left, I have no idea how this happened."

She had to ask. "Did you have sex with her?"

The waiter arrived with their plates. "Jesus, Edie." He winced, shaking his head. He pulled the plate toward him, took a taco in his hand. "Nothing bad happened while I was there. You have to lay off, please." His eyes rested on the table.

She despised herself for making him feel worse—she, the first person he'd called when he needed someone. "I'm sorry, I know. I'm just trying to understand. It doesn't make any sense."

"Maybe . . ." He stopped himself. She waited. "Maybe it was intentional." His voice was unusually shaky. "She could have been planning this for a while. She was struggling with depression, I'm sure you know if you've read her books. She was dealing with a lot."

Edie felt an urge to flip their little wooden table over, but when she opened her mouth, her words were steady. "A lot of us are dealing with depression. Just because her work examined her mental health, doesn't mean she took her own life." She hated that he was putting this all on Anaya, though of course she had considered the same.

Edie had not pegged Anaya as the druggy type but drugs were hiding in plain sight in San Francisco. Companies did acid on corporate retreats. You could get weed at your corner store. It was all fine, a way to spark creativity, to chill out, to separate from everyday stressors. But like the city itself, with its rainbow Victorians hiding a monumental housing crisis and mountainous landscapes on the verge of destruction, there was a darkness beneath. Drugs were a way to keep it all feeling cool, but she'd seen friends spin out over too much coke, have terrible acid trips they never recovered from. Weekends blurred into continuous highs with no purpose other than the hazy comfort of indifference to make days dedicated to the shape of the Join Now button feel like they mattered.

A long silence passed between them.

"She didn't say anything about being upset, or feeling hopeless when she asked you for drugs?" She tried to sound gentle, but her nerves were a wreck. "It's kind of an insane coincidence that it happened the very night you . . ." She stopped herself. It was all so bad.

His eyes were firm. "It had nothing to do with me." He took a bite.

It wasn't strange for Peter to assume he was right, but he had always been willing to entertain an argument, welcomed a chance to self-examine, if only to further prove his righteousness. With Peter, logic prevailed. This frustrated most people, Nicole most of all, but Edie loved him for it. If she could just present the right information, she could crack him, like her own personal puzzle, and when she finally did, her pride was overwhelming.

But tonight, he seemed closed off, refusing to consider the smallest possibility that he might have made even a minor mistake. He was using his well of confidence not to debate but to insist. And the more he refused to explore his involvement, the more Edie was drawn to it.

"You realize the police are going to check her phone, see you were there, and be on your ass in like a minute."

"I didn't text her."

"What do you mean?"

"It wasn't planned. I'd just left another date that went really well." He shook his head, a woe-is-me kind of shake. "After that, I wanted to tell her as soon as possible that I couldn't commit, so I biked over."

Edie could see it all play like a movie in her mind. She pictured the joy on Anaya's face, the excitement she must have felt seeing Peter show up unannounced at her door. Maybe she was in sweats, maybe her hair was a mess, but she threw on a good tank top before she opened the door, tossed her hair in a bun. Or maybe she didn't, maybe she was secure enough not to care—probably she was. Edie imagined her opening the door, the two of them sharing a smile, the rush of knowing the feelings she'd had for Peter were valid, that their connection really was special, it wasn't all in her head.

She imagined her considering drugs, thinking she wanted to have fun with this guy who had probably encouraged it, a guy who seemed like he could really, maybe, be the one, telling herself to stop being so uptight, to enjoy herself, maybe giving herself a pep talk in the bathroom. She imagined the crushing pain of realizing the whole visit was a breakup. That he didn't want to commit, after all, for no other reason than he didn't have to. That no matter how good she was, no matter how much work she put into herself, it was all out of her control.

By the time Peter was done talking Edie couldn't help it, she was crying under the bright taqueria lights.

Chapter Seven

ANAYA WOULD NEVER kill herself over a man, of course not. By the time she biked home from her stupid dinner with stupid Peter, Edie was mortified by her own theory.

The steady sensation of pedaling, wind on her face, had allowed her mind to spin in the way that dreams, even the half-awake ones, flush the day's thoughts clean. She thought of Anaya's unfinished book, *the biggest trauma of her life*, she'd said, and the answer the night they met that had seemed absurd, unbelievable at the time—*maybe never*.

There was a bigger sadness there. There had to be.

SHE SPENT NEARLY an hour searching variations of Anaya's name on Instagram but, like the first time she'd tried, found nothing. Anaya's only social media accounts were Twitter and Facebook, it seemed, the latter of which was oddly public, but sparse and out of date, like a relic from a past life. It made sense, if Edie put herself in Anaya's mind, which had become second nature in the past week, that Anaya preferred to avoid Instagram. Its reliance on imagery had never been good, a sea of comparison that called Edie in like quicksand.

She opened Twitter, instead. It felt wrong to see Anaya's photo, her bio, her location, all presented as if she were still here. She had just over three thousand followers, which, though far more than Edie's one hundred and two (mostly bot) following, struck her as low for someone with three books. Her pinned tweet, a link to her most recent book, had only twenty-eight likes. A profound sadness swept over Edie at the thought that the world had not appreciated her work.

A gust outside shook her window. She took Anaya's books into bed. They felt different now, ghostly. Her throat tightened as she read over the lines she'd marked with shy, almost invisible pencil. Like the first time she read them, she felt as if she were learning a language with each sentence, one that lived inside of her but had never found its way out. Like whatever made up the soul, or whatever, had found its way onto the page and in reading it now, she was learning who she was.

But now she wasn't just trying to learn about herself, she needed to learn about Anaya. Edie didn't like to admit it—she hated the thought of Anaya experiencing the day-to-day pain that would drive someone to take their own life—but, deep down, she hoped Peter was right. That her death had been planned. Not only because that would exonerate him, but because it meant Anaya had made her own choice.

She needed to know what had put her over the edge. And the question pricked at her like an itch in a cast, familiar, close, and impossible to scratch—why that night?

The wind outside was relentless. No one liked to admit that San Francisco was actually freezing unless you stood squarely in the sun so her shaded apartment was always arctic. She turned on her space heater and moved to the floor in front of it, brought her fuzzy blanket and books and computer, which she had reopened immediately after closing, with her. With each click through Anaya's old Facebook photos, Edie found herself searching for proof of sadness. She wanted to know that the deep sensation that made her own heart and nerves feel cloaked in a thick wet blanket most of the time was not weird or wrong, that Anaya had felt it, too, but more so—on a bigger, bolder level like everything else about her—and had made a choice.

Edie didn't want to kill herself, but she certainly understood the impulse. She knew that she could slip into the temptation because when she imagined it, she felt a deep encompassing relief. But she also knew that her mom needed her, so she tried her best to avoid the thought.

She was constantly setting rules like this for herself—concrete and enforceable. She refused to eat cheese or nuts, too fatty; just one bite and she'd never stop. She never touched a cigarette because even just holding one in her hand comforted her, like a baby with a bottle. Instead, she chewed three packs of gum a day, two pieces at a time. Though Peter had more drugs than he knew what to do with, she had never dabbled. It all seemed too good to be true and she was certain her life would spin out of control if she tried. Self-harm was in her blood.

It was almost 2 a.m.—a list of facts about Anaya's life and death organized into a tagged and sorted spreadsheet—when she reopened Twitter. Her eyes were tired but her brain couldn't rest. Most of Anaya's posts were re-tweets from other women writers and linked articles, which Edie saved to read later. But, then, just a week ago she had posted a link to a protest for abortion rights. Edie's eyes lingered on the tweet, the date, as if trying to bring her back to life. The protest was this coming weekend. Her tweet read "I'll be here!" As recently as a week ago, she had planned to be alive.

A sprawling sense of urgency spread over her. "That man will be the end of you," Alex had said when Edie crashed her bike trying to text him back. Alex was an intuitive person, with interesting friends and real, functional relationships. Surely, she was a better judge of Peter's character than Edie, who couldn't last a day without checking if he had any new followers. Edie didn't think he was *the reason* Anaya took her life. But maybe, there was a chance, he'd been the breaking point.

———

SHE WAS DRIPPING with sweat by the time she'd reached the Outer Sunset. It didn't occur to her to physically go there—asking Peter for Anaya's address was out of the question—until she'd spotted the street signs on a photo taken outside her house in an article that morning. And if she had the address, well, she needed a run anyway.

Of course, the tweet could have meant nothing. It wasn't like Anaya had some dire obligation to the two people who—god bless them—had liked the post. But the whole thing had left her so fundamentally unsettled that, on four hours of sleep, even the smallest indication that her death hadn't been intentional felt urgent.

Anaya's entire street was blocked off. It was a familiar run, up the Panhandle and through the park, but it was unseasonably warm and Edie had overdressed, so as not to show too much skin in front of the authorities. There was a sign for Oat Milk Matchas on the corner. The coffee shop had a new wooden exterior that looked out of place next to the chipped purple paint of the deli beside it. She ducked in to grab a cold brew with almond milk, hating herself a little for allowing her routines and tastes to be shaped by the trends venture capitalists had puppeteered, but she didn't have the energy to resist.

She caught her breath in the corner of the café, sipping her gentrified coffee steadily and watching the uneventful scene unfold as she plotted her next move. A man and a woman, both in police uniforms, were maneuvering cones around the street. It was unclear whether there was any real purpose to this exercise—the area was already blocked off—but it seemed to keep them busy.

A man, at least a decade older than Edie, walked over to the couple. He was wearing a suit, which felt absurd, like he was an actor on set but the rest of the cast had abandoned him. Police uniforms were one thing, but she couldn't remember the last time she saw a real business suit in broad daylight. It made Edie sad, that he still felt he needed to dress up like this for his job, which he probably hated anyway. He began talking to the cone-couple and they all started to laugh like old friends. It made Edie queasy, this playful, costumed performance in front of Anaya's house.

She walked toward the site.

"Hi, excuse me," she mumbled, first to the woman who had a kind, round face, but who either didn't hear her or was pretending as much. Then louder, to the man in the business suit, who turned to face her. "What's going on?" she asked.

"A death," the man said with a deep, gruff voice. "It's still under investigation."

"That's awful." She tried to act surprised. "What happened?" Though she'd practiced the lines the whole run over, as the words left her mouth, she felt both the need to laugh and a deep desire to run home. She bit her lip to get a grip.

The suited man walked toward her. On closer inspection, he looked nearer to her own age. She was always depressed to learn that real people with real jobs—doctors, police, whatever this man was, the people who made the world run—were her age, a reminder that she should be doing something useful. Instead, she was making Tixster Pages.

"Unclear," the man said to her as the other two officers continued to chat.

Edie swallowed a large sip of cold brew. She noticed the man's eyes glance down to her body and she realized how ridiculous she must have looked, a grown woman dripping with sweat, her curls damp and matted in a pathetically thin ponytail.

"Do you know how she died exactly?" Edie pried. She wasn't sure what she was looking for—a suicide note, the drugs she'd OD'd on—anything that confirmed it had nothing to do with Peter.

His eyes jumped back to hers. "So you know a little about this, then?"

"What? No. I just saw the tape and the cones."

"How'd you know it was a 'her'?"

Edie had to smile and this small crack of emotion felt like releasing a valve, as if she could finally breathe.

"I saw something in the papers about a woman who overdosed. I guess I just figured this must be it. It doesn't happen every day around here."

"You'd be surprised," he said, and scanned the block from one end to the next.

Edie followed his eyes but there was nothing to look at. "Was it a suicide?" she asked after a short pause. She didn't want him to leave before she got something out of him.

She could have sworn he rolled his eyes. "It's unclear if it was accidental or intentional. It's under investigation."

Unclear. Investigation. She tried to stay calm, think of something else to say.

He scanned her, eyes narrowed, then looked away. "If you hear anything, feel free to give me a call," he said, and with a movement so fluid she barely saw him take it from his pocket, he handed her his card.

She had never run as fast as she ran home; she felt it in her stride and confirmed it with her app once she'd reached her door. Her feet flew in a way that was only possible when her mind was absorbed, unconcerned with physical pain and the mundane inconveniences of her body. If the police were involved, then the cause of death wasn't clear, something, as Edie had suspected, wasn't right. When she reached her apartment, she read the card. *Ron Boilston, Lead Investigator.*

Chapter Eight

ALEX TAUGHT YOGA at Tixster every Tuesday, thanks to Edie's persistent plea to the HR department. At the front of an empty, mirrored room that reminded Edie of a dance studio for children, Alex bent her body with ease. Her voice was so different from the typical Tixster tone, a forceful competition of competency. Alex was both firm and indifferent, using a take-it-or-leave-it kind of voice so comforting that Edie nearly fell asleep in her pose. She appreciated yoga the way she appreciated stretching before a run—nice, but hardly exercise. But she had only gotten three hours of sleep last night due to her obsessive research and today she could barely manage a downward dog.

Alex was like a rock star at Tixster. Droves of young women who Edie didn't recognize—sales and marketing, maybe—raced up to her after every class, asking where she practiced, who her favorite teachers were. But Alex didn't actually care about yoga beyond the fact that people paid her to do it. She often complained that the whole industry had become a farce to make people feel good about themselves by throwing money at their health. She laughed at the women who spent hundreds of dollars on leggings and mats. All Alex cared about was her art. Her yoga mat was a hand-me-down, her clothes from Goodwill. This made Tixster women love her even more.

Edie watched them crowd around Alex, all but drooling, from her perch outside the mirrored room. Alex's head was nodding continuously until, eventually, she pried herself away.

"Good job today," Alex said, leaning into Edie's shoulder.

"Shut up," she laughed, knowing she had barely moved. The crowd that had previously encircled Alex walked past them like a group of schoolgirls. "Any of them asked you out yet?"

"Tixster women are not my type," Alex smiled.

Edie knew better than to feel insulted by this, but she did anyway.

"So, what the fuck happened?" Alex asked once they were out on the street, walking mechanically to their usual lunch spot.

"Al, it's insane. The woman he went out with di—" She didn't want to say it. "She OD'd. I still can't believe it." Her throat was tight. "It's terrible."

"Jesus." She put her hand on Edie's back and held her close for a few sidewalk squares.

"I'm so sorry."

"It's insane. They had just met, and she seemed amazing."

"And they were dating?"

"He wasn't looking for a relationship," Edie clarified. "You know, after Nicole. But they'd hung out a bunch. She was a feminist writer; you would have loved her. She was super smart, but warm, too, not pretentious or trying too hard. She was all about feminism but not in an uptight way, you know, she had a sense of humor about the world and herself." She was aware she was rambling but couldn't seem to stop herself. "And she just seemed interested in other people. Like she was genuinely happy to meet me and talk about women in tech, even though she probably talks about that stuff all the time being a feminist professor in San Francisco. I don't know, it's like it . . ." Edie trailed off, shaking her head, still unable to make sense of anything, feeling as if nothing was real.

Alex's eyes were wide. "You met her?"

"I know it's weird."

"Um, yeah. I don't know why Peter involves you in his life so much."

"It's not *that* weird. I had just finished a bad date and Peter wanted to get my opinion."

"He wastes so much of your time, E. And now my time." She pulled her fleece tighter. "Does he have any idea what happened? The poor woman."

"No," Edie started. She wasn't planning to tell Alex but it had been bouncing inside her and she needed to let it out. "Al, he was over at her house the night it happened."

Alex didn't flinch. "I fucking hate that guy. He has a real darkness, I'm telling you."

"Don't hate him," Edie begged, shielding herself from the bitter downtown wind. He could be shallow, sure, she'd give Alex that, but Edie never understood Alex's knee-jerk disdain.

"Technically, I said I fucking hate him," Alex clarified.

"He and I are like the same person. If you hate him, you essentially hate me, too."

Alex turned to her. "Don't say that. Please never say that again."

"We're very similar people. And he didn't do anything to that woman."

"Dude, I know he helped you with Matt, and you guys were like computer engineering buddies or whatever, but the way you've experienced the world and the way he has is entirely different. I know you want to believe you're made from the same cloth or something, but you are *not* the same." Her cheeks glistened and she swiped the remaining yoga sweat from her brow. "And that's a compliment." She smiled wide, revealing the adorable gap in her teeth.

The wind was always bad downtown but today it felt brutal. "Sure. I get that our lives are different. You don't have to remind me how spoiled he is."

"You don't find it odd," Alex went on and Edie could tell she was gearing up for one of her speeches, "that you both had the same exact major from the same exact school and he's a big shot millionaire at a tech giant and you're still paying back your student loans?"

Most of what Edie had learned about feminism she'd learned from Alex, but sometimes Alex took it too far, like she was giving up her power by blaming everything on men, like she had no free will. "I *chose* to leave tech and work at Safe Home."

"Exactly." Edie could see Alex raise her eyebrows through the corner of her eye. "Because you actually care about shit. In like a real, change-your-life, make-sacrifices kind of way. And you know why? Because domestic violence is a real thing *you* have to worry about. It's real to you in a way that Peter can ignore."

All Edie could think was that this sounded like the third chapter in Anaya's first book. Edie nodded. "Fine." Anaya would have liked Alex, she thought, a lump lodged in her throat.

They turned the corner and the sun popped through. Edie unzipped her hoodie. "Who knows what that man is capable of," Alex continued. "I'm just saying, he gets away with a *lot*. And most people can't."

"That's not his fault, Al." She appreciated that she could fight with Alex.

Alex laughed, low and breathy. "It is if he takes advantage of it."

THEIR USUAL SALAD place was packed. The neighborhood couldn't build bougie lunch places quickly enough. "I hate that I hate this city now," Alex said, looking through the glass window as if she were at the zoo. The line wrapped around the plastic tables like a snake. Alex took Edie's hand as they shuffled forward. "I'm so sorry this happened."

"Next!"

Edie didn't like to waste calories on lunch—or brain power on decisions—so had calculated the most filling, least caloric option—spinach, grilled chicken, veggies, and vinegar—and stuck to it. She scanned the faces in line while Alex studied the ingredients, then placed her order—everything except olives, ranch dressing. Everyone was around the same age, all slightly different versions of each other, most of them close to a decade younger than Edie. The people her age were either home with kids or making enough money to have someone pick up their food for them. Even getting lunch felt like failure.

The group in front of them was loud and wore matching sweatshirts stamped with a unicorn on the breast. There were a lot of self-righteous logos in San Francisco but to stamp a literal unicorn on your own shirt was bold, even for this city. They looked fresh out of college, unburdened. A tall boy with a pinched face was ordering in a louder than necessary voice. "Wait, you don't have quinoa?" He was looking up at the menu with cartoonish disbelief. "Are we even in California?" he scoffed. "This is wild!"

With a glance, Alex and Edie exchanged their unbearable embarrassment. But before he could continue, the woman closest to them pulled at his hood. "Aaron," she whispered, "shut up and order." The woman was sporting a unicorn hoodie, too, but somehow it worked for her, like an ironic prop. Edie stared at the back of her neck; her hair, short and clean, was the same cut she'd want if her hair wasn't so unruly. As the woman turned to walk away, Edie noticed her eyes, red and puffy, and hollowness in her face, as if she weren't all there.

"She's hot," Alex whispered as they walked toward their seats, not hiding the fact that she was now eyeing the woman intently. Edie gave a small grunt of agreement but it was always hard for her to distinguish between wanting to sleep with a woman or just wanting to be her. Having never tried the former she assumed her desire was simply envy or admiration. Edie had never thought she was gay, but then she had never really allowed herself to consider it. The idea of resetting her entire sexual framework after all the work she'd put into figuring out men was so exhausting she shut it down before the thought had time to settle.

Edie paid for the salads, then grabbed a stack of napkins large enough to reveal her East Coast sensibility and searched for Alex, who had snagged a table by the window.

"Thank you," Alex said, drawing out the *u* and taking her salad.

"Anyway, he had nothing to do with the death," Edie said, forcing them back to Peter.

Alex shook her head, not so much at that specific notion, but at the topic of Peter altogether. She picked a stray olive off her salad and placed it on a napkin. "So did you decide, are you doing the egg freezing?"

Edie had forgotten all about her appointment. "Shit, yes." She checked her phone. "Fuck. My first appointment is this week." Putting the kind of time and money that egg freezing required into something as simple as having children, something that seemed so easy for everyone else in the world, felt like a tax on her already miserable single status. "Would you consider it? Maybe we can do it together?"

Alex laughed so loud the guys at the table next to them turned. "Like I could afford that."

For all her degrees, Edie could be an absolute moron and, in that moment, she wanted to crawl under her wobbly plastic chair. "Sorry," she mumbled.

"Anyway," Alex continued, "kids are nothing but a resource suck, like all the other high-end hobbies in this city. Just something for boring people to throw their money at so they can feel less boring."

Alex was always involved in a dozen different art projects, paint cans and photo prints strewn around her loft. She scraped by on odd jobs—tutoring children, private yoga sessions—whatever she could find in the gig economy to pay for her art. Edie loved this about her. Not her art, necessarily, Edie couldn't tell a grade-school project from a masterpiece if she tried, but her ability to be fully obsessed with her own ideas. To be certain about what it was she wanted and do whatever it took to keep going.

Edie laughed, embarrassed; she didn't disagree. "I just want to squeeze all the money I can out of Tixster." She thought of her conversation with Anaya. *It took a long time for me to realize I didn't want kids*, she'd said. Edie had read accounts of women who definitively did not want children, and those who absolutely did. But there were far fewer stories about the grueling process of deciding. A new wave of grief, for Anaya's unpublished book, hit her as she shoveled down another forkful of spinach.

Chapter Nine

EDIE PULLED PETER into the corner of the party to tell him. The freedom of not having to worry about Nicole was intoxicating. She could be sloppy with the amount of time she let her hand rest on his chest, the way she grabbed his biceps to emphasize a point. She could swear he felt it, too, the way his eyes lingered on hers like no one else in the room mattered.

She'd apologized over text for getting so mad at dinner. He apologized in turn. He was going through a lot. He had cared about Anaya and didn't know how to process everything. He was looking forward to seeing Edie at the party.

She had chosen a colorful button-down top like the one Anaya had worn the night they'd met, although she didn't have the guts to button it to the top, so reliant on the idea of "showing skin" had she become. Patterns, jewelry, color, made her feel like she stood out, like she was trying to look pretty, which inevitably rendered her pathetic because she never really did. But tonight, she felt bold and feminine in her turquoise blouse with white and pink stripes.

Peter, as always, had brought a fancy bottle of wine, even to a house party, where no one knew the difference. But she couldn't be bothered with wine tonight. She grabbed a stray bottle of vodka from the party's drink table and lured Peter to the corner.

"There's a detective investigating the case," she whispered once they were safely in the far end of the living room, away from the DJ and the crowds. She took a sip of vodka. She had skipped dinner, knowing there would be snacks and that once she was drunk, she would eat them all, so the alcohol hit quickly.

Peter smiled at her like a father smiling at a toddler. "Makes sense. What's your point?"

Edie shoved him, letting her hands rest a little too long on his chest, the cotton of his shirt soft and familiar. "Peter, it could be serious. What if they want to talk to you?"

"Edie, stop!" He grabbed both of her arms, shook her a little, and chills ran down her back at the feeling of being touched. "Don't get obsessed with this case." He let go and scanned the room. "How do you know anyway?" he asked, leaning against the wall, opening up their conversation for all to see.

Edie stepped in front of him to close their circle. "I met him."

"What the fuck?" He was nearly screaming, all trace of his previous cool gone, and she felt ridiculous. "Where? *How?*"

"Dude, chill. I was jogging. I happened to cross the de—" She couldn't say *death*, as if uttering the word would make it worse. But it was already worse. "The site."

"You went to her house? Were you running a goddamn marathon?"

"You know I run a lot." Edie shrugged. Running was her loophole—a socially acceptable way to stay thin so she'd stop starving herself like she did back in college. Peter knew this, had always sensed when she needed help and had been there to listen, assuring her she was perfect as she was, but now he gave her a look—a plea of sorts not to bring her addictions into this.

"Okay, whatever." He sighed. "Just don't get involved in the case. I *beg* you." He knew what she was capable of.

She took another shot of vodka and felt his hand on her shoulder as she swallowed. He rubbed it a little in the spot she liked best, just left of her neck. She leaned into him, breathed in the scent that felt like home.

"It's tragic, obviously. But there's nothing to find out, is all I'm saying."

She pulled away, just enough to face him. "I just don't understand how you're not more curious about what happened."

"She had an interest in drugs, I told you she was asking about them. And I think she was probably struggling." He waved his hands as if they were playing charades. "Mentally, you know, emotionally." Edie shook her head. "It's terrible, but if there's an investigator, I'm sure they'll figure that out. I feel awful, but it happens."

The room was filling up. People were looking at them. If anyone was actually engaged in real conversation at one of these parties, people looked on with suspicion and envy. What generally ensued was empty chatter, shouting above the DJ, or just being quiet and dancing next to someone like it meant something. She smiled meekly at their spectators, then turned her back to the crowd. "Aren't you nervous, though, that they'll think you were involved?" The more sure he was that he didn't have to worry, the more compelled she was to fight him.

"I'm nervous about how much *you* think I'm involved. Does that count?"

"I'm serious." The vodka was making it easy for her to avoid the sadness that now flooded her unpredictably. "I would be freaking out if this happened right after I saw someone. It's shaking me now, and I didn't even *date* her."

Peter's face softened for the first time since it had happened, back to the Peter she knew. In college he was always the one who pulled the quiet engineers out of their video-game shells, cracking jokes at his own expense, digging for a thread of shared interest to open them up.

"Look, I get it," he said with a serious calm. "I told you I've been freaking out ever since I heard. I didn't go to work today. It's killing me. I had to take two Xanax to sleep last night."

Who was she to judge what his grief looked like, of course it looked perfect and painted on, he was perfect-looking. To think this didn't affect him was cruel, a betrayal.

"But she couldn't have died from the K we did together. I was there and she was fine. And I don't think I said anything hurtful." He looked at her with desperate eyes. "I can't let it haunt me. It's not my fault. I didn't do anything wrong."

It was a physical pain in her stomach, this inexplicable doubt in Peter's stance, that made her feel as if she might throw up. The vodka didn't help. She wanted to bottle up his assuredness and take it like a pill. She touched his chest, the pull of him overwhelming. Everyone she had ever loved she had also, at some point, wanted to be. She wanted Peter's confidence most of all. She knew if she were in his shoes, she wouldn't be able to *stop* asking herself what she did wrong. And she knew she wouldn't be the only one asking.

EDIE OFTEN FELL asleep playing back that night with Matt, wondering how she might have set him off. Peter was the one who begged her to go to the police—he almost walked down to the station himself. But she made him promise not to.

It wasn't until she graduated and moved to New York, got a job, settled into a normal routine, and started dating the gold-hearted Chris, that it came back to haunt her.

It was a regular day, sunny with the kind of cool, crisp air that's taken for granted in San Francisco but felt like heaven cracked open on a spring day in New York. She was ordering her regular coffee at her regular bodega on her way to work when she glanced down at the newspaper rack, as she did every morning back when people still looked to papers for the news. When she saw Matt's face staring up at her from the bottom corner of the *New York Post* she dropped her steaming cup all over the grimy linoleum floor. She jumped away from the rack as if there was a snake on the ground, apologized for the spill, and ran out of the store. With each step toward the train her feet grew heavier, slower, until she couldn't move an inch more. She hadn't made it a block before she turned back and bought a paper.

Three different women had accused Matt of assault and because his father was running for reelection, it was all over the news. Edie called in sick from the sidewalk outside the bodega, trying to fold the too-large pages into place against the light wind. Five years had passed since the night in her dorm room and she felt shamefully giddy reading their accounts, as if their words allowed her to believe herself, to admit the devastation she'd felt was real. At the same time, it made her nauseous, the idea that her own silence could have caused this.

Peter coached her back to life, repeating over and over, night after night, through the spotty service of their flip phones, that it wasn't her fault. He was the only one she could talk to about it, the only one who knew about Matt. She felt too ashamed to admit it to anyone else.

The papers stopped covering the case, so she submitted public record requests from the court and they mailed her updates when there was progress. She read about the women who testified. One worked at a bar and wore a "tight, eye-catching uniform," according to the transcript. Never mind that she was required to wear it for her job, the point was that she was signaling interest. Another woman was very drunk when it happened, as was Matt, according to his story, and it was impossible to tell what she'd communicated in the moment. The third woman had been seeing him regularly. The familiarity of her plea was so striking that Edie felt as if she were walking on ice as she read it. After two months of restless nights and distracted days, the case was deemed a mistrial. It would start all over again.

Edie switched her business school application from Columbia to Stanford. It wasn't hard, for all their prestige, the form was shamelessly similar. The idea of the West Coast had been in the back of her mind since graduation. She had been dating Chris for a year, he'd just told her he loved her and wanted to move in together. She didn't know what she wanted, but she knew she didn't want that. She saw their life play out: two people smiling at each other from opposite ends of the table, conversation fueled by logistics alone. She wanted someone with fire, someone she could fight with, someone who pushed her to be better, not just loved her for who she was.

Peter had moved to San Francisco after college. She watched his life grow like a plant in the sun, while hers seemed to stay the same, or maybe even shrivel. She couldn't imagine not being near her mother in Upstate New York, but Matt's case felt like an alarm; it was time to leave. Even if Matt was convicted, he was in the air, and she couldn't stay waiting for it to happen.

Chris begged her to stay, even proposed. But the more he begged the more confident she was in leaving. Anyone who needed her that much was not someone she wanted to be with. His love felt foreign and uncomfortable. Surely, this was rooted in her father, who she'd adored and then, in a sense, had abandoned her. But just because she knew she craved difficult, unpredictable men, didn't mean she could change it. For better or worse, she needed someone who would make her prove her worth, and Chris would never be that cruel.

She paid a fee to continue receiving alerts on the case, but for a long time heard nothing. Eventually she began to check her mailbox without dread. The air in California helped. It was sharp and fresh and felt like another planet from New York. She was almost a year into Stanford when she got a familiar envelope with a New York return address. Seeing it made her feel like she was being watched. She locked her apartment door and called Peter, opening it with him on the line. When she read the verdict, she thought she must be reading it wrong.

"What does it say?" Peter repeated.

He had only gotten two years—less, pending good behavior and community service.

PRESENTLY, PETER LOOKED at Edie with his big green eyes. "I have to let this go, E. Which means I need *you* to let it go." He bent his head down toward hers. "We can't blame ourselves for everything, we have to move on." His eyes said what his words did not. This was his case, not hers. If he didn't want to take this any further, she wouldn't make him.

Another shot of vodka, this time for both of them. Music was playing out in the garage, better music than when they'd arrived, which had mostly been some digitized synth stuff. But now hip-hop rang through the house and Edie wanted to dance.

"Garage?" she asked nodding toward the back.

"Definitely."

Peter snorted some coke and politely held it up for Edie but all she could think about was Anaya. They danced hard and grew sweaty. Every so often a woman eyeing Peter would cut in and distract him, but he always found his way back to her. Pressing against his familiar shape, she could not understand why this closeness between them couldn't extend beyond the walls of the garage, to her bed, for example, for the night and then forever.

The dance floor eventually emptied and Peter ordered them a car. Out on the sidewalk the wind was piercing and the car was late. He opened his arms, inviting her into his coat to shield her.

"Why do we ever come to the East Bay?" Edie grumbled, taking in his old Ivory smell.

"Seriously," he laughed. "We only talk to each other anyway. We should just dance on my couch like old times."

"Sounds perfect to me."

"Now that Nicole's not around telling us to keep it down." He peeked down at her.

She smiled up at him from the nook she was nuzzled in.

A shiny black car pulled up to the curb and he opened the door for her to slide in. She stayed curled against his neck, his hand around her shoulder for the length of the silent ride. When the car reached her house, she gave him a long hug goodbye and he held her with tight, steady arms.

"Night, E," he said into her ear.

"Night, Peter." As she turned, he took her hand.

"Please," he said, squeezing her fingers in his. "Drop the case. It's not healthy."

"I know." She smiled and hopped quickly out of the car.

ANAYA'S FACEBOOK PAGE had eight new posts, but nothing out of the ordinary. There were a few co-workers offering sympathy, two students, and then, buried in a reply to a comment, was a woman with the same surname—a family member, as far as Edie could tell.

Anaya was mostly raised by a single mom who died when she was a young adult. She had written about it briefly in her last book, but the details were never specified. This Facebook post was the first she'd seen or heard about a living family member. If she could understand Anaya's sadness, wrap her hands around it and see it, maybe her intention that night would become clear. She clicked the image.

This woman—Leah, according to her profile—was unmistakably related to Anaya. She had the same restrained smirk, and smiling, knowing eyes. But her hair was short, a pixie cut, and her frame was wider, boxier. She wore a button-up shirt with a blazer in her photo. She looked painfully familiar.

All of Leah's social media profiles were private. She couldn't see any posts at all. She could, however, see that Leah lived in San Francisco, according to her bio. Edie clicked back to Anaya's page and scoured it for any signs of this woman, but found nothing.

She typed *Leah Thomas San Francisco* into a new search window and found that she was a lead engineer at a tech start-up downtown. Datsta was some data mining company for advertisers. Edie had heard of it. They recently got a big Series A investment, and the concept had creeped her out. Their offices were in SoMa, like every other tech company, including Tixster.

Edie had assumed Anaya was an only child. It struck her as odd that she hadn't included much about her family in any of her books, given how open she was about everything else. But she supposed the repercussions of writing about the self were isolated, while inviting others into the story risked throwing them into a fire they had no part in starting.

Edie clicked back to Anaya's profile photo, which had also been her online dating photo, the photo Peter had sent only a few weeks earlier. She could almost make out the tiny pores on Anaya's beautiful skin, had nearly memorized the slight curve of her upper lip, as if she were in on a secret. Edie always smiled wide like a goon in photos. She practiced more tempered poses in the mirror but when it came down to it, she felt so ridiculous being photographed that she'd inevitably burst into laughter out of sheer embarrassment the moment the camera snapped.

Anaya looked poised, controlled. A chill ran through Edie as she clicked through her pictures until she got to the end and then clicked back again. She had performed this ritual dozens of times by now. Like an old mixtape, she knew the sequence by heart.

Chapter Ten

RON ANSWERED THE phone as if he'd just answered two hundred calls in row.

"Yeah?" he asked.

"Hi!" She could hear herself overcompensate for his gruffness with a grating friendliness. "We met at the crime scene the other day?" She swallowed. She didn't mean to say the word *crime*. "I mean, the site of . . ."

"Yep. What can I do for you?"

His tone was harsh and to the point.

"I was wondering if I could interview you about the case." She didn't want to get Peter in trouble, of course not, but Ron didn't have to know they were friends, and Ron had, in fact, given her his card, essentially asking to continue contact.

"Oh god. You're a reporter." There was something like disgust in his voice.

"No, no, I'm not," she assured him. "I'm just interested in these kinds of cases."

"So am I," he said flatly.

It was times like these that Edie wished she were the kind of woman whose beauty ingratiated her to other people. "I'd love to ask you just a few questions." She paused, and then added, "If that's possible, please."

"The case is confidential, lady."

She bristled. *Lady*, felt unnecessary.

"There must be some details that are open to the public." She knew this from Matt's case. It was shocking what you could find if you asked.

"Not much while the investigation is open," he grumbled. "But you can come by my office this evening. We'll talk." She couldn't tell if she'd been right and he actually had information to share or if he was just messing with her, wasting her time the way she was wasting his. Either way, she'd take it.

RON'S OFFICE WAS a living archive, like the deep corner of a library. He was heads down in papers and uncomfortably well dressed like the first time she'd met him. This time, though, his jacket was off, tossed over his chair, and his white shirtsleeves were cuffed. He looked better.

If she had any sense at all she would have dressed in something other than her gray T-shirt and stupid skinny jeans that looked like children's leggings, a rip around the belt loop where she'd pulled too hard getting them on. He looked stronger than she had remembered, more intimidating. If she was honest, she remembered him kind of soft, but now in the context of his desk, jacket off, she could make out the bumps in his upper arms, the lines in his forearms.

People rarely "worked out" in San Francisco. People were "active." Gym memberships were scoffed at but spending hundreds of dollars on a biking getup was commonplace. Up close, Ron looked like he hit the gym daily, like he was of another tribe.

Edie hung awkwardly in the doorway hoping he'd notice, but his eyes were glued to his papers, so she knocked lightly on the frame.

"You." It wasn't the greeting she'd hoped for. His eyes were lasers scanning her up and down, narrowing into slits. "You look different when you're not covered in sweat."

She forced an awkward laugh, grateful for what she allowed herself to assume was a compliment.

"Take a seat." He nodded to the chair across from him, which was full of folders. She stared at it wondering whether or not to move them until he noticed her hovering and transferred them sloppily onto his desk.

"Let's get one thing out of the way," he started, relaxing into his wooden chair. He looked at her the same way he had at the site, a playful, challenging look. "Why the hell do you care so much about this case? Was she a friend?" he added, as if giving her a hint.

She wanted to say yes and make it easy for the both of them, but she was a terrible liar. She had practiced her reason on the way over. She would tell the truth, just not the whole truth.

"I only met her once," she started. "But we really clicked. It's so hard making friends as an adult, especially in this city." She saw a nod from Ron. "When we met, I don't know, it just felt like we'd be friends for a very long time. You don't feel that often. And I'm a huge fan of her work." She caught her breath, crossed her legs. "I just want to know what happened." She could hear how weak it sounded, but what she could not say was that she worried her best friend had somehow, *maybe*—probably not, but she needed to be sure—driven Anaya to her death.

Ron looked skeptical, like he might kick her out. She pulled her seat closer before he could respond and took out her notebook. "Can you disclose anything about the case at this point?" she asked.

He exploded into laughter. "Oh lady." He kept laughing. "Of course not."

"Can you say what drugs she died of?" Edie tried.

"No."

"Is it possible to have a copy of the death certificate?"

He smiled. "If you want to wait two months, you can certainly request one. But if you think they'll list anything specific as the cause of death, you're dreaming."

She scanned the questions in her notebook, trying to find one that might open him up.

"Have any signs come up that she had a history of suicidal thoughts?" It seemed so unlike Anaya, but at least if this was a repeated attempt, it was less likely Peter was to blame.

"I'll tell you this because it's public knowledge. She had no history of drug use."

Edie's swallow was loud. Peter thought she had taken more drugs after he'd left. But why would she have drugs if she had no history of using them?

"And without a history of drug use, accidental overdoses are less common, which points to some intentionality. But there are a million factors that go into this, we just don't know."

"Can you tell me if anyone else was involved?"

He sat up straight as if a string had pulled him. "No comment on suspect." The use of the word *suspect*—not a dismissal of the idea but acknowledgment of it as a possibility—and the firmness in his voice made her jaw clench.

His office was decorated with certificates of merit, and she could see a gun poking out of the holster on his belt. He dealt with death all day. Edie imagined herself as he saw her and felt foolish.

"I'm sorry." She didn't want to take this route, but it poured out of her. "It's just scary." She looked down at her dirty sneakers. "To be a single woman and then you hear something like this and you wonder . . ." She stopped herself and looked up.

Ron's expression relaxed but only slightly. There were fewer lines on his face and his back no longer arched like a bow, ready to pop up and throw her out.

"Look," he said, throwing his feet on the desk. Edie pretended not to notice the cracks, worn deeply, on the bottom of his shoe. That he had to wear such a formal uniform, but could hardly afford a decent pair of shoes, filled her with tenderness toward him. "It was a pretty typical overdose. Maybe she intended it, maybe she didn't. Without a note it's hard to tell."

"So, there was no note."

He didn't like that. "Have you seen a note written about in the news?"

"No."

"Then no note has been reported."

"Got it."

He glanced at her notebook with what could only be described as pity. "If you ask me, a smart girl like that knew what she was doing. But families like to be sure about these things."

She steadied her breath. She had wanted to bring up Anaya's family and now he had done it for her. "Is her family in San Francisco?" She tried to make it sound like an afterthought.

He looked disappointed. "I'm not going to give you private information about the vic's family."

The single syllable made her feel exposed and desperate, like he knew she was a mess and was stabbing her with his professionalism. "What does her family think it might be?" They had real facts, they must, and if it was a straightforward OD, a bottle of Tylenol or something obvious, they probably wouldn't be asking so many questions.

"That's not your problem." An ambulance roared in the distance. He turned toward the window and she could see his face soften. "Suicide is very underreported in overdoses. We have to declare it unintentional unless there's hard evidence, and, unfortunately, that's often hard to pinpoint . . ." He trailed off, turned back to her. "But there are a few things that indicate there might be something else at play."

Edie perked up and uselessly wrote the words in her notebook. "Like what?"

He laughed again. She was getting used to being laughed at. "I'll indulge you because you seem desperate." She was more pleased than offended. "There may have been someone else with her when it happened." His brown eyes seemed to scan every piece of her as she registered this deliberately vague statement and she considered that he might be very good at his job.

She scribbled in her notebook as a distraction. "So, you're saying there was someone with her when she died, or when she took the drugs, or both?"

"The details are confidential. And to be clear, I said 'there may have been someone.'" He smiled and now seemed to be enjoying messing with her. She wondered if her tedious questions were the least disturbing part of his day.

"Even if someone was with her, it still could have been a straight-forward overdose, it doesn't mean they gave her the drugs."

Right, she reminded herself. Right. "And if they *did* give her the drugs?"

"Well, that gets messy. If they were administered without her knowing it, crushed pills sprinkled in who-knows-what . . ." His tone implied this was unlikely, but the black in his eyes watched her. "That's no good. But if the guy gave her drugs that she then took herself . . ." Her eyes widened and she saw him catching her catching him using a pronoun. "Dealers tend to be men," he added with a look that warned her not to use his own tricks against him. "Anyway, that's when it gets complicated, lots of gray areas."

"So you can prosecute someone just for supplying drugs?"

He looked at her as if she were a child. "Yes, hun." Ron checked his watch and Edie noticed he was not wearing a wedding ring. It was becoming increasingly rare to see someone her age without one. "If it's an intentional suicide, that's harder of course. Anyway"—he dragged the word out—"no info to share at this point." He stiffened as if he were playing a game of verbal musical chairs and the music had stopped. She wondered if this hot and cold was a tactic. She closed her notebook. It was almost five and he looked like he wanted to leave.

"I'm sorry again to bother you. Thanks so much for chatting with me, I appreciate it."

"Not a problem."

She hadn't decided if she'd actually do it, but as she stood up, her body reached for the card and she felt her mouth move. It was her last chance. "Can I leave my card in case you hear anything else you can share?" It was the first time Edie had used her Tixster business cards.

Ron looked amused. "Of course." As he took the small square, she could swear there was a twitch in his jaw, a clenching, before his eyes looked back up, warm, almost pleased.

She worried he thought she was hitting on him. "I'm just very interested in the case," she clarified.

"Right." He took his sports coat from the back of the chair as Edie stood. "I'm heading out, too," he said. "Any interest in a drink?"

IT WAS A terrible idea. At some point Peter would probably be questioned and if this guy found out she knew him she would look guilty at worst, psychotic at best. But she couldn't not say yes. The need to know more trumped all reasoning.

Ron was forty-two years old. He had married young and divorced early. He'd moved to SF from South Brooklyn a few years ago. He had dark features, a thick build, and, she realized once he got talking, the unsettled, cynical demeanor of an East Coast native. He had curly hair, like hers, but thicker, and he hid it under an unfortunate shellac of gel.

Edie had spent her whole life in New York—grew up in a small, dilapidated town Upstate, studied nearby at Cornell, moved to the East Village after graduation—and his anxious energy paradoxically put her at ease. His essence was at odds with the hipster bar where they sat, coated in cool, pastel tones and light wood. Not that New York was devoid of hipsters. But it wasn't the defining characteristic of the city. The hipster population in New York wasn't a feature as it had become in SF. It was, as they say, a bug.

He offered to get the first round but Edie insisted on paying for herself so he wouldn't get the wrong idea and expect something in return. She refused to date anyone more than five years her senior. This was a terrible rule since they were generally more mature and certainly more interested in her. But she refused to participate in a system of inequity, a system that allowed men to take their time figuring themselves out while remaining disinterested in women who did the same, then dip back into the pool of youth rather than explore someone with, god forbid, similar life experience. It was an unpopular stance that led to many arguments, including one with a guy at Tixster who'd married someone twenty-five years younger, that nearly cost her her job. Men dating younger women were so eager to prove that they weren't bad guys—that their love for these women was *real*—but she never tried to deny them their love. She simply couldn't respect the kind of love that prioritized youth over everything else.

"So, you've lived here for a while?" he asked.

"Seven years." She could hardly believe it'd been that long.

He took a sip of beer. "It's hard to make friends in this city, huh?"

Edie nodded. It was a great misnomer that people here were friendly. People here were nice, they smiled and said hello on the street, but they were cliquey when it came to anything serious. It was far easier to strike up a conversation with a stranger in New York; everyone was out there with themselves—not trying to be friendly, per se, but just being, living in public.

"I'm coming on three years and I tend to stick to myself. This job makes you want to be alone, but sometimes it's nice to pretend you're a normal person, having a beer with a friend."

For a moment, she warmed to him, the possibility that he was just trying to figure it out like everyone else, but then she worried he was just calling her a friend to bring her guard down.

"Why'd you move here?" she asked.

He jerked his head away from her. "Change of scenery."

Before she could pry, he asked what her deal was. Just like that, "What's your deal?"

"I work in tech," she said, and Ron stared at her as if she'd said nothing at all.

"For a company called Tixster. I'm a director of engineering." At one point in her life this would have meant something. The years she'd spent coding alone in her room so her all-male classmates, who had somehow been coding for years, wouldn't see her struggle. The strip clubs and dirty jokes she'd laughed along with at her first job, so her co-workers wouldn't ignore her code reviews. The smile she put on each day like underwear because to get mad was to be emotional and no one wanted that. She had wanted so badly to prove she could do whatever men could. But now that was all packed neatly behind her title, a title every other person in the bar probably shared. She could have been anyone else in the city. Her deal was pathetic.

"All right," he said, staring up at the game on the large screen behind the bar.

Everyone in San Francisco who didn't work in tech hated everyone who did. And half the people in tech hated themselves. "I don't like it," she clarified.

Ron turned to her. "So why do you do it?" he asked.

"It's not that I don't like the work, I love programming and problem solving and all that. It just feels pointless. Each app is dumber than the last."

"I'm with you there," he said, returning his gaze to the TV. She imagined a world in which she, too, could thoughtlessly gaze at a TV screen while talking to a stranger without a deep, paralyzing fear of being rude.

"I used to work at a nonprofit, right after grad school." Business school sounded too pretentious to say out loud. She only deployed it when she was talking to someone who thought he was superior. These people had usually also gone to business school.

He perked up, barely. "Doing what?"

"Safe Home Society?" His stare was blank. "They support survivors of domestic violence."

His eyes lit up. "You'd get along with my partner, then. She used to work on DV." He smacked his hand on the bar. "Man, that beat is rough. Worse than Narc."

She could hardly believe he was comparing the two. She opened her mouth to say as much, but the expression on his face was utterly raw. Violence and death weren't obscure concepts for this man.

"Domestic"—Ron shook his head, eyes back down on his drink— "it's bad."

Edie rarely admitted, even to herself, that leaving Safe Home was in many ways a relief. Working there, she'd frequently wake up with nightmares, lie awake replaying their stories. "I understand that," she said.

"Before this, back in New York," Ron continued, "I was in Murder."

"Jesus."

He laughed. "Yeah, it's a rough one. Does wild things to the brain, the way these cases get under your skin. Some people are good at letting cases go without a concrete solve, you kind of have to be in this business." He looked up and held her gaze. "But when I know someone's out there, responsible for an innocent person's death, I can't let it go."

"I can imagine," she said, trying to hold it together.

"My solve rate was shit because of it. I needed a break anyway . . ." He trailed off. "It takes a real toll on you."

She was about to ask more when he took his phone out from his pocket. "Sorry," he said, staring down at it with a shy smile. He turned his head away from her but she could still hear his voice loud and clear. "Down at the bar." Pause. A laugh, not forced, from the belly. "Yeah, I can stick around." Pause. "See you." He turned back to Edie. "Partner's coming by for an end of day debrief. I'm afraid we're going to have to wrap this up."

"Sure, of course. I really appreciate you taking the time."

Ron took another sip of his drink and nibbled on the Chex Mix that sat in a wooden bowl on the bar. "So, tell me, honestly." He paused, his eyes kind and questioning. "Is that why you're so into the case? You think it might be a domestic?"

"Oh god, no." She had never connected the two—the line connecting those dots would be Peter. She tried to play out the possibility but it didn't compute. Peter's role in Anaya's death felt more like a cog in a bigger wheel, not the wheel itself.

Ron was still staring at her.

She took a long sip of her drink. "No," she said firmly. "She's just the kind of woman"—Edie made sure to use *woman* and not *girl* or *lady*, but Ron didn't notice—"who seemed to really know what she was doing." She could hear how superficial it sounded and saw her ignorance reflected in Ron's face. "It seemed like she had a lot going for her and she could have had anything she wanted." She paused. "I just want to understand why it happened."

"Ever heard of mental illness?" Ron asked flatly.

Edie was glad Ron had to go. "I know I can't possibly know what was going on with her." Edie's battle with depression was long and layered, and she sensed from the quickness of his question that Ron might have had his own experience. But she also knew how much she would never know about other people's pain. "She just never wrote about suicide," she offered. "Not explicitly, at least. And she wrote about *everything*."

He looked at her skeptically.

"I've read everything she's published."

"That's right." He nodded, his expression unreadable. "You're a fan."

———

"I CAN'T TELL Peter I met him," Edie said shaking her head.

Alex was sprawled on her couch eating popcorn, the crumbs, Edie couldn't help but notice, also now sprawled on her couch. "Then I'll have to tell him I went down to the station and he'll think I'm a psychopath."

"At least he wouldn't be wrong." Alex shoved another handful of popcorn in her mouth. Half of it fell back into the bowl.

"I just don't get why he's being so weird about it. Like he refuses to talk about it *at all*."

"Because he's afraid you'll get obsessed and judge him."

Edie started to protest but that was definitely the reason.

Alex sat up straighter. "E, remember when I liked that girl, what the hell was her—"

"Calia, the vet." The rare woman who had given Alex the cold shoulder.

"Calia." Alex smiled. "You dug up her whole story. I mean, it was creepy, *for sure*, but I needed it, and you knew that."

According to a post Calia had been tagged in six months before Alex met her, by a woman whose hand was suspiciously placed on her hip, Edie uncovered that Calia had been through a brutal divorce. There were no photos of anything resembling a relationship on Calia's timeline (Edie assumed she'd deleted them since she and hip-woman no longer followed one another), but the woman who had tagged her was a "fiction" writer and her latest story had been about a horse doctor named Celia who cheated on her wife, the love of her life, in a really fucked-up fashion. From there the search got easier, a wedding registry on the Knot led to Calia's last name, which led to where she was from and the fancy college she'd attended, which led to her 2-star Yelp rating, which led to Alex feeling okay about herself because this Calia lady was clearly a dick.

"My point is," Alex continued, throwing a few pillows on the ground to make space for Edie on the loveseat, "throw me P-Fuzz, please!" It was Alex's nickname for Edie's pink faux fur throw, and she opened it up for them to cuddle into. "I know how you are. And I love you for it." Edie snuggled beside her and wrapped the blanket around them. "You're like me, a total psychopath when you let yourself be. But I'm telling you." She turned to face Edie. "You have to let this one go. It's not healthy."

Edie nodded, taking a pillow into her lap. "I know."

"Are you still taking your meds?"

Alex had urged her to try them a few years ago. When she'd told Edie, so matter-of-factly, that SSRIs had saved her brother's life, that Alex, too, had taken them for years, and almost everyone she knew took something, it felt like the permission she'd needed. Her depression wasn't a sickness to hide, but the opportunity to do something for herself, like Alex.

She nodded.

Alex squeezed her thigh, then got up and took a beer from the fridge. "Can I have this?"

Edie waved her hands. "Of course. You never have to ask."

"Also, the idea that you share anything in common with this woman you only met once is entirely in your little fucked-up head."

Edie laughed, the tickle of hearing herself described.

"She just seemed so great. It doesn't make sense."

Alex took a long sip of beer. "You never know that stuff, dude." She plopped back on the loveseat, her beer fuzzing up and dripping on the pink blanket. "The people who look the happiest are usually the saddest because they're working so goddamn hard trying to look happy."

Edie shook her head. "I don't mean it like that. She didn't seem happy exactly, just honest with herself, in control." It was part of what had stunned her when they'd met, what continued to stun her in Anaya's books.

"Peter said she was fine on the K, and that's all they did, right?" Alex asked.

"Yeah, she must have taken something after he left. I'm just afraid he said something to her. He can be so thoughtless sometimes, maybe he was too harsh when he broke it off? Or just said something idiotic."

Alex finished the handful of popcorn she was battling. "Dude"— she wiped her mouth—"do you really think your girl was that fragile? I know you think Peter is the god of all men, but you're giving him way too much credit. I'm certain he didn't break this badass woman in one night."

Edie hated the term *badass*; men were geniuses, while women had this tacky catchall.

"Give her some credit."

Edie nodded and got herself a beer.

"You said she wasn't an experienced drug user, right?"

"Right."

"She probably got some stuff from a rando and it was laced. Peter's guy always does those fentanyl checks, but there's a lot of bad shit going around."

She felt like an idiot. Of course that was what happened. Anaya had gotten drugs from a stranger, long before Peter showed up, she probably wanted to loosen up on K before going on a binge of her own, for any number of reasons, having no idea her drugs were laced.

Of course that was right.

But it didn't *feel* right.

Anaya seemed so strikingly self-aware, so thorough in everything she did. It didn't make sense that her life would end in an accident.

Then again, surely it never did.

Chapter Eleven

THE FERTILITY OFFICE was sterile and full of couples in neatly faded jeans and cashmere sweaters. Edie was suddenly conscious of the frizz of her hair, the sloppiness of her pilling sweatshirt, her big, dirty sneakers, unfit for a five-year-old, let alone a thirty-five-year-old. She shuffled up to the front desk, gave them her name and her birthday, mumbling the year so the others wouldn't hear. The woman behind the desk had thick penny-colored hair and glossy plum lipstick with a shiny diamond on her left hand. As this magazine-looking woman handed back her insurance card Edie couldn't help thinking she would never have to freeze her eggs.

She took a seat and picked up a *New Yorker* to signal, if nothing else, that at least she was a woman interested in the news. Her eyes gazed down, unfocused, scanning for cartoons until she was called.

The doctor's office was far bigger than her entire studio apartment and had almost nothing of medical relevance in it. There was a poster of the female reproductive system in the corner, with a glossy white male doctor explaining it. Mostly, it was a place to display photos of the doctor's perfect-looking wife and even more perfect-looking kids. Edie imagined his judgment—about her hair, her clothes, her grease-stained tote bag—scrolling behind his white toothy smile like a scene from *The Matrix*. No wonder she has to pay for more time, he was surely thinking.

"Being a woman is hard," he began once he was settled into his leather chair. "You have to make decisions quickly, and that will make you feel like you don't have control."

She nodded and laughed a little but not too much, because while it was ridiculous that he felt the need to tell her that, she couldn't disagree. He opened a PowerPoint slide to back himself up and continued as Edie nodded excessively, trying to look interested. She had had a million questions when she walked in but forgot them all as she struggled to respond to his pushy presentation in a way that made their situation feel normal.

When he was done with his explanation about being a woman, Edie waited for him under a robe on the exam room chair. When he returned, he shoved some kind of wand inside of her with such force that she felt like a lump of flesh, which, in a sense, she was. It had just been a long time since she'd felt that way. The sonogram displayed a shaky black-and-white image, like the kind she'd seen a million couples smile at on TV as they held hands and watched a heartbeat together. But it was just her eyeing the screen, which showed her ovaries, her follicles, no life other than her own.

On her way out she was directed to see billing, a small man who gave her an outrageous estimate. Tixster said it would cover up to ten thousand dollars, which she had assumed would be more than enough but was far from the sum the small man was now repeating. It would be cheaper if she froze her embryos, he explained for no reason at all, if she were doing it with a partner. This consultation alone would be $200. And it was not covered by Tixster.

She was told to sit back down, someone would come out and talk to her about next steps, so she returned to the soulless waiting room. She felt like a failed woman who now had to pay her dues. She didn't even have it in her to pick up a magazine.

It wasn't yet noon so she opened Instagram and navigated to Peter's profile. She clicked on his followers, two more than last week. He only had two hundred and eighty-five—seven, now—so it didn't take long, at least not very, to spot the newbies hovering close to the top of the list. One was a local bike company that Peter didn't follow, so it was safe to say they were vying for the attention of men who posted about biking. But the other was a woman, a pretty woman, who, by the look of the way the sun hit her bay window and a picture from just seventeen days ago in Dolores Park, seemed to live in the Bay Area. She had smooth hair, reddish and wavy, chopped into a shag, with bangs that looked wild but in a cool, compliant way: the kind of bangs some women had the gall to call "curly." She had a dog, and an average body mostly draped in expensive-looking linen. Her friends were also attractive and hip-looking, some from LA, most from the Bay, into cocktails and succulents, from the looks of their profiles. Apparently, according to a gorgeous photo from two years back captioned "home," she was from Utah. She'd also been tagged in a five-year Yale reunion pic three years ago, which put her, if Edie had to guess, at twenty-nine. A bus screeched to a stop across the street, pulling her attention away from Peter and his new, much younger follower. As if waking up from a dream she looked around the sterile office before closing out Instagram and opening Facebook.

Facebook was full of babies. Cute babies, which somehow felt worse. She navigated to Anaya's page and scanned the new posts. They were trickling in less frequently now, but someone had posted this morning. It was an older woman, from her hometown. There was nothing interesting about the post—*She was an incredible woman . . . bla, bla, bla . . . I'm so sorry for your loss.* Edie was about to close her phone when she spotted a comment from Leah, the woman with the shared last name.

Leah had replied immediately to the most recent post, thanking the woman for her words. She clicked on Leah's profile again and stared at her face, strikingly familiar like a word on the tip of her tongue. She had the same bright eyes as Anaya, but the feeling of recognition was more than resemblance. Edie clicked back to her comment and scrolled through old posts, condolences from strangers she'd already read a million times, the interesting ones—mostly from men who seemed to be exes—she'd copied into her spreadsheet, tagged them under "relationships" so she could query them quickly. But something had changed. Leah's name now peppered Anaya's Facebook page, a new comment from her on every post, all added this morning. Each message was tailored to its recipient, more sincere than polite. It wasn't until Edie got to the very end of the page, a comment she had made in the earliest hours of the morning, that someone had replied to Leah with something other than a "like." *You're a good sister, my heart goes out to you.*

She felt a surge of the kind of excitement typically reserved for children. The rush that comes from believing you're on the path to something bigger, a feeling most adults are incapable of after so many years of defeat. Anaya's sister was here, living in San Francisco.

"Edie?" a nurse called. "Here's my card. Call me to talk about next steps."

"Can't we just talk about it now? I took the morning off work. And I'm right here." Had she really been waiting all this time for a business card?

"I can't now." The nurse offered a patient smile. "Call me later this week," she said, and walked away.

EDIE WATCHED THE elevator crawl from the first to the second floor, pausing for an unbearable amount of time before finally making its way to where she stood.

"Edie?" said the woman inside when the doors opened. Her chestnut bob swayed as her head tilted, taking Edie in.

"Nicole. Hi." Her large brown eyes held pain, her oval face, now slack with indifference, looked transformed without its usual smile. The perfect side dish of a person Edie remembered had spoiled, and she couldn't help but think it looked good. "How are you doing?" She didn't mean to sound as concerned as she did.

"Fine, I'm fine. Better than I was in that relationship, if that's what you're asking."

It wasn't, but Edie was intrigued. "I'm really glad to hear that."

Nicole's lips tightened, an attempt at a smile. The elevator, which Edie was holding for dear life, began to beep loudly and Nicole stepped out with her black loafers and high-rise khakis, an enormous square leather bag over her shoulder.

"I know you and Peter are close," Nicole started, and Edie had no choice but to let her beeping escape hatch go. "But the number of years he promised that we'd try to get pregnant. He knew I wanted kids." Even Edie knew how much Nicole had wanted kids. "And he knew he didn't, not really, not with me. He just didn't want to admit it." She paused and Edie felt like she should say something but she didn't know what. "He's a fucking coward."

She realized, in that moment, hearing Nicole curse for the first time in her life, that she had never actually spent time alone with Nicole. Here in this hallway, she felt like a different person, which was to say she finally felt like a person to Edie. "He shouldn't have done that to you. I'm so sorry."

"He keeps you around because you revere him, but he's a waste of time."

The elevator dinged and Edie held it open as a couple walked out.

"Take care," Nicole said, and reached for the large double glass doors of the clinic.

Chapter Twelve

COMPOSING AN EMAIL to Leah looked exactly like composing an email to anyone at Tixster, so she could take her time without worrying someone would notice. It was easy to find her contact info, if you knew one person's email at a start-up, you knew them all. Datsta's email format was just the person's first name, as made clear by Brian, head of HR who was always eager to hear from the broader community, per their "About Us" page. And with only twenty people, chances were there wasn't another Leah at Datsta.

Edie said she'd known Anaya briefly, admired her greatly, said she was sorry, added *very* before *sorry*, then asked if she wanted to meet. Then deleted the line asking to meet—why would she want to meet? Then put it back in—why email if she didn't ask? She cut and pasted the line eight times before finally landing on paste and hitting send before she could change her mind.

Leah replied within minutes. Edie always thought the busiest people were the ones who were quickest to reply. She said she would love to meet. She wanted to be around people who knew her sister. She proposed coffee at three—that day.

———

LEAH WAS ALREADY at the counter when Edie entered. She wore a fitted T-shirt and jeans that were neither baggy nor tight, but lay on her body as if they were tailored. She had boots that laced up, no heel. Her hair was short and effortless. She wasn't skinny, but she wasn't not skinny, either. She was a perfect average of bodies, floating in the background of her other features. Edie could not let her body float in the background; her features were below average, her nose a little too big, her mouth a little too small. Keeping herself thin was all she had.

Something about Leah's posture felt masculine, not necessarily the straightness of it, she was kind of hunched. More like the space she took up, the lack of self-consciousness with which she held herself. Even her slouch felt confident. When they met eyes across the room Edie felt the same wave of recognition that hit the first time she'd seen her picture, lurking in her consciousness but too slippery to grasp. Leah waved across the café with a light flick of her hand and Edie sped over to meet her.

They greeted one another with a hug, which felt at once absurd and like the obvious option. It's a strange feeling, to meet someone for the first time and feel recognition.

"What can I get you?" Leah asked, fumbling for her card. Her voice was gentle and kind.

"No, please," Edie said, "let me get this," and before Leah could protest, she handed the cashier her card.

Edie noticed that neither of them had any makeup or jewelry on, and felt, however ridiculously, a sort of kinship. "I'm so sorry for your loss," Edie said once they'd settled at a table. It sounded packaged and cold. "I can't imagine how hard this must be."

Leah nodded. "Thanks, thank you. It doesn't feel real. It's just so . . ." She glanced around the room, not really looking at anything,

allowing herself to take her time. "It's very unexpected." Her voice
was soft and she returned her large dark eyes to Edie. "Are you with
the press?"

"No, definitely not. I knew her briefly. I admired her work, a lot."
She could barely believe she was sitting across from Anaya's sister.

Leah smiled with her eyes, then looked down at her tea. Despite
the boxiness of her clothes and angular chop of her hair, there was
a softness to her that didn't feel counter to Anaya, but was more on
the surface, exposed.

"Why, are you getting a lot of press requests?"

She continued to stare at her compostable cup and Edie wondered if she'd heard her. She looked tired. "No," she said at last, resignation in her voice, and Edie felt an urge to leave this kind, grieving
woman alone. "All my interactions with them have been bad."

Edie twisted her face into a frown. "I'm sorry. I've heard report-
ers can be insensitive," she offered, remembering Ron's disdain. She
wondered if he and Leah had met, realized they must have. She
didn't want to think about it.

"They're asking terrible questions." There was more confusion
than anger in her face. "They want to know about her drug use, her
depression, mental health history."

Edie nodded sympathetically, although she wanted to know all
of this, too.

Leah rested her head in her hands, staring down at the table.
"Anaya didn't do drugs." Every word sounded like a great feat to ut-
ter. "What are they *talking* about? That was not her coke." Her voice,
already shaky, cracked slightly and Edie's heart jumped to her throat.

"It was a coke overdose?" She could feel her heart beat faster.
Coke was Peter's drug.

"Whatever, ya." Her head, still in her hands, was now shaking
back and forth. "She had ketamine in her system, too, some other
stuff." The words came reluctantly, bitterly, as if they didn't deserve
to be part of Anaya's story.

"Were the drugs laced?"

Leah looked up and Edie felt as if she were staring at a child's face with an aging filter imposed on it. Deep bags under her large, gorgeous eyes, a strain in her mouth, and a dry emptiness to her face that didn't seem right against her otherwise impossibly smooth skin. "They're still running tests. But this wasn't her. She wasn't that kind of person. Not that—shit," she said, her face back in her hands. "Someone who OD's is not any one kind of person, obviously." She was talking to herself, lost in her own thought, and Edie could feel the likeness to her sister more than ever. "Anaya never bought drugs."

Edie's mind swirled. Maybe she and her sister weren't that close, surely not if she hadn't even written about her. Or maybe Anaya didn't want to burden her—who would want to worry this sweet, gentle woman who was now rubbing her left eyebrow so hard Edie worried it might bruise—so she'd kept her drug purchases secret.

"How do you know Anaya again?" Leah asked, shattering her thoughts.

"We met briefly one night, friend of a friend."

Her head twitched up. "You only met once?"

She'd planned for this after Ron's inquisition. She embraced her unease, leaning forward, fiddling with the lid of her cup. "I know it's weird," Edie started, "but when I met her, we had this connection. It's dumb, but I felt like I was meeting someone I would know forever. It's so rare as an adult, to click like that with someone off the bat," she said, conjuring the words from Anaya's email.

Leah nodded, long and slow.

"Her writing had a huge effect on me." She stopped, gauging Leah's openness to her admiration, noticing a softness in her face, almost a smile. "Your sister is brilliant. We weren't close, but I was—I *am*—a huge fan."

Leah stared back at her and Edie's whole body itched with the recognition of that face, familiar and impossible to place. Leah's lips stretched into a warm smile, but her eyes looked as if she might cry.

"She *was* brilliant." Eyes back to her tea. "She put everything into her writing. Never got the recognition she deserved. Never wanted to play into the dumb system, always rewarding the narcissist." She seemed as if she were in a trance, but Edie could hear Anaya's voice in her, the way we're all just shades of the people we most admire, and Edie knew, without a doubt, that there was no way they hadn't been close.

"The cops are hardly doing anything," Leah continued, voice shaky. "They're backed up and it's not a priority since there's no culprit or whatever." Though her voice was gentle, not like Anaya who spoke conclusively, with ease, there was an urgency behind it. She shook her head, staring at her boots, which Edie realized were tied loosely, knots on the verge of collapse. "It doesn't make any sense. Her phone doesn't say anything," Leah continued. "She had just fallen for this guy. She didn't have plans with him, they hadn't texted that night, but the police . . ." She looked up at Edie as if she were searching her face for whether or not to continue.

Edie felt sick. She opened her mouth, thought she might tell her everything.

"Sorry," Leah said, as if waking up from her trance. "I'm just—I don't know."

"Don't apologize," Edie commanded as if she were speaking to Elizabeth. Maybe because she was older than Leah, or maybe because she seemed as if she were barely hanging on, Edie felt in control of the conversation in a way she never had with Anaya. "I completely understand. And I agree. The cops should be investigating. That's insane."

She lifted her head slightly, then bowed it again.

Edie decided to jump off a cliff; she was getting better at taking these small, contained risks. "Do the police know anything about the guy?"

Leah shook her head quickly, looked around the room. "I don't actually want to talk about it anymore. Sorry. Or, not sorry. Whatever, you know."

"Totally," she said quickly. "*I'm* sorry."

They took sips of their now room-temperature drinks.

Edie knew if she didn't say something else, she might never see her again. "This is why I reached out," she continued and Leah looked up. "Something seemed off about the whole thing."

Leah's mouth twitched; the ends of her lips turned up slightly. "Thanks for saying that. I feel crazy right now. Like nothing is real. But something is missing."

"You're not crazy." She was startled by the confidence in her voice. "I know I don't really know her," Edie continued, "but I've read everything she's published."

Leah stared at her, truly looked at Edie for the first time since they'd sat down, and Edie knew she was wondering why she was really there.

"The law doesn't always work the way it should," Edie started. She hadn't planned to bring up Matt, but sitting so close to Leah's despair, he was all she could think of. "Years ago, I let someone get away who shouldn't have." She didn't want to imply there was someone to blame, but she wanted to give Leah a real, honest reason for why she was there, without telling the full truth. "I'm sorry I reached out, but when I saw what happened, I just couldn't let it go."

Leah's eyes closed for a moment, and Edie worried she'd made this about herself when the last thing this woman needed was a competing story of trauma.

"They just came out with a profile of her in the *Examiner*."

Edie let out a breath, as if she'd passed a test. Then felt a jolt of panic at the idea that other people were reading new details about Anaya before her. Her search alert hadn't come in yet and she'd only had time to check the *Chronicle* this morning.

"It was not good—basically her résumé with some old pictures."

That seemed perfectly normal to Edie.

"The press is set on this story of an *accomplished* woman hiding her demons."

A crowd of men in Patagonia outerwear streamed into the café, the tall one with wire-frame glasses asked what the others wanted. Leah eyed them for longer than was appropriate. When, finally, their order was in, she turned back. "Sorry, I forget what I was saying."

Edie knew she should let her stop talking. "The press is painting her as a woman with—"

"Right, no. Just because Anaya is out there with her issues—not like we all don't have them, it's so silly—pulling quotes from her books, using her own words against her . . ." She paused, grabbing a paper napkin for no reason, it seemed, holding it tightly in her fist. "They imply, they say they don't but that's bullshit, that the overdose was a cry for help. They say it as if they care, talking about how un-derreported suicides are, how much more mental health support this country needs. Of course . . ." She looked up at Edie as if needing her to understand. Edie nodded. "Obviously, we need more mental health services, I *know*. But no one wants to believe that maybe she actually liked her life, despite how messy it was, that the messiness was what drew her to life, the attempt to make sense of it, and that maybe this was all someone else's fault." Her lips quivered and she sipped her tea, as if needing something to steady them.

In a different world, Edie would have leapt out of her seat, thrown her full weight around Leah's short, boxy frame, and hugged her as hard as she possibly could. But in this world, she stared ahead, trying desperately to make the ache in her heart visible on her face.

"I'm not saying she didn't have real problems," Leah continued. "Her issues weren't just a thought experiment. She struggled with depression and anxiety and was always wrapped up in bad relation-ships." A small grunt, almost a laugh. "You'd think a woman that smart would know better."

Edie felt awakened to action and shook her head firmly. "Not at all. Smart women look for challenges. It works for us in other parts of our life, but definitely not in relationships. At least hetero relationships," she added, remembering that Anaya always made that distinction. "I think ambitious women who chase what they want are often tied up with difficult men."

"You sound like her." She smiled, but her face fell quickly, like she didn't have the energy to keep it in place. "She has terrible taste in guys," Leah laughed and then caught herself in Edie's eyes. "Had," she said softly. "But she was excited about this new one."

Edie coughed for what felt like a lifetime. When she looked up Leah was staring out the window, watching men in fleece walk away with their cups.

"I just wish I could have spoken to her. There's no way she would have done this without talking to me first. No way." Her hand was resting lifelessly on the table and Edie felt the urge to reach for it but she looked down into her cup and nodded instead.

"When was the last time you spoke to her?" Edie asked.

"That night," she said quickly, a tremble in her voice. "We had dinner."

Edie's eyes shot up. She noticed a tear had escaped through the corner of Leah's eye. "Did she seem off to you?"

"Not at all."

Her hands blurred, the table where they rested rocked. What was she doing here, in this overly lit coffee shop, talking to this beautiful stranger about what was very probably the most devastating event of her life?

"She seemed happy, actually." Leah was staring out the window again. "Anyway, she had to go home early to work on her book, she was sending the final draft to the university press that night." Her voice trailed off as if losing steam. "And that . . ." She paused, swallowed. "That was it."

Edie's heart raced. "I'm so sorry." She didn't even think this time, her hand reached for Leah's which still lay lifeless at the center of the table. She didn't move away.

"Thank you," she said.

Edie opened her mouth to ask about the draft—the trauma she

was writing about, if it would ever be published, surely her sister had answers—but Leah's eyes were heavy and distant and Edie couldn't bring herself to make her talk for a moment longer. "Thank *you*," she said, "for meeting me."

"Of course." Her eyes were so earnest. "Most people don't actually care about things. They'll share an article but they're not *really* interested." She let out a small sigh. "You can't blame them, there's so much tragedy. You hear and then you forget."

Edie nodded. She was usually one of those people. "I'm always free to talk. I work just a block away at Tixster."

Leah's forehead wrinkled for a fraction of a second. "Share your culture," she laughed, the saddest laugh Edie had ever heard. It was Tixster's tagline.

"God," Edie groaned. "It's the worst."

"It was good to meet you," Leah said, and pulled a hoodie from her bag. As she zipped it Edie noticed a cartoon unicorn stamped on the breast. Of course she looked familiar, Edie had seen her before.

Chapter Thirteen

EDIE HAD FOUND a fertility clinic that was cheaper (and didn't run the risk of bumping into Nicole), and started her egg freezing treatment that night. It was absurd how much trust the medical system put in random civilians. After nothing but a blood test she was shipped off with an unholy quantity of drugs and needles and a link for how-to videos. Each morning she had to get her blood taken at 7 a.m. and they'd call her each afternoon to inform her of what dosage to inject. That part seemed fun, like a secret agent receiving her mission for the night's operation. Then, each night for ten to twelve days, she'd inject herself with a cocktail of hormones.

She'd watched the videos for an hour before mustering the courage to shove the first needle into her stomach. And before she did, she'd practiced a dozen times on a grapefruit. It wasn't hard, but it wasn't normal, plunging a needle into your gut. The vats of medication spread across a towel on her bed like a science experiment. She still wasn't sure if she'd done it right, but either way her stomach was bruised and bloated as she walked to meet Peter.

Before she entered, she felt a buzz in her pocket and grabbed her phone, worried Peter was bailing. But the text was from Ron. **Thought you'd find this interesting,** he wrote, opening with a goofy hand-wave emoji and linking to the article about Anaya. It was odd, even suspicious—was he flirting?—but a relationship with Ron could be useful. She thanked him with an exclamation point, and asked, with a smiley face, **do you really think I don't already have this memorized?**

Peter was waiting at their usual drinks spot, a dark bar with bad drinks that hadn't yet attracted the young San Francisco mobs. He sat in a large booth and wore his usual hoodie. He had the same hoodie in seven different colors. For a long time, he'd assigned each color a day of the week, but Nicole had demanded he abandon his system, which she deemed goofy and inflexible. Today he wore maroon, but today was Tuesday and maroon used to be Friday so, clearly, he hadn't picked it back up. The two white strings hanging from his hood nearly glowed in the dark.

Edie recalled the first time she saw Leah, in her unicorn sweatshirt. How both she and Alex—though she hoped to god she'd been more concealed than Alex—had ogled her at the salad shop. She'd been reminding herself since she left the coffee shop yesterday afternoon, that that was before she knew she was Anaya's sister. Now, there was no attraction whatsoever. Now, there couldn't be.

She went in for a hug, her face pressed against the soft maroon cotton. "Did you see it?"

His face was blank.

She threw her jacket off. "They had a full write-up of Anaya in the *Examiner*. I thought that was why you wanted to talk." Anaya's face had been enlarged as the header: an image Edie recognized from Facebook a few years back. It looked childish and inaccurate, like an old school picture.

She saw his reaction before he had time to hide it. The closing of his eyes, a quick shake of his head. She had broken their pact. He was mad.

"I missed it." He exhaled, then looked up, renewed, with his familiar Peter grin. "I don't read the *Examiner*." No one read the *Examiner*. "I didn't think you did either."

"Peter, reading an article about Anaya is not the same as obsessing over the case." With a nod of his head, he gave her that. "You should read it."

She must have read the profile twenty times. The more she read the closer she felt to Anaya, a strange and twisted replication of friendship. Leah had been right; the piece implied it was intentional self-harm. Again, it mentioned that Anaya's mother had died young but didn't specify how. She craved more information, to fill in all the gaps of Anaya's life and create a model of her mental framework, a schema of her psyche so she could think exactly as Anaya would have.

She thought of her own mom, the night Edie received the call that she'd been hospitalized. How it felt as if Edie's body had stopped working, frozen, then gone into overdrive—zero to one hundred—it was only one or the other during that time. The idea that the only person in the world who really loved her might no longer exist turned everything dark, a cold and impossible world.

"I'll read it," Peter said in an exaggerated defense. "Of course, I'll read it," he continued. "I just didn't know about it." His eyes rested on hers, the kaleidoscope of colors—specks of gray and yellow and brown mixed against a backdrop of green—she could draw with her eyes closed. "I still think about her all the time."

She felt ashamed. "I'm sorry."

"Don't apologize." The softness in his voice soothed her. "Thank you for telling me."

She imagined Leah needed someone to blame. But Alex's explanation made the most sense: It was an accident, the drugs were laced, and if it was an accident, then they weren't Peter's drugs. Of course Leah was suspicious of the mystery man in Anaya's life. But Edie knew this man, she had gone over every detail with this man, she trusted this man.

Their drinks came. The vodka soda cooled her nerves. Drinking had no effect on egg freezing, according to the research, which she preferred to the mind-numbing scroll of rules in the advice blogs.

"Wait." She turned to him. "If you didn't want to talk about the article, what's up?" His text had seemed urgent.

He paused, hung his head over his pint glass, then looked up. "Don't judge."

"Never!" Peter loved being judged. As far as she could tell it stemmed from a deep-seated guilt, as if he knew he had lucked out—his life was nearly perfect and his looks were more or less impeccable—and felt undeserving. Not that he would ever give any of it up. But he relished the opportunity to defend himself.

"So the date I just left was great," he started.

She didn't know whether to be confused, horrified, or impressed. It was only six o'clock on a Tuesday. "You already had a fucking date?"

"I know, it's impressive." He smiled. "She's an artist so we both have weird schedules."

Peter wasn't cool enough for an artist, was all Edie could think. "You don't have a weird schedule. You just don't really work." She was aware that her love and her hate for him ran violently at equal and opposite speeds. On some level she knew they countered one another, resulting in something that was neither love nor hate but closer to obsession.

Peter laughed. "I go into Primals most days. Anyway, we met up for lunch."

"Long date." She took a sip of her drink.

"She was great," he continued. "Fun, smart, *tall*."

Edie tried her best to appear encouraging despite the fact that all she could think was that she, too, possessed these seemingly pivotal qualities. Her desire for him—this smart, attractive man sitting inches from her, who knew her better than anyone else in the world, and she him—swept aside her thoughts about Anaya and Leah in a way that felt like relief. She would have given him anything and he couldn't even see her as an option.

Peter looked giddy. Edie signaled for him to keep talking the way you might up the intensity of an electric shock machine—just to feel the pain.

"We had sex."

She swallowed, long and hard, then searched desperately for the bartender, who refused to look in her direction. "On your first date." She needed it to sink in. "And it was a *lunch* date."

"I know." He slammed his hand on the bar. His smile stretched the full width of his face. She recognized this look from when he'd met Nicole. The moment he saw her from across the party, back when people still met at parties, he told Edie he wanted to be with her, like Babe Ruth calling his shot.

He's a fucking coward, she'd said in the clinic. Edie had done her best to forget their brief encounter, but Nicole's words had lingered.

"Was it good?" she asked, trying to forget the unfamiliar gravity in Nicole's face.

Peter's head nodded up, then down, in slow, exaggerated movements.

She finally caught the bartender's eye and signaled for another. The young woman making her drink wore a tiny tank top stopping just above her belly button, like what Edie wore to parties in the early aughts. She wondered how the woman could afford this city, given the only people who could live here anymore were either grandfathered into rent-stabilized apartments, or making at least six figures. As she handed Edie her drink, Edie noticed a silver bracelet with a fancy logo and the name *Emma* engraved in a heart, and remembered that some people had very rich parents.

Like Peter. Peter's greatest point of pride had always been *not* taking money from his doctor parents, as if their constant offering was some burden to battle. Edie stared at him wondering how her life might have been different if she knew she had money to fall back on, if she considered herself deserving of wealth.

"Of course dating is easy for you," she said, turning back to Peter. She, too, used to have those instantly passionate, never-ending dates back in her twenties. When you met someone who, within seconds, you knew you were on the same speed as, where your eyes lingered on one another a little too long and the conversation never veered to interview-like questions, but floated like a stream, choppy with laughter. She remembered nights with these men, sure, afternoons sometimes, too, that feeling in her stomach—possibility. But they'd all ended in disappointment.

"Come on. I'm sure it's not that bad for you, either. You're amazing, E." He reached for her hand and she couldn't help but give him a smile. "You're just too picky."

"I'm not picky!" Obviously, she had standards. But it was all within reason.

Peter raised his right eyebrow.

"If I don't enjoy talking to a guy, I'm not going to keep him around just to have a warm body next to me."

He lifted a shoulder, tossing her comment aside. "I'm just not that picky."

"Clearly!" She laughed, but in truth she'd never imagined that Peter would act like this. It felt like an alternative universe where the guy she loved had a creepy twin.

She leaned toward him, elbows on the table. "You are, though. You're just not picky at first. My pickiness is consistent and upfront. I don't sleep with a guy if I don't want to date him. But men will definitely sleep with a woman, and then decide they don't want to date her." She pointed at him for effect. "Guys just get picky *later*."

He laughed, caught out, and admitted, "That's right."

Those two words felt so good. "Look," she continued, on a roll, "if you had to go out with the female equivalent of the men I put up with, you wouldn't last a day."

He nodded, abandoning his grin and seeming almost apologetic. This touched her; she hated when he was kind.

"At our age, guys have the power," she explained. "It's just how it is." She thought of the sixth chapter in Anaya's latest book, about men wanting women who fit into their lives and women wanting men who expanded theirs. It made sense that men were less picky up front, that they often weren't searching for someone outstanding, necessarily, just easy, and as it got harder, as compromise became essential, they pulled away.

"Well, she wasn't our age."

Edie looked up.

"That's the part I thought you'd judge. I actually thought you'd be impressed with the afternoon delight."

"Don't ever say that again. How old was she?"

"Twenty-five?" he said through a tight, nervous smile.

In a slight, sick way, his smile endeared him to Edie, an acknowledgment, at least, that he was in the wrong. She'd always laughed when she got in trouble as a child, tickled by the idea that she wasn't behaving the way she should, though terrified and ashamed all the same. "That's disgusting," she scolded, and he tried harder to hold back his smile. She ran her fingers through her thin, curly strands, but stopped as soon as she started. It was impossible to get them through.

He sat up straighter. "She's in her midtwenties, she's not a child."

The noise that came out of Edie was deep and guttural. "Is that your bar now? At twenty-five your frontal lobe has literally just finished developing."

He's a waste of time, Nicole had said before turning away.

"I'm just having some fun."

So he didn't actually want kids if he was out dating twenty-five-year-olds, she wanted to say. He actually *had* wasted Nicole's time. He really was a fucking coward. But it was too soon to bring up the breakup, not even two months since it'd happened. And yet, he had clearly moved on, so why shouldn't it be fair game? And by not saying something wasn't she just enabling him, letting him feel like he'd gotten female input, or, god forbid, *approval,* without actually interrogating his actions? Did he really just keep her around because she *revered* him? No. She had to stop. Obviously not. They'd known each other for fifteen goddamn years, and most of that time his relationships with women were respectable, admirable, even. Nicole was just bitter and Edie couldn't blame her. Clearly, she'd wanted to lash out against Peter, tear down his image to the people he still kept close. But Edie had known him far longer and she relished their dynamic—he wasn't perfect by any means, but he was *good*. Nicole didn't understand.

"So do you, like, *like* this girl? Because there's a power imbalance there whether you want to admit it or not. She's going to be into you, and you need to be upfront if you're not into her."

"It's very unfeminist of you to assume women aren't also in it for the sex."

She had to laugh. "The only time men genuinely care about equality is when they're defending women's right to sex." In Anaya's second book, she'd blasted hookup culture, a culture Edie had been steeped in, having entered adulthood at the turn of the century, racking up sex stories like little badges of honor, drinking to the point of oblivion so she wouldn't have to notice. "I know some women just want casual sex, but you're at an age when most people assume you want to settle down, Peter. And if you're taking her on romantic dates and acting like a boyfriend—being all kind and responsive, I know that's how you are—and aren't super clear up front, women are going to assume you want a relationship."

"You really are an expert at projecting," he said, but she could tell he was taking it in.

She wasn't in the mood to laugh it off. "Yes, Peter, when I was twenty-five, I *was* always trying to be the chill, down-for-anything girl and had way too much sex because I was taught that's what guys wanted. And then I'd get fucked—literally, then emotionally—and you *always* told me I deserved better, that those guys were jerks."

His eyes shifted to the table then back up, warmer.

"Don't turn into one of those guys."

"You're right." He nodded. "I'm sorry, E. I think I was clear with her?"

Edie shook her head.

"But I'll make sure, promise." There was a pause. "Maybe I shouldn't tell you the other stuff, then."

"Fuck you, tell me." She couldn't help but laugh. She could judge him, and she could argue with him, the more the better, but to *actually* get upset felt impossible. He wasn't a pig, he was just high on his new situation playing the part of one. And she was willing to wait until he got bored and knocked it off. It was the same with her father, an inability to get angry, to not reflexively make excuses for him, to know—really believe—that he was at fault.

"Well . . ." He paused. Sadly, she was out of vodka. "I had sex this morning, too."

She felt it in her gut this time, a real churn. "Peter, this is insane!" It was happening. He was turning into every other single thirtysomething guy. She wanted to shake him. Like a kid who just got the keys to his very first car, he wanted to ride all over the place, didn't care what happened. She expected it would be bad, Peter finally single, but not this bad.

"Peter, you do realize that when women have sex with you, they do it because they like you. And when they let you into their vagina, the assumption is that you like them back."

"You're projecting again, E." He shoved his head into his pint.

"I'm informing you of a perspective that I have and you lack. Call it projecting, or call it helpful, your choice."

She considered excusing herself to the bathroom and texting the data scientist from Tinder, or maybe Ron for god's sake. She could have a boyfriend, or even just some random sex, if she wanted to. It still sat somewhere, ingrained, that empowered women had lots of sex and she visualized Anaya's words—women getting what men want is not the same thing as women getting what women want. The truth was, it wasn't that she didn't want sex, she just didn't want what was offered to her. As Anaya had put it in her second book, at some point in her thirties, she had begun valuing herself more than society valued her. In terms of dating, that meant she was operating at a deficit. Her options didn't interest her. It had stopped being fun.

"Just use protection if you're having sex with this many people."

"Of course." He looked up at her. "Hey." He put his hand out on the table, palm up, and she placed her hand on his. "We just set a date for the charity event I'm organizing for Primals. It's late July." His eyes were bright and lingering. "Be my date?"

Anytime Nicole couldn't attend one of Peter's fancy work events, Edie stood in. She appreciated that this hadn't changed. "Sure. Is this the climate change thing?"

"No, still working on the details for that. I'm on too many god-damn committees."

"Probably because you don't do any work."

"Whatever," he said with a smile. "No, this is a Women in Tech event. We're getting some great speakers, I thought you'd enjoy it."

At the corner of the bar a couple was on a first date. She could spot one a mile away. The woman was all smiles, her head rested on her hand, her legs were perpendicular to his, her knees touching his thighs. He looked straight ahead, talking, glimpsing over at her every now and then to share a laugh. They were performing for one another, guessing at each other's desires to distract from how little they knew about their own beyond the all-consuming need to feel desired, a performance so practiced that it felt real, to the other person and themselves in turn.

"Sure," she nodded, eyes lingering on the couple. "I'm in."

RON HAD GOTTEN in the habit of texting her, his lack of friends in the city becoming quite transparent, and she didn't tell him to stop. Innocent, innocuous remarks about his life peppered with just enough commentary on the case to keep it interesting. It wasn't much but it was a thread tying her to the investigation and that was enough. The only explanation she could think of was that he was gearing up to ask her out. And while she had no interest in that—he was too old and anyway it was too complicated—she figured there was no harm in letting him think he had a shot. So when, in their latest exchange about the decaying state of Market Street, he asked if he could buy her a coffee, she quickly agreed.

She threw a fake meeting on her calendar and walked over to the new café on Brannan Street. She had been waking up at five every morning to get to the clinic for her blood tests and could barely keep her eyes open by noon. But the worst part was her body. She was at risk for something called overstimulation, which meant that if she wasn't careful her follicles, which now felt like gigantic, fragile melons because of the drugs, might bump into each other and burst. She couldn't move much, let alone exercise, which meant no running.

Her five miles a day were the only part of her life she could point to and say with certainty, *that was productive*. Without running, not only did she feel ugly, she felt unmoored and undeserving—of food, of joy, of life itself. Of course, this was something to "work on," but it was also one of the few manifestations of addiction that was accepted as healthy, even congratulated. At present, she needed an alternative outlet for her obsession.

Ron stood out like a sore thumb at a coffee shop that looked more like an Apple store, everything white and unblemished. It was as if he only had one outfit, the same white button-down shirt, cuffed to the elbows. His jacket tossed over the back of his barstool. In fairness, Edie was wearing the same hoodie and T-shirt, only in different colors, that she'd worn the last time they saw each other.

He got up when he saw her but she didn't go in for a hug. It seemed important for him to buy her a drink so this time she let him. Four dollars for a black coffee was ridiculous, but it wasn't enough to make her feel guilty.

"How's Tixsty?" He asked with a playful smile, handing her a cup that didn't feel very hot. She knew single drip coffee was supposed to taste better but all that dripping took too long. No matter how good the bean was, or whatever, the best coffee was simply steaming hot.

"Tixster," she corrected. "It's amazing. Saving the world, one hipster-with-something-to-prove at a time."

He laughed.

"How's the case?" she asked.

He raised his eyebrows, like she shouldn't be asking but she just grinned back coyly, an unspoken *please*.

"Slow," Ron said. "The office and labs are all backed up right now."

"Busy season?" Edie joked but Ron nodded as if she were serious.

"Long days." He stared out the window, eyes alert, then back at Edie. "But we finally got the tox reports back."

She felt a deep, overwhelming sense of relief. "And?"

"There was a lot in her system, too much."

His ambiguity was unacceptable. "Were the drugs laced? Is that what caused it?"

He shot her a stern look. She stared down at her coffee.

"Not that we can tell."

"Wait, there was no fentanyl?" She focused on breathing. Bad drugs would have cleared it up—tragic, but straightforward—an accident. Peter would never have given her laced drugs.

Ron shook his head. "But we have a lead on where they came from."

She had nothing to lose. "Where?" She knew Peter's dealer, an old friend from college. A responsible guy, a good guy, who lived up in North Beach. His drugs—according to Peter at least, he had reassured her every time he'd offered—were top quality, pure. Especially the coke. He always ran a fentanyl test and Peter had been buying it from him for over a decade.

"Looks like a Silk Road situation."

"What?" It sounded like something from *The Wizard of Oz*.

"Dark web, the site's been blowing up with transactions."

Her whole body relaxed. That was not Peter.

"You're a tech person. Were any of Anaya's friends real good with computers? It's not straightforward, buying drugs online."

She thought of Leah, but dismissed the idea as quickly as it came. "Like I said, I didn't really know her. She could have bought them herself," she offered. She hated when people assumed women didn't have the capacity to do something technical.

"Could have, but a few signs point to that being unlikely."

She waited for more, but he just sipped his coffee. "So, what do you do for fun when you're not investigating local crimes?"

She didn't like the subject change, but learning that the drugs were from the dark web—not from Peter—satisfied her enough to move on. "House parties?" she offered. "These days I mostly just sit in my studio and read."

"Sounds wild," he said with a smirk. "I haven't been to a house party here yet."

Edie wanted to end wherever this was going and quickly. The last thing she wanted was for Ron to ask her out and then have to reject him and then where would she be?

"Trust me, they're overrated. So," she started, pivoting, "you're still investigating the case, then. Seems like it's pointing more to something intentional if the drugs weren't laced?"

"You're relentless." She could tell he didn't mind. "Yes, still open. And I have my own reasons for prying into this one."

She stared at him, hoping he'd continue. A tall, skinny man walked in and ordered a nonfat latte. It wasn't crowded and Edie could hear every word of his order. She wondered how a place this large, with nothing more than a stale scone on display, could stay in business.

"My old partner," Ron started in a low voice that made her wonder if he'd also clocked the clarity of the man's order, "my best friend." He snorted loudly. "Best friend doesn't do it justice. Sounds like a kid at a sleepover. He was my *partner*." He looked up at her and his eyes were soft. "Like a sibling, knew him in and out." Eyes back to his coffee. "Well, he OD'd."

"Ron." She took a breath. "I'm so sorry." She felt an urge to touch his forearm, resting close to her hand, to hug him, even, but they barely knew one another and she didn't want to give the wrong impression. "Is that why you shifted to Narcotics?"

He looked up at her. "Miss detective over here." He was mocking her but she didn't mind. He looked relieved to have lightened the moment. "You got it. It's also why I left New York. Anyway, he'd done it before. We were on Murder together. I won't even get into what that year looked like for us." He shook his head. "They called his OD accidental, let him out of the hospital with nothing but a goddamn pamphlet, not even a meeting with a therapist. The force wouldn't give him time off, or god forbid the resources he needed. No one took it seriously back then." He took a sip of his coffee. "I tried to talk to him, I . . ." His voice went high and he stopped. "Anyway, he did it again the next month. This time, it worked."

Edie could see the veins in his hand as he gripped his cup.

"We like to chalk things up to chance." He turned to her. "But most things, if you dig deep enough, aren't chance. Not really. If someone dies, we shouldn't shrug our shoulders and call it an accident. Anyway . . ." His tone shifted, eyes scanning the room, and, though she had a million questions, she knew he was done. "Have *you* heard anything about the case?" he asked. Their running joke was that she was a detective-in-training.

"I read the profile, but that's it. I don't know why it's still being investigated if everyone thinks it was an intentional overdose."

Ron shook his head, like he was tired of the whole conversation. "Look." He leaned in closer and she mirrored his movements; their heads were nearly touching. He stared at her for what felt like a long time. "Her apartment showed signs of struggle." He studied her face, which she was trying hard to control.

"What?"

"Things were knocked over. Maybe it was . . ." He paused. "Maybe it was just a fit of some sort while she was high, who knows, but it needs to be checked out." He took a sip of coffee while Edie's heart pounded. He looked up at her again, the way he had before, examining her. "There were signs of distress."

"What?" Her brain felt locked, inaccessible, all she could do was repeat this one word.

"They found bruises on her body." His eyes were relentless. "Marks on the neck."

"Wait, what? Was she hurt?" Something in her stomach pinched.

"Nothing to worry about," he said firmly, "just something to look into. Do not repeat this."

"Of course not. I'm not a journalist."

"Right." He sat back in his chair. "You're a fan."

"I've read everything."

He raised his right shoulder, a half shrug.

"Except the book she was working on," she ventured. The unpublished manuscript still circled in her mind.

He looked up at her, curious. "Yeah, some interesting stuff in there. A shame it won't get published."

"Right." She remembered what Leah had said, that the draft was due that night. "So, you've read it?"

"It's part of the investigation."

Her mind spun, she had scoured all of Anaya's writing for signs—drug habits, suicidal thoughts, anything that might lead to an explanation—but came up empty. "Did it—"

"I can't talk about it, so please don't ask." He stared at her with a sympathy that made her uncomfortable. He wasn't unattractive but all she saw across from her was a man who took his time and now felt he was owed someone younger.

"Sorry I keep prying about this stuff," she said. "Thanks for entertaining me."

"Yeah, well it's a little sick, but it's nice to have someone to talk to." He smiled. "What do you think of this joint?" he asked, scanning the room.

"Not exactly my scene." She flicked her eyebrows up. "It's very West Coast."

"Certainly is." He smiled.

They were both lonely, it was harmless. She would let it go until he crossed a line, which hopefully wouldn't happen until after the investigation if she played it right.

SHE PICTURED THE bruises as she sped home, purple and blotchy, fingerprints on the inside of Anaya's upper arm, a redness around her wrists. She didn't have details, but her own memories from her job at Safe Home filled in the gaps.

She was a block from her house, music in her ears—an old Radiohead album she liked to bike to at night, she felt too old to keep up with anything new and whenever she tried, she didn't like what she found—making the world feel like outer space, a backdrop of blankness. She passed her block. She kept pedaling, inhaling the scent of eucalyptus that marked the Panhandle. One song floated into another. She knew she shouldn't. She didn't know what she'd even say when she got there. But she had to go, her legs wouldn't stop.

She remembered exactly where her department building was. It hurt to remember how she had searched for Anaya on her runs, hoping she'd see her on her way home, to know there was no chance of that now.

The door was open but the halls were empty. She walked from one door to the next, her footsteps, even in her sneakers, echoing through the cold tiled hall. Finally, she found the main office and cracked open the door.

A young woman with a bun on top of her head and large wire-frame glasses looked up at her from behind a large desk. "Can I help you?"

"Hi," Edie stammered. "I was curious if I could speak to someone about Anaya Thomas?"

The woman's welcoming face dropped instantly into a hard, suspicious stare. "We're all very saddened by what happened to Anaya," she said coldly. "What's your interest in her?"

"I'm a big fan of her work."

"We all are. Or were," she said, softening slightly. "No, are, we are still all fans of her work. Always will be."

"Of course." Edie nodded. The woman was still eyeing her with some suspicion. "I was wondering . . ." She felt ridiculous. "I was just curious if she had any work that you might be able to share. Work that maybe was in progress or unpublished?"

The woman looked at Edie as if she had just asked her for gold, both appalled and amused. But Edie had nothing to lose besides self-respect, and she was very practiced at giving that up.

The bun remained perfectly still as the woman continued to stare at Edie, searching, it seemed, for a reason to trust her or even just like her. Edie couldn't provide much on either front and looked down at the tin of pens, the only thing on the counter aside from her own hands.

"She was working on a manuscript," the woman said after a long pause. "But I believe her sister halted the publishing process due to recent events."

"Leah?" Edie blurted, and whatever trust the woman was developing seemed to evaporate.

"Yes," she said, and turned to her computer screen.

"Why would she do that?" Edie said more to herself, her head down, eyes on her shoes.

The woman clicked away on her mouse. "The contents of the book," she said without turning from her screen, "would be inappropriate to publish given the circumstances." She turned to Edie, who was clinging to each word. "We would never do that to her."

Edie was shocked not only at her answer but that she had answered at all. "Was it done, the manuscript?"

"Yes." She could see the sadness in the woman's face, bursting behind her suspicious eyes.

"Didn't she want it to be published?" Staring at the tin of pens, she wondered if Anaya had stood here, if any of them had rested on her fingers.

The woman's eyes narrowed. "We may share pieces of the work with students and researchers. But that's all." Eyes back to her screen.

Edie took a pen from the mug, clicked it open, then closed. Her father always carried a retractable pen in his back pocket, never went anywhere without one. She quickly put this one in her pocket before the bun woman looked up again. It was clearly time to leave, but she was unable to move. "She wanted me to read it." Her voice sounded more desperate than she intended it to.

"What?" Her look was incredulous.

"I can show you." She reached for her phone and searched her email for Anaya's name.

"That's not necessary, I don't—"

"Here." She handed her phone to the woman with Anaya's email open. "You can see, she sent it just days before."

After a minute, the woman looked up, uneasy, and handed it back.

"She's had a profound effect on me. I would call myself a researcher."

The woman's face had softened slightly.

"Is there any chance I could access a copy for further research? I'll keep it confidential."

The woman, petite with glowing skin and a thick gold necklace, stared at her. "No, I don't think so." She glanced back to her screen and Edie, now mortified as the whir of adrenaline faded, zipped her hoodie in resignation. "But I'll ask my director." Eyes back to Edie. "Write down your contact info." She handed her a yellow pad and

Edie wrote everything—her name, her email, address, phone, she didn't care—with a trembling hand.

She raced to her bike. *Inappropriate to publish,* she repeated over and over as she sped along the Panhandle's generous bike path, opposite the stream of commuters on their way home.

THE LAST TIME Edie *really* thought about suicide—the idea crossed her mind more than she'd like to admit but she generally shut it out as quickly as it came—was two years ago after a phone call with her mother. She was in a frantic mood, the heat and cable had stopped due to unpaid bills, and to top it off a raccoon had knocked down her bird bath. Getting her mother to calm down was impossible, even Lolly couldn't cheer her up. She could hear her dad yelling in the background. *Don't try to get her on your side. You're an idiot if you think she cares.*

She had just quit her job at SHS and signed her offer at Tixster. Over the phone she heard her mom shout to her dad to leave her alone. "I don't want to be here," her mom said, as defeated as she'd ever heard her. She was nearly inaudible, as if she didn't want Edie to hear, which was how Edie knew she wasn't kidding.

The thought of losing her mom felt as if someone were putting a vacuum to her insides and literally sucking the life out of her. It was also, a small, shameful part of her whispered, a relief. It meant she, too, wouldn't have to keep going. "You can come live with me, Mom. I'll get you your own place soon."

"No, I don't want to be here at all." Her voice was thin and hollow, a shadow of a voice. "I'm so tired." Her dad's voice in the background. "I have to go."

Her mom hung up before she could respond and Edie went back to Netflix. The sadness didn't overwhelm her, pour in like a busted faucet, until later that night. She was an hour deep in a text chat with a new match on Tinder. He was funny, playful, responsive. It was so perfect a distraction it barely registered as one. But as she waited for his reply to what she thought was a witty question, he unmatched her. It wasn't dramatic. There was no alert or notification. He just never answered, and when she went to write him again, just bite the bullet and ask him out, he was gone. No message thread, no picture. As if he never existed at all. And that, the quick flick of a button by a stranger somewhere on the far end of the city, toppled her.

She thought about how she would do it. Opened an incognito window in her browser to compare the details—pain, cost, time. Her body relaxed at the thought of escape. She closed her computer and wrote each scenario down in a notebook. Her planning was precise. She made herself confront the particulars with extraordinary care. In the time it took to write it all down her thoughts invariably wandered to her mother. She took twice as many sleeping pills as usual that night, and waited.

OBVIOUSLY, EDIE'S OBSESSION with Anaya's death stemmed from the fear that something in her was capable of irreversible self-harm. But in her quietest moments she knew it wasn't fear at all. It was something more disturbing, too dark and shameful to acknowledge most of the time. Her fascination was driven by a deep loneliness. Suicide, depression, mental illness in any form, weren't acknowledged in San Francisco, not really. Stress was allowed, about work, at least, but it was a masked form of pride. If someone was really feeling down, they strolled to the park, smoked some weed, bought a yoga membership, downloaded an app.

Sadness lurked around the city like a deep-sea monster, growing, untouched, in its invisibility. Reading Anaya's words, she felt briefly free from her shame, a state so chronic and perpetual it mostly went unnoticed. Edie was desperate to be close to someone who, maybe, could have understood. And she wanted to show Anaya, in spirit, if nothing else, that she, too, was not alone.

Her eyes were heavy in bed, but not yet closed. Anaya's words were a blueprint of sorts, and she needed to understand where it led. If she *did* take her life, or even if it was a bender-gone-wrong, was it related to her mother's death? If so, why *now* when she'd lived with that death for years? Anaya had been writing about the "biggest trauma of her life," had the writing process triggered this? But then her whole career was personal writing and she had worked on this book for *fifteen years*. And what, if anything, did Peter have to do with all this? Why, the one night that her best—and *druggiest*—friend happened to stop by to end it with Anaya, did this otherwise together-seeming woman take her life?

Edie grabbed her phone and opened the screenshots of Peter's profile, the ones she'd snapped on the toilet the first day she saw him on the app. She had barely been able to look at them then, but now she studied them. The photos were familiar; she had seen them on his Instagram and had even taken a few, the one with him in the beer garden in that goofy hat and the one in Joshua Tree. He only had one selfie, and he was smiling, though not too hard, a warm and effortless smile, in all his pictures. The last shot was the text of his profile—short, witty, and to the point. She almost put her phone away when she realized there was another shot, one she'd forgotten she had taken, of their compatibility score when she found him on OkCupid—a devastating 68 percent. She scanned the categories. Relationships: He was less traditional; ironic, given that Edie had almost never been in a traditional relationship and he had almost never not been. Artsy: She was artsier and she felt a sharp shot of pride. And Sex: He was kinkier.

It's not that Edie knew every detail of Peter's sex life, but she knew quite a lot, and he had never mentioned kink. There was that one time, Nicole bought handcuffs for Valentine's Day and Peter admitted he enjoyed it, so much, in fact, that he couldn't get into it. He was too disturbed by how much he liked the idea of Nicole tied up. He didn't want to be that kind of guy. They never did it again.

She thought of the bruises on Anaya. Edie always had stray bruises—from her bike, her coffee table, some simply inexplicable. Anaya could have fallen that night; clearly, she was not okay. But. She opened her laptop and searched *BDSM bruises*. Clicked "images" then clicked away, unable to look. *BDSM bruises on neck.* No images this time. *Erotic asphyxiation,* she'd heard of it, of course, but here were stories, people wondering how to hide it from co-workers. *BDSM play choking.* How to do it safely, why it was so arousing, how the restraint of oxygen leaves you light-headed and high. She asked the internet who liked it more, men or women, and found that choking was now so common in sex that men no longer felt the need to ask for consent. She read about choking as a form of orgasm control and couldn't help but picture Anaya and Peter, she didn't want to but it was impossible not to, until, halfway through a sentence, she slammed her screen down.

Most of the time, Edie believed it was all an immensely tragic accident. She did not believe Peter would intentionally harm anyone. But the question of whether or not he had *something* to do with it, no matter how unintentional, kept her spinning. It was what kept her awake, that night and every night since it happened.

Chapter Fourteen

PETER ARRIVED LATE with a bottle of Edie's favorite red. It was her last night of egg freezing, the night before the retrieval operation, which would hopefully result in many, many eggs. The "trigger shot" had to be administered at 9:15 p.m. exactly to coincide with her surgery appointment the next morning. She had given herself dozens of shots in her stomach in the last ten days, but the trigger shot had to be in her butt, and according to the nurse who had marked the spot with an *x*, someone else had to do it for her.

Alex was teaching a class that night, and Peter had jumped at the chance to be helpful. He was always there for her when she needed it, brought her soup when she had walking pneumonia last year, biked over with a backpack of groceries when she tore her Achilles. He was usually her emergency contact. In so many ways, they were already each other's partner.

It wasn't the way she had pictured him seeing her butt, but he would see her butt nonetheless, and that felt like progress. She'd chosen simple, black underwear for the occasion.

"Sorry I'm late," he said, placing the bottle on the counter and opening her far-left drawer for the bottle opener. She found herself noticing his movements, direct and forceful, and thinking about Anaya, the knocked-over items in her room.

"It's fine. I knew you'd be late so I told you an hour earlier."

"Ouch." He wore his green hoodie and his hair was damp; he'd just showered.

"Peter, this has to happen at nine fifteen exactly. I told you that."

"It's eight forty-five! We have all the time."

"We have to watch the videos." She opened her computer to line up the instructional videos.

"Wine?"

"Not until after the shot." She felt the size of an actual balloon. She hadn't worn pants with buttons in over a week. The hormones had given her PMS times a hundred. Taking a shower made her cringe, she had to look away from her stomach as she washed her body.

"It's awesome you did this," he said, taking a seat on her couch. "I can't imagine having kids anytime soon."

"That must be nice," Edie said behind a clenched smile. "To know there's no rush."

He looked surprised. "But that's my point. Now there's no rush for you, either."

She had gone through this torture so she could think like Peter about children, which is to say not think about them at all. But she knew it didn't really work like that. Peter spoke of having children as if it were like going on a long vacation or buying a new car, another thing to have, something exciting to play with when he got older. To Edie having a child sparked nothing but terror, a noose around the small chunks of freedom she was slowly cobbling together. Not that she was too busy; her life was objectively quite empty. It was freedom from other people's expectations, the ability to access her own wants and needs, and panic gripped her as she imagined entering a life of servitude anew.

"It, like, totally removes the timeline." His legs were encased in slim-fitting denim.

She didn't have the energy to argue. His excitement was nothing he could help. His advantage, this time, was deeper than anything she could argue against. It was biological.

"Let's watch the videos." She opened her laptop and navigated to the page. "I've been watching them every night. They're cheesy, but helpful. I'll play it a few times. It took me a while to remember."

"Fun," he said with a sip of wine. His presence on her loveseat made it feel as if her apartment had shrunk.

She got the needles in order on the coffee table. There were three different medications. She retrieved the one from the fridge and measured the others. The video playing on her small computer screen, the one for the trigger shot, featured the same lady as her nightly videos, but the steps were different. She flinched as one lady stabbed the other in the ass.

She brought over a grapefruit. "Here, you can practice on this." But Peter was heads down on his phone, thumb moving rapidly left to right.

"Are you on Tinder?" She nearly screamed.

"Sorry!" He laughed. "What do you need me to do?"

"Did you even watch the video?"

"Sure," he said with a goofy smile. It was this combination of irreverence and care, his ability to do whatever he wanted, while still remaining utterly confident in the task at hand, that made her love him.

"Peter, if anything goes wrong tonight, I will literally kill you. Do you know how miserable this has been? Going in at seven a.m. every morning, feeling like an actual whale for two weeks?" She was mortified by her own voice, shaky and shrill. "And there's no way Tixster will pay for another round." She felt as if she might cry.

"I'm sorry." He threw his phone on the couch but he was still smiling, amused or maybe convinced, she couldn't tell. "Let's do this then!"

"You have to watch the video!" She smacked his arm and as he held his hand up to stop her, she noticed a bulge in his pocket, a plastic Ziploc sticking out. "What is that?" she asked.

"Nothing," he said, turning away from her.

"What's in your pocket?"

"E, you're so intense!" He was laughing but she wasn't. "It's drugs, if I go out later."

She almost asked him to leave. Would have, if she didn't need him. It felt like a betrayal, of Anaya, of *Edie*, who he was supposed to be spending the evening with. Old Peter would never have done this. "Don't bring drugs on your fucking dates." She grabbed her computer to restart the training video but by the time she looked up he was back on his phone.

"Peter! Stop." Something in her chest hurt. It wasn't funny anymore. "You're addicted."

"I'm not," he said, but his eyes stayed down. "These videos are just *very* boring. I saw it. I know what to do."

It was infuriating and offensive but she knew this was why she'd chosen him. Whether he watched them or not, she trusted him because he so fully and unequivocally trusted himself. And more important than technique or practice was the confidence to shove a needle into someone's flesh without flinching.

"Here." She handed him a grapefruit. "Show me what you can do." It wasn't that he *needed* to put in effort, it was that she wanted him to.

"You want me to inject this?"

"It's practice. No liquid, just stab it."

He shoved the long needle into the grapefruit quick and steady. Perfect.

The clock crawled toward 9:15. Edie was too nervous to think of anything other than how to make sure nothing went wrong, so conversation was thin and Peter continued to swipe. When 9:12 came, she double-checked the dosages and handed him the needle. "Right where the *x* is." The nurse had marked her like an animal. She could feel her palms sweating as she pulled down her pants. She wasn't sure how she could have thought this was a good idea.

"Got it," he said.

She'd barely felt it.

"Now have a glass of wine with me. *Please.*" His pour was generous, hilariously so, almost to the top of the glass. "I'm sorry it seemed like I wasn't taking this seriously. Is anyone going with you tomorrow? I'll take you."

No way would she let him see her like that. "Alex is picking me up. But thanks."

His phone buzzed on the table. This time he threw it in his pocket with an apologetic glance. "Okay, so I've been dying to talk to you about Juicegate." His eyes were shining the way they always did when he presented a topic that he knew she'd love, like an offering.

"What's Juicegate?" It felt good to fall back into their usual rhythm, to finally have his full attention.

Juicegate was the latest tech scandal—a $700 juicer found to be completely useless. It produced the same result as squeezing a lemon by hand but had somehow amassed over $100 million in funding. He knew she loved examples of tech bros elaborately wasting money, large-scale proof of the small transgressions she felt daily.

"Okay," he started, "what's the most ridiculous idea for a start-up we can think of?"

She considered for a moment. "A remote-control shoe tie-er? Like, for adults."

Peter's face lit up. "But fastening it to your shoe takes more time than actually tying your shoe, of course, and you have to refasten it each day."

"Exactly, but you can track how many times your shoe goes untied, so . . ."

"Totally useless data—but *data!*" Peter's laugh was loud and free, a laugh she knew well, but one that didn't come often. "Do you think it's unethical to market a useless product as life-changing?" he asked.

Any tech product she could think of fell into this category, Tixster being no exception. "Life-changing is subjective. So no, it's fine, as long as you're not all-out lying."

He cocked his head. "Just because you meet the bare minimum of legality doesn't mean it's ethical, right? I don't think it's okay to hide facts that people would want to know."

He was often more idealistic than her. "Right, but all of marketing is about selectively hiding facts—changing the color of a shampoo bottle and calling it new and improved."

"Fair." He smiled. "So, all of capitalism is unethical is what we're getting at, then?"

"Exactly." She was so tired. "You know what else is unethical? Starting philosophical debates after nine p.m."

"I feel like ten p.m. is a more accurate cutoff for our age? But then age is just a construct, so the question becomes what's the right curfew for our *state of mind*, you know?"

She threw a pillow at him.

"I hope you sleep well, E. Tomorrow will be great." He took their glasses to the sink. "Text me if you need anything." He zipped his hoodie in the doorway, then turned to her. "And I'm sorry for messing around earlier. You know you can always trust me."

She wanted to grab both his hands and tell him that she trusted him more than anyone in the world. That he had been a beacon of sorts, while the rest of her life had flailed. She decided enough was enough. Why did a seemingly endless stream of random women get to be with Peter Masterson while she sat watching? "If you want something, make it known," Anaya had written in her second book. At least then you can move on. It was ridiculous to wait for Peter to make the first move. Maybe he *did* want to be with her—he was always in her orbit, requesting dinner, inviting her to parties—but was also torn about admitting it. After the surgery, she would tell him how she felt. It was silly to wait any longer.

———

THE WAITING ROOM was ice cold. It was strange being there alone, naked in a paper towel of a robe while the other women held hands with the person beside them. The secretary looked at her with concern when she said she was there by herself. "You can't drive home," the woman behind the counter scolded. She explained that Alex would be there soon.

The wait was long but the procedure had been quick. She'd been knocked out and didn't remember a thing, but apparently, they'd "retrieved" a dozen eggs, which left her feeling like some sort of commercial chicken. Her body was wobbly but generally fine except for the occasional spasm, like an electric shock up her butt that left her paralyzed for a few long seconds. The doctor assured her that was perfectly normal.

AT HOME, ALEX followed her inside with a bag full of soup ingredients. She chopped up vegetables while Edie lay on the couch. It was so hard to quiet the noise, the guilt of not moving, the largeness of her limbs. The discomfort was helpful, something else to concentrate on, an excuse.

"How's the project coming along?" Edie asked. She didn't need to shout or even raise her voice. The counter and the couch were only a few feet away.

"It's not working," Alex said, shaking her head, eyes on an onion. She was working on a photo series of empty office spaces, so dark and desolate they looked like graveyards. She was framing the photos in old window frames, a nod to the changing city. She had spent months searching for frames. Edie had seen a few and they were chillingly beautiful.

"You've been working on this forever, I'm sure it's amazing."

"I think it's too cheesy, like it's trying too hard and not saying enough. It feels cliché but also not strong enough at the same time, I don't know. It's not working."

Edie wished she had more to offer in the realm of art. Unfortunately, she was impressed by pretty much everything Alex did. If someone created something that wasn't there before, she was in awe. So different was it from the world of Tixster, constant consumption, the only output being lazy posts of other people's art. She had never met a person who worked as hard as Alex, who put so much of themselves into the world.

"Al, the pieces I've seen are beautiful." She was so nervous when she spoke to Alex about her work. She didn't know the words of the art world. "The concept alone is brilliant. And the windows you're making, they're stunning. I can't even explain it."

"Thank you," Alex said. "The other problem is that window frames are *so* hard to find! I need at least a dozen more and I feel like I've searched the whole city." Her voice was perkier now after the compliment. This was how it always went, she just needed a little prodding, deep down Alex knew her work was good. "It just feels like it's brilliant one day and then the next it feels like the dumbest thing in the world."

"You say that about every project."

Alex laughed.

"I think you kind of have to feel that way. At least that's what it seems like from watching you. Your craziest ideas will inevitably feel absurd. But they're your best ideas!"

Alex slumped on the couch next to Edie. She had finished chopping vegetables and the soup was simmering. "Thank you for saying that. It's helpful just to have a reminder that I'm not completely crazy."

"Well, you *are* completely crazy."

Alex gave her a look—that gap in her teeth.

"How is *your* project going?" she asked playfully.

Edie appreciated the interest, even if she was mocking her. "The drugs weren't laced."

Alex looked genuinely surprised. "Oh, weird. What do they think it was then?"

"I don't know. She had K and coke in her system, and potentially more."

"Was she taking medication? Antidepressants are twice as common in women."

"I have no idea, but probably, right?" Edie wasn't about to admit that she'd started skipping hers, hoping—stupidly, she knew—that her old mania might fuel progress on the case.

Alex nodded, thinking, and it pleased Edie to finally see her taking it seriously. "A lot of people do CK on antidepressants, that couldn't have been it. But I guess it all depends on dosage and temperament?"

"CK?"

"Coke and ketamine, it's a pretty common combo."

Edie was mortified by her own ignorance, but she was used to that around Alex. "They won't give me details. But they did say the drugs probably came from the dark web."

"Sounds like they *are* giving you details." Alex looked at her, dubious. "A surprising amount of them."

"I think the detective might be into me. Or maybe he just feels sorry for me. We should invite him to your next loft party, he seems lonely."

"Okay." Alex drew out the last syllable. "Thank god it wasn't Peter's guy."

Edie nodded, groggy from the painkillers. "Can you get my water?"

Alex brought over water. "I hope you're not trying to find the dealer. Aside from the fact that the dark web is crazy, prosecuting dealers for overdose deaths just supports our state of over-incarceration." Alex was still standing, as if teaching a class. She was often didactic, but most of the time Edie appreciated it. "The suppliers aren't the problem, it's a way to avoid the actual issues in our country—total lack of support for people in need." She sat on the couch, taking Edie's feet into her lap.

"I know, I'm not trying to find the dealer, don't worry." Edie had been researching similar cases. There was no clear precedent, the outcomes were always different based on how many resources the defendant had, race was almost always a factor, and there was significant research indicating that the increase in prosecution rates for overdose deaths was not going to solve the drug problem. "I'm just curious what was going on for her, how it got to that point. It doesn't feel right." She knew how silly it sounded. "Thanks for indulging me."

"Today you get a pass, because of this"—she waved her hands at Edie's lifeless body sprawled across the couch—"whole situation."

Edie took a long gulp of water. She hadn't been allowed to drink or eat anything since midnight the night before. She finished the glass and handed it back to Alex, who took it wordlessly and filled it back up. "I met her sister."

Alex turned, mouth open.

"She works near me!" Edie laughed and couldn't stop laughing, partially because of the drugs, partially because Alex had stared Leah up and down at the salad shop, though Edie wasn't about to reveal as much, and partially because of how silly and sad it all was.

Alex burst into laughter, too. "Like that has anything to do with it."

"I saw that she lived in SF and wanted to pay my condolences."

"Uh-huh." She was not convinced. "So you didn't ask her about the case, then?"

"I mean, we talked about Anaya if that's what you're asking."

"Right." Alex nodded. "Does Peter know you're doing this? I don't like him, but you're being particularly creepy."

"No. And don't tell him!"

"Like I'd ever willingly talk to that man."

Edie wished that Alex would at least try to put in an effort with Peter. "I'm going to tell him how I feel."

Alex raised her eyebrows.

"Obviously there is something between us. And I know him, he wants a real relationship. But he's been going on all these dates." Peter's words flooded back to her, the smug look on his face against his ugly leather sofa. "He has sex with a new twentysomething like every—" She shook her head, as if trying to wake up her common sense postsurgery. The last thing she wanted was for Alex to hate him even more. "Anyway, that's not who he is. It feels like he's changing and I want to talk to him before it, I don't know, gets too far."

"Gross. So, when are you telling this wonderful, clearly moral and honorable man that he's the love of your weird, twisted life?"

"This Friday." Edie didn't have it in her to argue. "We're going to a party. You should come!"

Alex rolled her eyes.

Chapter Fifteen

SHE SPOTTED HIM right away, in the back, by the food. In the end, she was glad Alex had stayed home, it meant her attention to the task would be undivided. The house was old and crowded. You had to walk down a long narrow hallway, made even narrower by the rows of people lining the smudgy white walls, to get to the party. Most people crowded in the living room and overflowed into the kitchen. A handful of familiar faces peppered a sea of strangers. It was the thirty-sixth birthday of one of Peter and Edie's mutual friends. Neither of them knew her that well, they both found her a little too boring and a little too energetic, but she had a huge apartment and knew how to rally a crowd.

The moment Edie locked eyes with Peter she knew he was happy to see her. He was resting against the counter by the sink, talking to a woman with red lips and a blue dress that hugged her curves. The woman was clearly interested, but by the eagerness with which he caught Edie's eye, Peter did not feel the same. He could engage people better than any man Edie had ever met, but she knew he despised the routine laughter and mindless affirmation at parties like this.

Edie got her drink, said hello to a few friends, took her time making her way over to him, where she knew she would stay for the rest of the night. She had promised herself she wouldn't bring up Anaya. Not only would it upset him, it was too risky. She planned to get very drunk in order to finally tell Peter how she felt, and so she had to set clear and strict rules, lest she reveal how psychotically she'd been pursuing the case. She kept herself busy, talking to whoever was nearby, while he finished up his chat with the blue dress. Minutes later he appeared by her side and threw an arm around her shoulder.

Without a word they made their way to a far corner so they could discuss everyone else at the party without worry. On the opposite end of the living room a group was playing Balderdash and just the sight of it made Edie want to crawl under the couch, or simply die. "Want to play?" Peter asked with a wide grin. He knew how she felt about games, a tool for the uninventive.

According to Edie, any adult who needed a board game to stay entertained at a party was distressingly dull; it was a substitute for real connection. This stance delighted Peter because he fundamentally disagreed with every bit of it. To Peter, games were not an excuse to avoid connection, but an added layer, another dimension of it. Games allowed people to get close to one another in ways that would otherwise be impossible. Edie took the point. But the people who relied on games for bonding were not people Edie cared to bond with.

"So all you want to do is talk all the time?" he asked. "Nothing else?"

"Exactly."

"I reject that argument, there has to be something else you like doing with people." There may as well have been no one else at the party, they were both so immersed in their own dialogue.

"Nope," she said flatly. "I hang out with people so I can get to know them, learn from them. If we're not talking, I'd rather just be alone."

"Then you don't like seeing movies with people," he said confidently, like he was on the verge of a point.

"No, I guess I don't."

He looked at her skeptically. She always saw movies with people.

"I see movies with people because it's more socially acceptable. But I'd just as happily go on my own. I prefer to watch Netflix in my house."

"But you get to talk about it after!" he protested, and Edie flushed with confidence.

"Exactly. I like the talking. We can both see movies on our own, and then when we want to talk, I'll join." It felt like being home, this affectionate push and pull.

He took a sip of his drink, taking the point and thinking harder. A moment later he was smiling again. "Then you don't like dancing?" His smirk tightened. "Can't really talk when you're dancing." He had found a crack in her stance.

"Fine." She smiled wide, shoving her head into his chest. "I like dancing."

They strolled onto the now crowded dance floor at the far end of the house in some poor soul's bedroom. The mattress was propped up against the wall for space, who knew where everything else was. The DJ had set up shop atop an old Ikea dresser. It wasn't long before Edie and Peter were pressed together, groin to groin, dancing sloppily to '90s hip-hop. Seeing who could go down the farthest, then stay down, one of them, usually Edie, toppling over, and Peter scooping her up. They were sharing a bottle of bourbon, Peter's favorite, passing it from one to the other. Bourbon gave Edie nightmarish hangovers but she was too happy to think about tomorrow tonight.

The room was dark and no one else mattered. Peter was high on coke, his movements sharp, his laugh quick. "These drugs are potent tonight," he said.

"Did what's-his-name get a new source?" She had no idea what language to use. "What's that guy's name again, North Beach guy?"

"Greg."

"Greg!"

"Greg had a kid and moved out to Walnut Creek." He mimicked a crying face. "So lame."

"Super lame," she repeated absentmindedly, her thoughts suddenly stumbling through the haze of the bourbon. "You found a new guy?"

"*Actually* . . ." He raised his eyebrows as if impressed with himself. "I got it online."

It was as if the party had melted beneath her. She felt an urgent need to grip Peter by the shoulders and ask him at the top of her lungs what the fuck happened that night with Anaya. Instead, she swallowed and steadied herself.

"You're buying drugs online now, too?" She tried her best to sound aggravated but playful. They regularly debated about the importance of face-to-face interactions. Edie argued physical shops were essential for human development and an empathetic culture. Peter ordered everything from TVs to toilet paper on Amazon, arguing that saving time shopping allowed people to be more productive in other, more important ways.

"Dark web, baby. Super easy and actually really safe. If I never had to buy anything in person again, I'd be happy."

"We know." She forced an eye roll. "How do you buy drugs online anyway?" she ventured. "Can they track the purchases back to you?"

"No, it's really cool, actually, this thing called onion routing. You know when you interact with a website"—she could tell by his tone he was launching into an explanation—"you send an encrypted message so only that site can read it?"

Edie nodded. She didn't technically know, but she had a sense she should, being an engineer, and it sounded right.

"So, on the dark web, there's a layer on top of that, encrypting *that* message with an encryption key for another server on the network, chosen at random, then wrapped in another encrypted message directing it to another node with another key, so it's like this ball of messages and each destination knows where it came from and where it's going next, but it can't be traced back to the sender of origin." He was grinning, he loved playing teacher.

"Okay, layers of encryption; hence the onion," Edie said, actually kind of impressed.

"Exactly. So if you 'unpeel' the outer layer, the inner layers aren't readable by anyone, no one knows who you are after that first node."

"But, like . . ." It was a dumb question but she'd spent enough time in tech to know the seemingly dumb questions were always the ones worth asking. "What website do you go to? Like how do you even get started?"

He smiled, pleased. "The website is the tricky part." This was how it was with coding, the simplest things, like setting up your terminal and doing your first code push were impossibly annoying. Coding itself wasn't particularly hard, but only super confident people didn't feel like they were doing something terribly wrong in the first few steps. Edie always thought it was an intimidation mechanism—someone could make the process easier if they wanted to—but like finance and its unnecessary vocabulary, it made the whole ordeal feel exclusive.

"You have to download this special browser, Tor, and then enter in a totally insane website. The websites, like Silk Road, for example." She nodded, feeling a desperate urge to swallow, but not wanting to seem tense. "They're always changing, and there's no directory tracking them. The website creates a node on the network and asks it to broadcast what website it is and how to reach it so you have to find that."

"That sounds insane." She didn't care anymore. All she cared about was that Peter now purchased his drugs on the dark web, just like whoever gave Anaya her drugs.

"Oh, it's totally insane. And the URLs are actually digital signatures so they're crazy-looking and a lot of fake sites pretend they're the real site, essentially mirroring it to get your info. You have to compare the URL in the captcha with the actual URL to make sure you're on the real site. And the load times are ridiculously slow and always timing out because of the onion thing. And you have to use Bitcoin to pay, so that's a whole thing."

"That sounds like a nightmare." She took a sip of her drink, wishing she could mute him.

"It is. But it's also pretty cool and the drugs tend to be safe because dealers care about their reputation on there, anyone can see what people say about them."

She had to ask. She had to know. She needed to keep believing he had no part in Anaya's death. "When did you switch over?" She could feel, even as the words left her mouth, an intensity in the question that didn't fit the moment.

His head cocked slightly. She should have indulged him longer. "Just recently." He looked away, scanning the room. "Everyone does it now."

Right. Of course. There were thousands of people in San Francisco buying drugs online. Anaya, or someone she knew who wasn't Peter, was one of them. Surely, she had been in San Francisco long enough to befriend a hacker. Peter's new source meant nothing. He'd said she was fine. He'd said it wasn't his fault.

Another sip. And another. She had to make the thoughts stop.

Edie saw other, more beautiful women eye Peter and then her. A few of the bolder ones tried to join them, hovering around the periphery. Edie let them. She knew the drill. Peter would entertain their interest, darting glances at Edie as whoever he was with danced to the actual beat, hips moving rhythmically. He couldn't keep up nor would he try. When the song ended, he'd return to Edie so they could bounce around ridiculously. Too old to care.

After a long time, they escaped to the kitchen for air. They felt each other's shirts as they left the room, comparing whose was sweatier—Peter's, always Peter's—and leaned against the sink as Edie poured them both water. Peter chugged his like he'd just finished a race.

Edie's body had metabolized the alcohol well, she was buzzed but not sick, thanks to the dancing. Suddenly she remembered her hair. It must have looked crazy, sweat or moisture in any form did not go over well. She felt her wrists for a tie but they were bare, it must have slipped off. Peter had finished his water and was staring at her, amused. She patted her hair down frantically, trying to comb it into place behind her ears.

He pulled a thin black hair-tie from his pocket. "Looking for this?"

She jumped on him, wrapped her arms tightly around his lean frame.

"It fell earlier," he said when she let him go. "I knew you'd need it later."

There was no way he couldn't see how right they were for each other. She was certain—would have bet millions if she had it—that she was the single person he liked spending time with most. He handed her the water. "Drink a lot of this or that bourbon is going to get you tomorrow." He knew her hangovers as well as she did. "You want food?"

"No, I'm okay." She drank the water and plotted her next move. They were both leaning against the counter, watching the party play out like a movie. A group of nearby women surrounded a tall guy in thick glasses with a substantial beard, arguing about something in a playful way. Two of the women were laughing, while one couldn't have been less amused. The man was smiling like a child, but stole glances at the disapproving woman, clearly seeking her approval.

"I can't believe this is the first time we're both single," Edie said finally, filling her glass back up with water for something to do with her hands.

"I know!" Peter said, eyes still glued to the party. "That relationship was such a trap."

Edie turned back to him, landed by his side, her shoulder touching his arm. "Not all relationships are traps," she ventured. "You just have to find the right one. It has to feel natural." The setup was good. She looked up to catch his eye and intuit what she was really talking about, but when she searched for his smile, she saw nothing but the back of his head. She followed his gaze to a girl, or more accurately, a child, who seemed to have just arrived. Her leather coat was still on, and beneath it she was wearing barely anything. Her dress would have been a shirt on most women and barely covered her ass. It was ridiculous to wear in San Francisco, a city that dropped to freezing as soon as the sun set. When she took off her coat as she walked toward the kitchen, Edie realized the dress also did very little to cover her freezing, hard nipples. Her hair was thick and blond and the waves ran down her back like a waterfall.

"Peter!" Edie nearly screamed. In an instant she felt unbearably old, like a quilt better off in a closet. That Peter thought he was in the same conceivable category as this child felt absurd. She called his name again. He turned. "Don't even think about that."

He smiled mischievously with a twitch of his eyebrow. A smile that acted, simultaneously, as a dare. A smile Edie knew well.

"She's a *child*, Peter."

"She has to be over twenty-one."

"Shut up." She shoved him and wobbled a bit in the process. He held her arms to steady her. It felt good. "Don't be that guy," she grumbled, leaning into his chest.

When he looked down at her the mischief in his eyes was gone, warmth taking its place. "I'm just fucking around. What were we talking about?"

A weight lifted. She took a breath, steadying herself. "We've never both been single," she started again, mapping out where to go from there. "It just"—she paused—"it just feels really nice."

"Yeah, it's really fun," he stated matter-of-factly, not even meeting her eye, and Edie felt as if a wave of cold air had entered the room. The momentum from their dancing was wearing off. She had to act quickly.

She put her hand on his arm, glided it down to his hand. She always got handsy when she was drunk, it didn't feel weird. She leaned against him, his body a plank steadying her. "Do you ever think we should maybe try to be, like . . ." She paused. There was no way to say it without sounding cliché. "Like, more than friends?"

She could feel his muscles twitch. His hard abs getting harder, her head, once resting on his chest, suddenly bereft as he pulled his body back.

He stared at her, his large green eyes piercing into hers. She wanted so badly to look away. He didn't have to say a thing, she knew what was coming. "That's not a good idea."

Her eyes shot to the ground, she was terrified she might cry.

"We're too good of friends, E. You're my best friend." Even in his rejection, this touched her. "That would be a terrible idea." His voice was lighter now, his arms wrapped around her. He began to laugh, and, strangely, she appreciated it. She could write the whole thing off as a funny experiment. "It's not worth the risk. And I really don't want a relationship right now."

"I wasn't asking for a relationship," Edie yelped. "I just said more than friends. You're sleeping with everyone else these days. Why can't we sleep together?" It wasn't the direction she planned to go but it was the only one left.

Peter tilted his head as if mentally checking her in place. There was no possible world in which Edie would want to be fuck buddies with Peter and they both knew it. And yet if that was all he could give, she was willing to take it. She turned to the sink to fill up the cup that was giving her life and gulped hard as she contemplated her next move.

When she turned back she saw the girl, standing next to Peter. He was handing her a red cup. Edie's eyes narrowed and she waited until they met Peter's, which took longer than she would have liked. When they did connect, he didn't abandon his conversation with the child, who was apparently named Maggie, but invited Edie into it.

"Maggie's cousins with the birthday girl," he said to Edie as if she might actually care. "She just moved to San Francisco."

Maggie nodded along. "Now I just have to find a job."

Edie made no effort to hide her reaction, a concoction of disgust and disappointment, which she directed at Peter in what she hoped was a razor-sharp glare.

"Where do you live?" he asked turning back to the girl.

Edie walked away with no destination. She circled the room, eyeing the crowd. Everyone seemed to be in their twenties. She only felt old in the presence of the young. It wasn't a matter of their skin or the lines on their face, Edie could barely make those out under the dim lights. It was the sloppiness with which they approached the night that gave them away.

She spotted a familiar face, a man whom she'd met through friends. She vaguely remembered sharing a joint with him at Dolores Park. She knew he was in his late forties, had gotten divorced a few years ago, and was by far the oldest person at the party. He asked how she was while simultaneously trying to pull her onto the dance floor. If she'd answered he wouldn't have noticed. He was sweaty and on drugs and Edie pulled herself away from his needy grip.

When she finally returned to Peter he was still impossibly engaged with the girl. She watched them for five minutes—she counted—like a creep, she was too drunk to care. The party felt more like an amusement park or a video game than real, actual life. Not once did the girl chime in with more than a laugh or a question. Peter's mouth ran on and on.

Finally, Peter caught Edie's eye.

She twitched her head to the side to indicate she wanted to leave.

He shot her a patient smile and said goodbye to Maggie.

"I'll get us a cab," he said, throwing his arm around her. Edie fetched their jackets from the pile.

"Someone's not feeling very friendly tonight," he said as he threw on his coat.

She shook her head. "She was a baby, Peter. An actual fetus."

"She's actually a recent engineering grad from Stanford. I'm sure you two would have had a lot in common." This stung. He knew it would.

"I'm not saying she's dumb. God, Peter." They squeezed through the narrow hallway, even more crowded than when they'd entered, until they reached the clearing of the stairs. "I'm saying you're both in very different stages of your life. Your experiences and context and maturity are *so* different."

"Or not."

She stared at him, searching. She had stopped walking but he went down a few more steps before noticing she'd stopped. He turned and stared up at her.

"If you really are perfectly matched with a woman that young, you should ask yourself why."

"I guess I'll just have to see when I take her out."

Edie's eyes itched. She blinked quickly but it was too late, she could see a flash of recognition in his face, an awareness of how much she cared. She'd tipped from teasing into hurt and she hated herself for it. He reached his hand out for hers and she took it. He held it tightly as they walked to the black car waiting outside.

SHE STARED OUT the window as taquerias and shiny neon bars streamed by on Valencia Street. Nearly nothing remained from her first few years in SF, less than a decade ago.

The car turned sharply up Eighteenth Street and Peter fell into her. His body felt warm against her chilled skin on this annoyingly cold spring night. "E," he whispered. "You okay?" He hadn't shifted his weight back into position so his face hung inches from hers.

"I just think we should have sex," she blurted, the world still wobbly and dreamlike. The words were tight coming out of her mouth but it felt so good to set them free.

He sat up. "Edie." The muscles in his face were pulled tight, controlled. "I'm telling you, that's not a good idea."

She fell back onto the window, forcing a smile to keep the whole disastrous attempt light. "You literally have sex with *everyone.*" She pushed out a laugh, to make it sound more like a joke than a plea, but it came out hollow and desperate. "You're so dumb," she said, moving her shoulder up to look like a shrug. "It'll be fun."

He was silent for a minute. "It won't end well."

This hurt. How sure he was that he could hurt her. She stopped being playful, crossed her arms and looked out the window of the Lyft. Anger was all she had left—her last move. "You're not attracted to me, are you? You can just say it." She had thought it all her life. That Peter would never go for her. Her hair was too frizzy, her features too bland. She was thin but not hot. She wasn't striking, she was mediocre. She wanted to hear him say it, to see how harshly he would reject her, how mean he could be.

"That's not it. I just really care about you."

"Right," she said, eyes still on the window. "So you're a feminist, but you only date twenty-year-old models. Very cool."

"Don't be a dick, Edie."

She wanted to jump out of the car. She hated herself.

"E." He took her hand again, rubbed it slowly with his thumb. "You know I'm attracted to you." It was the matter-of-factness that hit her. It was an *of course.* She actually believed him. "I just don't want to ruin what we have. It means a lot to me." She didn't turn right away, but when she did his eyes were pleading.

"So if I were a stranger," she started, now unable to hold back her smile, "and you just met me at that party . . ." She trailed off, distracted by his nodding. "Then you'd sleep with me?"

"Totally." His face had softened, eyes sincere.

She rolled up the window, shoved a few pieces of sweet-mint gum in her mouth, and stared through the foggy glass. She hadn't expected it. She hadn't even thought, in all her planning for this moment, to ask the question. But it was all she'd needed. It was better, even, than actually sleeping with him, which would have introduced a whole new set of worries. She could sit tight knowing she was just as desirable as any of the women he pursued. It set her free.

When she finally caught hold of her consciousness, which was painfully slippery from all the bourbon, she stole a glance at him from across the seat. He was heads down, face lit by the glow of his phone, typing away. He reminded her, in the soft digital glow, of a mouse on a wheel. Was it really possible that this was all it took? A simple verbal validation, the ordinary assurance of her attraction. There was, and she looked, she really tried to feel, no inkling of attraction left. Let her hair fuzz to its heart's content, her sagging face rest naturally where it landed, her energy, once directed at Peter like a laser, spread like gas. She rolled down her window and laughed hysterically out into the fog. For the first time in as long as she had known him, she felt no desire to sleep with Peter Masterson.

Chapter Sixteen

S HE WAS TRYING to decide where emailing Leah landed on a scale of deranged to normal when her name flashed across Edie's screen. She assumed she was hallucinating, surely more likely than Leah actually reaching out, but there it was. A real, clickable email from Leah Thomas. Apparently, she'd read something about Tixster in the news—they were partnering on a local music festival in Golden Gate Park—and it made her think of Edie.

The opportunity to correspond was too good not to take advantage of. She would invite her out. Not coffee, no more coffee. She would suggest a drink. Leah's response was as quick as the first time. Was Edie free tonight? She canceled her Tinder date. Of course she was.

LEAH WAS SITTING at the bar, a few sips into her drink. Edie loved this place—the white tablecloths, the small lit candles, the bowls of crunchy Asian snacks peppered around the room—and was pleased Leah had chosen it.

They greeted one another with a hug and the pressure of Leah's hand against her back shot a chill down Edie's spine. Leah wore a crewneck sweater with a denim collar peeking out from the neck.

Her slim jeans lay neatly over her leather boots. Edie, unsure what to wear to impress a woman, wore a fitted black sweatshirt, distressed mom-jeans, and her white Reeboks. Her curly hair had always made her feel incapable of glamour so she put effort into trying to look as if she put in no effort. If she couldn't be beautiful, she could at least try to be cool.

Edie wasn't typically into the woo-woo culture of San Francisco, but the only way she could describe the unearned ease between them as they greeted one another and exchanged stories about their days was to admit they shared a similar energy.

Leah was drinking an amber beer. "What do you want?" she asked.

"Tequila soda." Edie had recently read it had fewer calories than vodka.

Leah shook her head, a strange smile across her face. "That's Anaya's drink."

Edie remembered the night they'd met, their matching glasses, clear with a lime, and felt a childish pang of pride at another shared connection. She nearly laughed at how desperate she was for affirmation.

"Half the time she forgot the soda, she was always sipping tequila on ice."

Edie's drink was served.

"I'm sure this is a dumb question . . ." Leah started, and Edie was immediately grateful, so rare was it to sit across from someone with humility. "But do you get to go to that music festival since you work for Tixster?" She seemed different from the first time they'd met, weeks ago now, more present, almost playful.

"That would mean there was something cool about my job. And I assure you, there is nothing cool about my job."

Leah laughed.

"Are you going to it?" Edie asked.

"I am. I'm kind of a music festival junkie."

"Nothing wrong with that," Edie lied, tearing at her coaster. She was suspicious of people who liked crowds.

"Um . . . it can be a pretty annoying crew."

Edie smiled. "What kind of music are you into?"

"I like most things, but I'm really into the house scene. Electronic festivals, ambient electronics are my favorite."

It sounded like Edie's nightmare. "That's cool."

"I'll send you one of my favorite events," she said, typing something into her phone. "What kind of music are you into?" she asked, placing her phone in her pocket.

Edie let out a breathy laugh. "My exploration of music stopped a decade ago." It wasn't that she didn't care about music, jogging to her running playlist was close to a religious experience, but the music that moved her was from a time when she had the capacity to be moved. A time that felt like forever ago.

She didn't want to talk about herself. She wanted to talk about Anaya. But she couldn't talk about Anaya when Leah finally seemed to be doing okay. Although, any detail of Leah's life was, in a way, a detail of Anaya's life. "Do you ever write your own stuff?" Edie asked.

"God no," Leah laughed. "Anaya is the creative one. And my mom. They both loved to write." She seemed lost in thought again and Edie regretted her selfish prying. "Anaya was my mom's golden child. I just blasted my music and played with the computer most of the time."

The mention of her mother made Edie's breath quicken. She wanted to whip out her phone and her spreadsheet of questions.

"Naya hated my festival addiction, but she tagged along every now and then. She loved that I had something I loved." Leah was staring down at her drink. "She had her writing, of course. She always said that me, my mom, and her writing were the loves of her life." Leah laughed to herself and it finally made sense to Edie why she had invited her out. She was desperate to talk about her sister, and she needed someone to listen. "You know, Anaya hated writing as much as she loved it—opposite edges of the same sword. It made her miserable."

Edie raised her eyebrows, asking for more.

"She always said it was torture, trying to figure out what she thought, to get it just right. She was so alive when she was writing but she was also tortured. The joy came after."

"Wow," Edie said, genuinely surprised. "Her writing feels so effortless. I always thought it just kind of flowed out of her."

Leah let out a gruff breath.

"How are you feeling with everything?" Edie asked.

Leah studied her face. "They found bruises on her body. Marks on her neck."

It wasn't new information but just hearing it out loud was enough to make her gasp.

"They think it was from the guy she was seeing." Her voice didn't waver but her eyes were pained. "Apparently, he was over that night."

Edie's eyes shot up and she noticed Leah notice her surprise. "How do they know?"

"His DNA was all over the place." She stared at Edie as she spoke. "And inside of her."

Edie stared at her damp, torn coaster, unable to move. The revolting alcohol-soaked heap of shreds was the only thing that made sense. Peter could be an asshole, but she'd asked him if he'd had sex with Anaya that night and he'd said no.

Hadn't he? He'd shaken his head, she remembered that, he'd made her feel like a monster for even asking. But then she remembered the waiter had interrupted them. He had taken a bite of his taco. And he hadn't *actually* said no. She did remember. The words had lingered with her since that night. *Nothing bad happened while I was there* was all he'd said.

The bar was near empty but a group burst through the door, loud and laughing. Leah's hand was lying inches from Edie's on the bar, smooth and perfect, and she wanted to grab it, to tell her she was sorry, but she went for the coaster instead, ripped at the biggest chunk and continued to tear it into a million little pieces.

"So, he's the top suspect."

"Suspect?" Edie asked quickly, too quickly. "They don't think it was . . ."

"He could have given her the drugs, pressured her into it."

"Can they find out whose drugs they were?" She wondered if she'd listened to Peter's big, dumb dark web explanation for nothing.

"Maybe." Leah put down her beer and turned her body toward Edie's so her knees grazed the outside of her thigh. "Peter Masterson." Leah dropped the words like marbles.

"Who?" A wave of self-hatred flooded over her; she forgot why she was doing any of this. She had to tell Leah everything she knew about Peter. Certainly that she knew him, and well.

"That's the guy's name."

But what could she say that would actually help? That he was in an asshole phase, sure, but that wasn't who he *was*. That he did drugs, but everyone in the Bay did drugs. That he was spoiled, of course, but deep down he was kind, a *good guy*, he took care of her. "Does he have any prior offenses?" Edie stumbled, buying time.

Leah exhaled a sad laugh. "No. He's a rich white guy who works at PrimalSearch."

Edie flinched. It was like she'd skimmed the top layer off of him, like a warm cup of milk, and threw everything else—the good part—out.

She felt an animal urge to defend him. She knew she couldn't tell Leah the truth without jumping to his side, and she didn't want to put that distance between them. "Maybe he can help put the pieces together?" she offered.

Leah's dark eyes clung to Edie, searching. "I hope so."

There was a long silence and a Radiohead song shuffled onto the speaker. She thought of her bike ride home, the cold wind against her face, images of bruises, the university receptionist with the bun.

"I've been rereading Anaya's work," Edie started. It was a sharp turn, but enough silence had passed that it felt like an open field, clear enough to move in any direction. "I think she mentioned she had another book in the works?" Edie kept her eyes on her drink, her hands wrapped tightly around the cold, dripping glass.

"A draft was due that night." Leah's jaw clenched. "She worked through a lot in that manuscript. She'd worked on it for years."

"She mentioned that." *Fifteen years*, Edie remembered. "She said she was writing about a trauma." She paused, hoping Leah might chime in, but she sat still and quiet. "She was actually going to send me a chapter. She emailed me a few days before." It felt good, to conjure Anaya in this way, to admit they did actually share a past, if only briefly. Still, no response. "Do you think it'll ever be published?"

Leah shook her head. "I don't want to talk about it."

"Eventually, though, right?"

Her face was stone.

"It's just"—Edie felt tipsy, but it had to be said—"well, her writing changed my life." It sounded pathetic. She knew it did. But it wasn't a lie. And Leah was smiling. "It opened up how I see things," Edie continued, "like I was living under a blanket or something. She must have done that for a lot of women."

The warmth in Leah's eyes returned. A look of gratitude, and happiness, yes, but more than anything, a look of understanding. "I don't know who I'd be without Anaya," Leah said, then swallowed hard and looked down at the bar.

The song switched. Edie needed to change the subject before she stepped on any other mines. She needed to be someone Leah could turn to.

"So what do you do at Datsta?" she asked.

"I'm an engineer," Leah said with enthusiasm. "I really like it. Heads down, keeping to myself. Knowing there's an answer for everything if you just think hard enough."

There were few people Edie envied more than woman engineers who loved their jobs. But she understood. She used to love that, too.

"And I get to mine through people's data all day!" She raised her eyebrows at how bad it sounded. "It's great."

"Sounds super important and totally legal." She remembered the bowl of snacks on the bar and grabbed a few, relaxing slightly. After a drink she cared less about calories, which was partly why she liked drinking.

Leah laughed. It occurred to Edie that she hadn't seen real joy in Leah's face since she'd met her. She really was beautiful. "It *is* legal." She took a sip of beer. "Barely."

Edie's phone, which was stupidly lying face up on the bar, buzzed. She flipped it over.

"Tinder date?" Leah asked.

Apparently, she hadn't flipped it quickly enough. "A match," she smiled. "It doesn't matter. Tinder only matches me with freaks."

"Let me see."

Showing her friends the monsters she was matched with was a common party trick. But it hit her as Leah grasped for her phone, that not only did she not want Leah to know how little she was valued on these dumb sites, she didn't want Leah to know she was straight.

"Come on, it'll be fun." Something in her eyes, the steadiness, made Edie trust her. Not about the fun part, but that it didn't matter who she dated, that Leah was interested regardless.

Leah held the phone for no more than a second before she burst out laughing and Edie laughed along, she didn't need to see whatever profile she was looking at, she knew how bad they were. As their breath steadied, Leah slid the phone along the table and back to Edie.

"So that's what it's like to date guys," she said, not trying to hide her relief.

Edie nodded. "These days it is. I really hit a wall at thirty-five. The dangers of filters."

Leah laughed. "That's exactly what Anaya said." She rested her elbows on the table and cupped her chin in one hand. "So do you only date guys?"

Butterflies was the only way to describe the buzzing inside her, and she realized with sadness how long it'd been since she'd felt them. "That was the plan." She leaned her head in her hand, elbow on the table, mirroring Leah's pose. She was properly buzzed and the words just came out. "But I'm thinking that might change." Peter had served as her mold for so long, anyone she was interested in had, in some way, been a version of him. But now he was gone. Her interest was free to spread into its own form. How much had she closed herself off to?

"I hope it does," Leah said with a quick twitch of her lip.

The only problem was that she was afraid of women; the thought of their rejection felt unbearable. Not to mention the thought of hurting a woman, being lazy with her emotions the way she could be with men because men had hurt her for so long. And then the biggest fear of all: If she couldn't make a relationship work with a woman, either, then she couldn't blame everything on men.

THAT NIGHT, EDIE found herself, once again, rereading Anaya's books. Like a children's story, the passages soothed her. Her words felt like the familiar voice of a mother, a steady pillar to lean on. The chapter she'd turned to tonight was titled, rather dramatically, "The Drug of Male Approval." Just seeing the word *drug* made her shiver. She had scanned the digital version of her books for the word *drug*, of course—it was one of the first things she'd done—but the mention of it was rare; appearing only in obscured forms, like the title she was reading now. Edie's eyes were starting to close around the words when she heard a buzz, angry and intrusive, against her wooden nightstand.

She reached for her phone but a small part of her already knew what was waiting. **Talking to the cops tomorrow. Will let you know how it goes. Dinner after?**

She wasn't surprised that he'd had sex with Anaya that night. But she *was* surprised that he'd kept it from her. She didn't reply right away, she wanted him to feel alone. She wanted him, for once, to believe that everything might not be okay.

She texted Leah that she'd had a great time, then navigated to the Tixster link that Leah had sent her at the bar, energized at the possibility of new information. She scanned the page. Lots of neon, one of those silly silent discos, audio samples that felt like a head-ache.

Edie almost never went on Tixster outside of work, but she quickly navigated to Leah's profile. Thrillingly, she saw that Leah was now following her and was what they called a "super user." Edie browsed her page, studying her concert history, trying to understand this person who enjoyed Women and Non-binary Electro Morning Bike Meetups, how to act around her in way where Edie might not feel utterly dull, until she clicked on a bluegrass festival two years ago and froze. Her name hovered on Edie's screen. Leah had tagged her sister.

She clicked to Anaya's page, her fingers shaking with anticipation. But it was empty other than that one tagged festival. Nothing but her profile photo, one Edie had never seen, hastily snapped in a bathroom mirror.

Staring at Anaya, unguarded in her home, wearing the leather jacket she'd seen in person just a month ago, she felt an overwhelming affection toward her—beyond affection, something like devotion. It was a nice photo, intentional, at least, and why would she care what her icon was if she never used the platform?

Staring at the small phone obscuring her beautiful dark eyes in the mirror, Edie noticed the image was smaller than Leah's, the text

on her profile was from the old design template, her background image was Tixster's standard yellow, not customizable. Anaya had not
upgraded to the new version of Pages, and any users who hadn't up-
dated to the new version of Pages were considered inactive, all posts
older than three years were automatically archived. Her Page was
blank, but that didn't mean there was nothing there.

Chapter Seventeen

SHE'D FORGOTTEN HOW to export a user's history so Jim would have to do it. She explained—nervously, somewhat inaccurately—that her friend had recently passed away and she was helping with an investigation.

She wasn't searching for anything in particular, she just craved information, little hits of discovery. The need to know more was the only thing that mattered. It was impossible to stop unraveling the thread, the way it was impossible to not eat her Nutri-Grain bar each morning or run her five miles each night. There was no world in which she would not keep going.

Maybe if Anaya had attended events where drugs were rampant, it would imply she had other people besides Peter to give her drugs and the overdose would make more sense. There was a whole language of coded emojis that the Trust and Safety team regularly scanned for—chocolate bars, bananas, diamonds, dragons, and, of course, the snowflake—that loosely veiled drug activity. Jim promised to get her the list soon, which, for Jim, meant sometime next week.

She propped her phone beside her keyboard so she could see it while she worked on Tixster's two-year roadmap, mapping out the future of the only thing she could control. She was waiting for word from Peter, or Leah, who distressingly hadn't returned her last text. But when the screen finally lit up in a heart-stopping glow, the name on the screen was not the one she was expecting.

"Ron?" she whispered, cupping her hands around the receiver to hide the noise of the open office. "What's up?"

"You know I can't share details about the case," he started. It was funny to hear Ron's voice, deep and rough, soften now that they'd grown closer. "But if we questioned a suspect, you know I'd *want* to tell you, right?"

She felt guilty for declining the past two times he'd asked her for drinks. She liked having him circling without having to actually see him. "I know you'd want to, Ron. Yes."

"It's unfortunate I wouldn't be able to."

"Riiiight." She let the *i* drag playfully. Why couldn't she just suck it up and date an older man like every other woman her age? "That is unfortunate," she said, proud of how good she'd become at acting, how natural it felt. "I'd be very curious how it went."

"Not great for the guy."

She grew tense, not with fear, she realized with something close to horror, but excitement.

"But good for the case." He didn't specify who "the guy" was but he didn't need to.

"What'd he say?"

Ron laughed, his chuckle loud and unrushed. "Nothing," Ron said. "Which is the only reason I can tell you anything because there's nothing to tell. He was a jerk, totally silent. Our questions could have been over in a minute if he'd appeared more . . ." He paused, searching for a word. "Human? If he gave us anything. Now we have to dig around, the whole nine yards."

It wasn't like Peter to withhold. These days he felt less like the person she knew better than anyone, and more like someone she barely knew at all.

"Look, once we start finding actual evidence, don't expect any calls. But we have a thread to pull at least, thought you'd be happy about that."

Edie's hands were shaking.

"So," Ron started, "any house parties on the horizon?"

She didn't have to think, the words just came out. "Ron, I'm sorry. I'm not looking for anything serious right now." It was so easy, a familiar script. She deserved her turn to say it.

"Huh." He sounded more confused than disappointed. There was a pause, as if he were calculating something. "I wasn't asking you out, Edie. Just trying to make a goddamn friend."

"Sorry," she stammered, racing through their interactions, wondering if she had really gotten it this wrong.

"This fucking city." He laughed. "Enjoy your day." She felt more drawn to him than ever, but he hung up before she had a chance to say more.

She shoved her phone into her bag, as if by making it disappear, she could make all the dumb things she'd ever said disappear with it. She stared at the spreadsheet, the *roadmap*, taking up her entire screen, each cell a color-coded date, like she could predict how every day would go for months on end. It was what she was paid to do, pretend she knew how things would play out. She nearly cried at how ridiculous it all was, how little it mattered.

She reached for her phone. She wouldn't admit she knew about the questioning. She would just ask how Leah was doing, and mention, casually, that she'd love to see her. She sent the text quickly before she had time to change her mind. She watched her phone, lifeless, for nearly an hour until it was time for her next meeting.

HER WEEKLY TEAM meeting was in Dave Matthews. Elizabeth, who set up the meetings, was too young to have any relationship to the band and had chosen it ironically. But Edie had lost her virginity to Dave Matthews—"Ants Marching," specifically—in Matt's twin dorm room bed and the conference room served as a constant, sinister reminder of how much she hated her job.

Her team went around in a circle to give their updates. Leah was mere blocks away, probably in a room just like this, hopefully with a better name. She checked her phone, still blank.

"Edie?" Elizabeth asked, and she realized everyone was staring at her. "Is it okay if I move forward with the interactive social feature? It'll be more work but I'm willing to stay late. From what I calculate, putting those extra controls in the nav bar will give us a twenty-five percent increase in engagement."

Edie had to smile at how much Elizabeth cared. She, too, had worked that hard at her age. "Let's do it. I love it." She couldn't remember the last time she used the word *love* and now she was using it on a social media feature in a global navigation bar.

"Great! If you have any additional changes, please send feedback. We can work it in." Her speech, her posture, her freshly pressed T-shirt tucked into her polka-dotted skirt, were as polished as her baby blue nails. Edie wondered if it took as much effort as it looked like, or if somehow this came easily for her. Either way, Elizabeth would do well—in life and in love. The world rewarded neatness in women.

"I trust your judgment." It was how Edie had learned to manage at Tixster—how Derek had managed her since she'd started—not at all. He said he liked to lead with trust, but as far as she could tell, he did very little with his days. Edie had worked tirelessly that first year to prove her worth and secure her title, a title she should have been hired into in the first place. But that was done. Now she did what she had to at Tixster, and nothing more.

The meeting ended, and Elizabeth approached Edie before she reached the door. "Jim mentioned you were looking for an archived user."

Stupid Jim.

But Elizabeth looked concerned. "I'm sorry about what happened to your friend. Jim was busy, and you know how he is." They had never talked about Jim directly, but they shared a knowing smile. "I pulled it for you, told him not to worry about it."

"Elizabeth . . ." She was genuinely grateful. "That's so nice of you. Thank you."

"I'll send you the file when I'm back at my desk but, so you know, her event log is pretty much empty."

It was a long shot, thinking Anaya was some secret party animal, stupidly posting her outings on Tixster. "Good to know. Thanks anyway, just thought I'd try." She shut her laptop and headed toward the door.

"I did find something, though," Elizabeth called. "This wasn't archived on her account, but you know we take down posts that violate our policies. One of hers was removed just a few months ago."

Edie stood in the doorframe, too shocked to move. Shocked that Anaya had posted, and so recently, yes, but also that Elizabeth had outsmarted her. "I hadn't thought about that at all. What was the post?"

"Here," Elizabeth said, clicking open a text file on her laptop. Edie stood beside her, staring at a format she knew well:

<user_num="21517">;<event><title> Women's Refuge Circle</title>; _{A wellness group for women grappling with depression, anxiety, and suicide.};<desc> We provide space to discuss the emotional and practical challenges of this time for female-identifying persons, and help one another with coping skills, education, resources, and emotional support.</desc>; <user_note> There's no shame in needing help, and profound bravery in asking for it.</user_note>; admin_flag ="triggering";</event>

It was dated two months ago. There were no other tagged users at the event; Edie figured Anaya had wanted to respect their privacy. How foolish she was, assuming she could possibly under-stand Anaya's pain, that they were somehow the same. Books were intentional pieces of work. Edie had no idea what Anaya was actu-ally going through, how much she'd been struggling.

"There's no reason support groups like this should be taken down," Elizabeth said, disrupting her thoughts. "Just the other day the Trust and Safety team crawled the site for AA meetings because it was 'off-brand.'"

The words hit her suddenly. That leather jacket, her clear, bubbly drink. *I've noticed that,* she'd said when Edie complained about this very thing. *Tech companies design apps to exploit. They suppress what makes us human.* "Everything is so curated here," Edie blurted out, furious.

She imagined Anaya getting Tixster's dumb take-down template after posting something so vulnerable, so necessary. "We should be able to handle this kind of complexity. We have half a billion in rev-enue, it's insane."

"What if," Elizabeth started, and Edie took the seat beside her. "We launched a kind of trigger warning feature, or something, maybe not that wording exactly."

Edie nodded for her to say more.

"Users could self-filter, real-time or in their settings, and opt to only see 'art' posts if they want, but could see more sensitive events, too, instead of our T and S team just removing every post that makes them uncomfortable. Sorry, it's probably dumb. I'm sure there's a rea-son we do it this way."

"Elizabeth, I love that." How had they not been doing this all along? "'Content warning,' I think is the preferred phrase." Anaya had written about the phrasing in her first book and Edie was thrilled to be putting it to use.

"Yes, that's better." She looked uneasy. "I'm pretty sure Derek will crush it. He's always making fun of that kind of thing."

"Derek's an idiot." It felt so good to say out loud. Women helping women is a super power, Anaya had explained in her first book, a dated mandate by now, but Edie remembered when it hadn't been. The first ten years of her career, feminist talk got you nothing but eye rolls. She'd come up in that culture, rolled her share of eyes as well, and knew competition still fueled most of her instincts. "You're amazing at your job, Elizabeth," she said with a kindness she hadn't mustered since Safe Home. "You know that, right?"

"Thank you." Elizabeth looked genuinely surprised. "That means a lot coming from you." She closed her computer. "I'll draft up requirements and send them over to you."

There was an energy between them, an alliance that she remembered from when Elizabeth had first joined. Somehow, she had forgotten what that felt like.

PETER ANSWERED THE door in his oldest hoodie, his favorite, she knew. He had gotten it when he first moved to SF. It had a stain on the chest from when he painted his bedroom blue, and holes in both cuffs. The string had been lost years ago. Looking at him, she was stunned at how little she felt. His smile, which was wide, did not spark one in her like it had for the past fifteen years. It looked goofy and entitled. His hoodie didn't look cute and understated, it looked pathetic. Not that she was above old clothes, but she would gladly replace all of hers if she had the means. Peter wore his old hoodie like a badge, as if he didn't need nice things, and yet he had access to all of them.

She eyed his mostly empty floor-to-ceiling bookshelf and realized he had definitely never read any of Anaya's books. For a moment, she regretted coming. Why couldn't she be the type of woman with boundaries, who cut toxic people out of her life, and all the other maxims social media touted about self-respect? But if Peter had really looked her in the eyes that first night and hidden so much from her, what else was he capable of hiding? She had to confront him, but first she had to make him comfortable enough to let his guard down, and their last interaction had been anything but comfortable.

She followed him into the living room where he had a pinot waiting for them on the coffee table. He shut off the television and poured her a glass, his leg bouncing in place.

Edie took a seat on the far end of his couch. "Don't be stressed, Peter. You said yourself it's standard for them to investigate." She wanted him to talk to the cops. If he wasn't going to tell her everything, she was rooting for Ron. She needed answers.

"It's just silly that they're asking me now. It happened over a *month* ago."

She thought of Ron's office, the stacks of papers, his stiff, heavy suit, the funding challenges he'd griped about. "I'm sure the police have a lot to deal with. It's probably standard procedure. It would be negligent of them to *not* talk to you given the circumstances."

He rolled his eyes. Took a sip of his drink. Everything in Peter's life was on-demand. When he wanted something, it happened. "It's just all so inefficient. These government agencies waste so much money it's ridiculous. They just showed up at Primals first thing in the morning."

She thought Peter had gone down to the station. She pictured Ron in the colorful walls of Primals all suited up, pulling Peter out of a meeting, and tried not to smile.

"I need my lawyer with me, you know?"

She didn't know. She tried not to think about lawyers, who had always felt like a luxury. Even just talking to one, as far as Edie knew, would cost a grand she didn't have with no promises of resolution.

"Now I have to go down to the station tomorrow." He took a sip of wine.

She watched him on his leather couch, the only seating in the room, wondering why he had been so withholding in questioning. Their conversation felt distinctly weird—silences a bit too long, eye contact a bit too short. For the first time, they each had secret lives they knew the other disapproved of.

The door buzzed and Peter took a large brown bag from the delivery girl. As he disappeared into the kitchen, a pay request popped up on her phone with a chopsticks emoji and a smiley face. She was used to Peter splitting nearly every bill to the cent, his idiotic way of treating her as an equal. But his request was for $25.42 and her chicken basil, she knew, was only $11.50.

"What did you get?" she yelled into the kitchen.

Peter came in with a pile of containers stacked in his hands and spread them out on the table. "I got us dumplings and a salad. I hope that's okay."

Arguing over money with Peter was a battle she had worn herself out on years ago in his early days of discovering libertarianism. When she began working at Safe Home, her debt mounting, he had just cashed in on Primals and only once had he ever treated her for dinner without needing something specifically in return. It never bothered her too much; he viewed splitting the cost of dinner with the same analytical precision he applied to everything in his life, and he didn't owe her anything. But increasingly he was becoming frivolous about it, not caring what he spent while still demanding they split the bill. If he was going to be precise about money, she would, too.

"My thing was only twelve dollars, why am I paying twenty-five?"

He looked offended. "You don't have to eat the dumplings. I thought you liked them. I was trying to be considerate."

"If I'm going to have to pay for something, I'd like to know about it in advance." She forced it out quickly, but her anger was impossible to hide.

"Geez." It was the worst kind of tone, declaring her hysterical, ceasing further discussion. "I won't charge you for the dumplings or the salad if you don't want them."

"Thank you," she said. Tension filled the room and she fought every instinct not to diffuse it with an apology or a self-deprecating joke. Instead, she took short measured breaths as he dramatically tapped a new payment request into his phone.

"Done."

It occurred to her that if their positions were swapped, the first thing she would have said, probably for weeks on end, would have been "Sorry." If she'd ordered the dumplings without consulting him, she'd *insist* he eat them, as many as he liked, without taking a cent. Instead, he was the one offended. Her anger did nothing but make him angry in turn, and, as Anaya had explained in every one of her books, men's anger was always the priority.

"I just don't know why you're always so adamant about splitting the bill," she said when he sat back down.

Peter looked up like a deer in headlights. In a flash his face hardened as if he were ready for battle and she knew she should have kept quiet. "First of all, obviously eat the dumplings, I don't care at all."

There was no fucking way she was going to eat the dumplings.

"Second of all, you didn't have to work at a nonprofit. That was your choice. We have the same degree. You actually have one *more* degree than I do. Other people shouldn't have to pay for your decisions." He took a bite of his dish, and then, barely audible: "I thought you wanted equality."

Something burned in the pit of her stomach. "I worked there because I was trying to do something good for the world. God forbid you ever considered that."

He rolled his eyes.

It was not a debate. It was a fight. A real, actual fight. With a quick sorry, an easy laugh, she could make it okay. But she was tired of always being the one who made it okay.

She swallowed the hurt, along with her dry chicken. The silence spoke for itself and though she wouldn't apologize she decided she would at least move them on. She had too many things she wanted to cover.

"Still having an insane amount of sex?" she asked, knowing it would appeal to his ego enough to forget about the money.

Peter lifted one shoulder, not hiding his smile. The tension eased slightly.

Her stomach twisted with a new kind of excitement. She realized she wanted every excruciating detail, needed them as justification to side against him. If he didn't want her, she wanted to soak in all the reasons she didn't want him, either.

"Is the sex different than it was with Nicole?" she asked and couldn't help but smile. It was so easy to egg him on. "Like kinky? I know Nicole hated that stuff."

Peter laughed nervously. "Kind of, actually."

She nodded for him to continue.

"Lots of the women I've been seeing like it." He paused. "I don't even know how to say it."

"Just fucking say it," Edie said, forcing a smile.

"Rough, you know? Like, really rough."

"What, whips or something?" She felt so old.

"Actually, yeah, this one girl had a whip. But more like just hard, dom type stuff."

Hearing Peter say *dom* made her want to throw up, the idea that he was rationalizing his bourgeoning misogyny with some kind of progressive sex term, but she nodded along.

"Like choking," he continued. "Not that I mind. Nicole and I never did that stuff, but turns out I'm pretty into it."

She could see how excited he was. Living in San Francisco, she knew the BDSM community was typically safe and dry and had clear lines of consent, and even she was turned on by a good power dynamic. But in the drunken hookups that made up Peter's new dating life, with women ten years younger and eager to please, she couldn't help but think it was different.

"And you don't think it has anything to do with the insanely violent porn these women grew up watching? You're sure they actually like it, they're not just doing it because that's what they think you want them to do?"

"Look, I'm not here to tell a woman what she should or shouldn't want." He put his hands up as if she were physically attacking him. "If they say they like something, who am I to argue?"

His hair fell in his face and he flicked his head back to get it out of the way. The Peter she knew in college was not this man. That boy was shy and curious, interested in others and eager to make them laugh. He was learning about the world and his part in it. The man in front of her, stretched out on his too-large leather sofa, tanned from days in the sun, shaped from nights in the gym, had learned about the world. He'd learned he was smarter and better looking and more successful than most of the people in it. He'd learned he could get whatever he wanted if he tried hard enough and so he assumed everyone else could, too.

For a moment she wished he'd shed this version of himself like dead skin. The Peter she knew must be living in there somewhere if only this ugly shell would die. But instead, he seemed to be leaning into it, not shedding that layer but growing more of it.

She thought of her recent internet searches. "You're doing after-care at least, right?" This had come up on multiple sites and she'd wondered many times since if he'd checked in with Anaya that night.

"Woah, okay then. How do you know about aftercare? Tell me everything."

She shot him a pointed look. "No, I mean I haven't experienced it but I don't live in a literal hole."

"Oh. Well, don't worry, it's not that big a deal. Choking is standard these days."

"It's really not, Peter." Her eyes rested on the rug. She had been playing with her hair, a nervous habit, and imagined it was now puffing out in every direction. When she looked up his face had relaxed. He looked closer to the Peter she knew.

"If I'm being honest . . ." He paused, looked at Edie. "Can I be honest?"

She nodded.

"I'm scared of doing what I did to Nicole to someone else." He was staring down at the gray shag carpet that, ironically, Nicole had chosen. "Women my age want to move fast. And that makes total sense." He sounded earnest, even pained. "They have a timeline. They should be with people who are ready to go at their speed." He shook his head, eyes still on the rug. "I'm just not ready."

"That's not fair," she said, barely audible. She wasn't talking to him, there was no debate to be had. Whether something was fair or not was not a good argument. And he was right. It would be awful to do what he did to Nicole to someone else. What was fair was beside the point.

But why was she letting him off so easy? Sure, biology wasn't fair, but he couldn't honestly call himself a feminist while thoughtlessly perpetuating an unfair premise. It was more work, of course it was, to grow up, but he could do that work if he wanted to, the way so many women had to. Fuck his women in tech events, his supposed allyship.

"How's dating going for you?" he asked, snapping her back into the room. They hadn't talked about the night in the cab, not a single mention of it. Mostly, Edie was grateful, but a small part of her wanted him to acknowledge it had happened, that her feelings were real.

"Nothing to report," she replied flatly. "I think I'm taking a break from online dating." She surprised herself when she said it. The break wasn't planned but she hadn't touched the apps in days. Her thoughts spun on Anaya and Leah. "I feel a little more dead inside after each date."

"Well, good. I'm happy for you." He stood up and walked to the closet by the door. "Hey, I got you something."

"What"—presents were not Peter's thing—"the fuck?"

He pulled out an Amazon box and placed it in front of her. She looked at him as if he were insane before ripping it open.

DVDs. Her favorites. The DVDs they'd watched endlessly in college before streaming was a thing. Tom Cruise's profile on the little plastic *Mission Impossible* box stared back at her. The first Matrix movie—the exact poster she'd had on her wall—came next. And then—was it really?—by far the most underrated Sandra Bullock movie of all time, *The Net*.

"Peter." There was a lump in her throat and she hoped to god he couldn't see what felt like wetness behind her eyes. "You bought these?" As presents, they were cheap and dumb. But they were parts of her, parts she'd had to move on from but parts he still loved and celebrated.

He sat beside her on the couch. "You seem so stressed lately, E. I know how you spin on things, and I know the Anaya stuff has been hard. Plus, everything you're doing for your mom. You need a break." He held Sandra Bullock in his hands. "I mean truly, they don't make them like this anymore."

She fell into his shoulder. A tear slipped down her face. "Do you remember . . ." she started.

"I know." Face in his hands.

"Who knew you had to press play a *second* time?" she burst out.

"How long do you think we were laying there listening to the *Mission Impossible* theme song before I realized you had to select the movie from a *menu*?" He mimed air quotes. DVDs had just come out and they'd stared at the intro image for close to twenty minutes before realizing that, unlike VHS, you had to actually select the movie from a menu for it to start.

"Oh *you* realized? That sounds like revisionist history."

"I'm sorry things have been so weird between us. Stay over, we'll watch one. Your pick."

It was a familiar swell. The feeling of being chosen, of someone like Peter Masterson showing her kindness. She didn't want to hate this man.

MISSION IMPOSSIBLE WAS ridiculous, but as far as entertainment went, it held up. Tom Cruise was a total psychopath but he was also, undeniably, a movie star. When she woke up perpendicular to Peter on his sectional, she noticed that his hair did, in fact, still curl in the morning.

It was early. She let herself out without waking him and walked home, then plopped back down among her pillows. In bed, she performed the standard nighttime procedure she'd missed the previous evening—scrolling through Anaya's social media. She was rereading an article Anaya had shared four months ago about the origins of female monsters and how we, as women, might reclaim the narrative over time, when a notification popped up reminding her to pay Peter for dinner.

She was brought to his profile on the payments app. Like some sort of sociopath, he had his transactions set to public. She had never noticed and laughed to herself. What kind of society was full of people so desperate to be seen, they even made their monetary transactions something to "like"? She wondered if the director of this payments feed hated themselves as much as she did.

Nevertheless, she was interested. The most recent charge, she noticed, was from a woman named Maggie R. Her icon was too small to make out but her hair was long and blond like the woman at the party. Next to the charge was a goofy-looking squid emoji. Without thinking—it was autopilot when she got in this mode, searching and clicking for a shred of information, something to cling to, an action to take—she searched the internet for *squid emoji*. Overwhelmed by the uselessness of the results, she corrected to *squid emoji euphemism meaning*. More helpful, but boring: sea life, seafood. The most suggestive association she could find was cuddling. Innocuous as it was, her heart pounded at this girl's sorry attempt at flirtation. At the thought of Peter, surely eating it up.

She kept scrolling. More transactions with Maggie R, the first of which was two days after the party where he'd met the blond girl. Each exchange had a different dumb animal emoji. Did she think that was cute? Some desperate display of quirkiness? How childish that full-on adults sent little creatures to one another with something as simple as a payment. She looked up every annoyingly twee icon, queasier with each search. There was a thrill in the discovery, a hit of energy that made her alert, alive. She continued to scroll in a trancelike state—more women's names. Little hearts next to martini glasses. Women in red dresses dancing next to men doing disco. And then, her name. Anaya T. Had she really had her profile set to public as well? It felt too hard to believe, but maybe she had wanted their transaction to be seen? Because there it was: Anaya T. to Peter M., with prayer hands and a heart emoji, that night.

Chapter Eighteen

THE WEATHER NEVER changed in San Francisco. At least not day to day, only hour to hour. The cycle—from a crisp morning to a sunny afternoon to the cold chill of sunset—remained both unpredictable and routine.

The weekend dragged on. She didn't reach out to Peter. Nor did he reach out to her. Instead, an eerie, unfamiliar silence spread between them. She was positive he would never have charged Anaya for what he claimed was just a tiny bit of ketamine. He wasn't cheap with dates the way he was with his friends. There was more to it.

Leah, on the other hand, had not ghosted Edie like she'd assumed after she didn't reply to her last two texts, but had been in Tahoe, understandably craving an escape, and was now wondering if she maybe wanted to go out next week. Edie immediately confirmed.

She'd spent the weekend inside, despite the sun, leaving her house only for her nightly run. She'd moved on from Anaya's books and was now reading the authors she'd mentioned as influences—Edie had listed them all in her spreadsheet and was working her way through.

They were always the same—authors published by independent presses with meager followings and brilliant tweets. It was absurd how much talent was wasted on the internet. She'd spent the full weekend clicking from one essay to the next, reading ebooks, and listening to podcasts featuring the authors where she could find them. It had become clear that she'd missed out on an ecosystem of thought up until now, that her rubric for "good" and "bad" had been based off of men's for so long she'd never realized its distortion.

Edie called her mom as she walked to Alex's loft. She called her mom whenever she walked anywhere, if only for the chance to hear her voice, to know there was something, somewhere that sounded like home. But the second it rang she remembered how late it was on the East Coast—after all these years the time difference still slipped her mind. She was about to hang up when her mom answered with a drowsy hello.

"Sorry, Mom. Are you awake?"

"I can be. Everything okay?"

"Yep, sorry. I just wanted to say hi. See how you're doing."

Her mom groaned then laughed a little. What was there to say?

"How are your legs feeling?" Edie asked, more specifically.

"Well, your father wouldn't help me with the groceries so I tripped on the stairs trying to carry them to the house. Everything fell on the sidewalk. The apples rolled down the porch." There was a sadness in her voice but she was laughing. "At least Lolly made out well."

"Jesus. I'm so sorry."

"It's not your fault. He nearly knocked me down the stairs trying to go watch the game. Obviously drunk. You know how it is, a dream vacation over here!"

"Mom, four months. We're almost there. We'll road-trip together, you won't have to fly."

"You know . . ." she started. There was a trace of excitement in her voice, foreign to Edie, and beautiful. "I saw a house I like. It's in, what is it called? Oaktown?"

"Oakland! You looked!" Her mother never let herself get excited unless she was sure something was happening. "Send it to me."

"I told you I don't know how to do that, sweetie." Her mother's voice was kind but Edie felt a sharp pain at the thought that she might have made the strongest person she knew feel inferior because she didn't know how to copy a link.

Her mom recited the street name and number, so Edie could search for the listing.

"Oh it's perfect! And in our range." An adorable blue cottage. In need of new floors and a paint job, but a big porch with sunflowers out front, and two decently sized bedrooms. It even had a small yard that Lolly, who hated walks or movement of any kind, would love.

"Oh, sweetie, your dad wants to talk to you." Edie could hear his voice, low and hoarse, in the background. "You don't have to," her mom whispered.

"It's fine." He was likely drunk by now, but she knew the colder she was to him, the harder he was on her mom, and she really did like talking to him most of the time. "I love you," she said when she realized her mom was getting off. It was a weird tic from childhood like holding your breath when you passed a graveyard, if you didn't say it something bad was bound to happen, but it came out a beat too late.

She heard her father breathing on the other end of the line. "Hi, sweetie. How are you? How's work going?"

"Hey, Dad. I'm good. Work is fine, we're releasing a new version of Pages next month," she offered, concrete progress he could be proud of. Despite everything, it was impossible for her to express anger toward her father. He had always been her biggest fan, encouraging her to stay in engineering when she thought she wouldn't make it, to ask for more money when she negotiated her salary at Tixster. While her mom reminded her to be grateful for what she had, he assured her she deserved anything she wanted. Her earliest memories were all with him, hunting around the garden, recording clips, as if the simple bloom of a flower were a monumental finding. Mostly, he'd showed her nothing but love. There was only one night when she was young and poured all his beers into the sink, partly as a prank but mostly so he'd stop drinking, that he'd grabbed her arm so hard she cried and warned her not to do it again.

"That's great, sweetie!"

"Ask her if she set up her 401k," she heard her mom say in the background. "I've been meaning to ask her about it."

"They're very lucky to have you there. I'm sure you're doing great."

"Robert"—now louder and she wished her mom would stop— "please ask her the question. She needs to start saving."

"Shut your goddamn mouth." It was swift and steady, like a snake bite.

Edie froze as if she were fourteen again, trying not to move a muscle in bed as the shouts rumbled downstairs. She would give whatever it took to transport herself to her mom's side, wrap her arms around her, and suck the shame from her like venom. But she was stuck across the country, unable to even console her with a glance, and confronting her father would only make the situation worse. So she stood still, breath caught in her throat, on the cold San Francisco sidewalk.

"I'm very proud of you, sweetie." His voice had transformed, fluffy and round again.

She was three blocks from Alex's. "Thanks, Dad. I'm just getting to my friend's house."

"Not a problem. I just wanted to say hello. Have a nice time with your friend."

"Thanks, Dad." It was impossible not to say it. "I love you."

ALEX'S LOFT WAS a slice of heaven. When she rented the space in what was now known as SoMa there was nothing within a mile of it. But just as she'd gotten used to it, started to feel safe in her neighborhood, the neighborhood had started changing. At first, Alex welcomed the changes, a bar that served drinks in mason jars, a wine store, a dance club with an ironic hotdog counter. It had turned from scary to cool, and Alex didn't mind cool. But a few years later tech was sprawling around the city like a colony of mold, and it had chosen SoMa as its center. Every time she left her house she saw college grads making more than she or anyone in her family had ever made. But her space was not only her home, it was her studio, her gallery, her income.

Photos hung everywhere. Edie was in awe of how their seemingly haphazard placement, no two frames in a row, looked so precise and intentional. Coming here felt like visiting another world.

Alex was sketching on her desk, an old wood door propped on legs, just like Edie's dad's, when she entered. Edie threw her jacket on the couch, then plopped herself beside it. She took out the bottle of wine she had brought, placed it on the scuffed wooden coffee table, and spread her legs over the green velvet couch. It was a rare Craigslist find, as was everything else in the apartment, that Edie had helped haul from the East Bay years ago.

"How's the collection going?" Edie asked, noticing a few window frames in the corner that looked old and haunted and beautiful.

"Awful!" Alex came over and joined Edie on the couch. "How is it so hard to find window frames in this fucking city? There is literally construction everywhere!"

"Where do you even go to look for them?"

"Fuck if I know. Dumps, Craigslist, construction sites. I've been trying everything." Edie could never be an artist. It required a certainty in her vision that she would never have. If something went even a little bit wrong, there was nothing in her that would say keep going for the sake of the art itself. She needed a more tangible mission; she didn't trust herself.

"How are you doing?" Alex asked. "Did you talk to Peter?"

"About the investigation?"

"About your feelings! Didn't you say you were going to tell him?"

Edie pulsed with embarrassment. "He's a mess right now. It's weird, Al, but I think I might be over him."

"I'll believe it when I see it."

"You know they're questioning him."

"Shall I open the wine in celebration?" Alex smiled. "Are you honestly worried?"

She wasn't ready to tell Alex everything, not yet. "I mean, I don't think he killed her. But he might have given her the drugs . . ."

Alex nodded, considering this. "Yeah, that wouldn't be good. But he only gave her K, right? Didn't you say it was a coke overdose?"

"Both were in her system. I'd just be nervous if I were him. I have this feeling that if it wasn't for him, it wouldn't have happened. Like, I'm haunted by it."

"It's like you're feeling blame on his behalf. It's not healthy, E."

"I'm starting to realize that." Her phone buzzed and she grabbed it quickly, hoping for Leah, but it was dumb Bumble reminding her there were matches waiting. "Are you hungry? Want to order food?"

"I'm good," Alex said, but Edie could hear a slight hesitation in her voice.

"It's on me, please?"

Alex smiled. "Okay, sure. The usual?"

Edie nodded. "The sickest part is that I'm kind of enjoying seeing him squirm," she continued, tapping their falafel order into her phone.

"Really?" She could hear the pride in Alex's voice.

"Ever since he left Nicole he's been sleeping around like crazy." Edie caught herself. "I know there's nothing *wrong* with having lots of sex. I just feel like he's treating these women like a game, seeing how many he can get." She could tell by Alex's face that she was reaching her limit of Peter-talk. "How's it going with that woman you've been seeing?"

Alex smiled. "Chloe. Great. Really great, actually. She's an elementary school art teacher. And she's really kind and supportive and *funny*. We're going to the hot springs this weekend." She paused. "E, I'm really falling for her. It's weird." She did seem happy—her skin was always enviable, but today it looked particularly glowy, her brown eyes seem rested, brighter.

Edie tried to smile but all this news did was depress her. She had the feeling that it was always great with Alex and the women she was seeing. And a part of her she wasn't proud of thought, because of this, Alex didn't deserve to talk about her relationships, like her happiness was its own reward.

The sky was dark outside the floor-to-ceiling windows. When Edie didn't reply, Alex filled the space, but the energy in her voice was drained. "How about you? Any dates this week?"

"Actually, I'm meeting up with Anaya's sister."

Alex's whole face burst into a smile and Edie felt terrible for resenting her happiness just moments ago when Alex was so clearly pleased by Edie's. "You're so fucked-up," Alex laughed.

Chapter Nineteen

L EAH WORE A green T-shirt with a denim jacket and she looked good. They had been exchanging messages frequently—sometimes about Anaya but not always. Leah had commented on the new sushi burrito place between their offices—was a sushi burrito really necessary, she wanted to know, and Edie was steadfast, if she could eat everything in burrito form, she would. Edie had asked her how Tahoe was—not worth the traffic, she'd replied, and Edie wondered if it ever was. She couldn't help but think their exchanges were flirtatious.

They hugged when Edie approached the bar. Leah asked how work was going but Edie promptly switched the conversation back to Leah, who described a concert she'd gone to last weekend, a movie she'd watched in the park the night before, and a trivia tournament her team recently won. She was the opposite of how Edie pictured Anaya, a creature of bed and books, like she was becoming.

"As you can tell, I'm drowning myself in distractions. Probably not the healthiest approach, but it's working." Her smile was bright but her eyes looked tired.

Edie ordered them another round. Leah had gotten the first and Edie was eager to return the favor. "Whiskey and beer for me," Leah said to the bartender and Edie turned to her. She had never seen her drink hard alcohol, not that she was anyone to judge.

"Distraction." She smiled.

The conversation had come to a natural pause. They sat looking at one another, shy smiles on both their faces. "I like your hair," Leah said. It was a particularly humid evening and Edie knew she was saying it out of discomfort, a tell that it was out of control. Leah moved to reach for her curls but Edie flinched.

"It's crazy," Edie said shyly, sipping her tequila. "So frizzy."

"It's not crazy," Leah said, trying to catch her eyes. "It's curly."

The notion that there was nothing wrong with her, that her hair was simply curly, moved Edie beyond belief, and she let Leah touch her fuzzy curls.

"It's so soft, like baby hair."

This was code for *thin* and Edie hated hearing it. "Crazy," she repeated, looking away. How could she ever think this beautiful woman was flirting with her. Leah's hair was smooth and thick. She wore no makeup. Edie had dotted her face with concealer but Leah's skin was even-toned and smooth. She had lines around her mouth and at the corners of her eyes but they made her face look more interesting, not less.

"Well, I love it," Leah said, catching Edie's eyes and gently pulling at her edges. And for the first time, Edie let herself believe this might be true.

Two drinks in and Edie was having such a good time she was willing to avoid the topic of the case altogether. Maybe not everything had to be a fact-finding adventure. Peter was her oldest friend, she had to stop obsessing. She would leave it to Ron to figure out.

The next round arrived. Leah was drinking twice as much as Edie—who was no lightweight—but it didn't feel like Edie's place to intervene.

"So they've been questioning that suspect," Leah said, taking a sip.

Well, if Leah was going to bring it up, she wouldn't stop her. "And?" Edie asked.

"Seems like a real jerk." She slid her finger up and down her pint glass, the moisture dripping onto her hand. "I think they're going to prosecute this guy." She threw the statement down like a rock and watched closely as Edie's face rippled. "They think he gave her the drugs."

She felt her lips curl and realized her first reaction, an instinct that bubbled somewhere beyond her consciousness, was joy that Peter was finally, maybe for the first time in his life, facing consequences. But as quickly as the joy came, a maddening urge to protect him surfaced. "But it's not like he did anything intentionally, right?"

"So, if you just carelessly give someone drugs and that person dies, that's fine?"

"No, I mean . . ." She needed to phrase it cleverly, how Anaya might have. "Don't you think she had agency in this? The drugs weren't laced. She took them."

"Of course Anaya had agency," she said as if Edie were a child. "I'm not saying he roofied her, but if we can prove he gave her the drugs, and I know for a fact she didn't intend to die, he should be charged." She looked at Edie. "Don't you think?"

She didn't know what to think. "I don't know anything about him," she said instead, wading deeper into her lie like an idiot, but, in a way, it felt more natural than telling the truth.

"I can tell you." There was an unusual stiffness about her that made Edie tense. "I've been doing research. He's very attractive. Six foot three." She sounded like she was reading a grocery list. "A multimillionaire." She stole a glance at Edie, who, now also quite drunk, was starting to enjoy the game. "He owns a three-story Victorian on the edge of the park."

Leah shot Edie an I-told-you-so glance, the kind of smile she used to give Peter when he'd had a point she couldn't contest.

"Sure," she agreed, "he sounds terrible. But none of those facts are *evidence*." None of what she'd said had anything to do with the case.

Leah turned her whole body toward her, rested her head on her hand and looked at Edie, earnest and confused, it seemed, as to how she could not understand. "Anaya didn't use drugs." Her vowels were longer than usual, but her voice was resolute. "She would never have done this on her own." Their playfulness was veering into combat, and they were balancing on a tightrope in between. "This guy, *Peter Masterson*, gave her the drugs that caused her death."

"But how do you *know* that?"

Leah moved closer, ran her fingers through her hair, and Edie wanted to kiss her.

She raised one shoulder. "The cops found coke and K in his system around the same time as Anaya's death. Plus, the charge from him on her Venmo the night she died."

Edie tried to steady her breathing. It made sense.

"And his phone records." Leah's head tilted slightly toward Edie, her gaze firm, lips tight. Edie watched her face: unguarded, curious, and even—endearingly—apologetic. In that moment, Edie knew she knew everything.

"I'm sorry I didn't tell you." The words barely came out. She couldn't swallow.

"I snoop on people's data for a living." Leah's eyes scanned and probed every inch of her face, Edie felt like she was in an operating room, surgical lights glaring down on her. "You really thought I didn't know?" She finished her whiskey.

"I'm so sorry." Her voice shook, her thoughts were jumbled. "I don't know how I was so dumb." She really didn't. "I care about Anaya. I want justice for her. I was afraid if I told you, I would try to defend him." She was rambling.

Leah looked up at Edie. "Are you trying to protect him? Is that why you reached out?"

"Not at all. No. I wanted to know what happened to Anaya. Everything I said was true."

"That's literally not true," Leah said, eyes wide, and like the clouds had parted for a brief, beautiful moment, she cracked a smile.

"Leah." She gripped Leah's hand with both of hers. Leah didn't pull away. "I'm so sorry I didn't tell you. It was idiotic and wrong and I feel awful. I was trying to stay out of it, but I wasn't thinking. I will never lie to you again."

Leah shook her head, eyes on her boots. "Do you trust him?" she asked.

"No," Edie said before she had time to think, surprising herself. "I mean, I thought I did. When you and I met I did. But I really don't. Not anymore. I just want to know what happened."

Leah looked up and searched her eyes. "Why didn't you *tell* me? It's so fucked-up, Edie." She looked like she might cry as she signaled for another round. Edie quietly waved the bartender away, mouthing *water* instead, and wishing she had done so sooner.

"I know. I'm sorry. I thought you wouldn't talk to me if you knew how close I was to him."

The right side of Leah's mouth curled up. "Well, that's true. I wouldn't have talked to you."

And then, because she had no other choice, she told the truth. "I like you, Leah. I really like you. And I care about your sister. I'm so sorry."

Leah turned to face her. "Well, I'm talking to you now." She let go of her hand, but not, Edie couldn't help but notice, before squeezing it slightly. "Tell me everything you know."

So she did. She went all the way back. Edie told her about college, about Matt. How Peter not only saved her that night but all the years after by being there over and over again. She admitted how much she'd loved him and for how devastatingly long. How she thought he was the only person in the world who would ever really know her, no matter how lame that sounded. He'd seen her at the lowest point in her life. She couldn't imagine letting anyone else come that close.

She told her about Nicole and the breakup. That she'd felt him change since he'd been single. Like something in him had snapped, he'd become greedy, careless. Maybe she would always love him, but she hated him, too. She had always admired his success as something he had achieved, but now she saw it for what it was, something he took.

Leah listened for a long time. It occurred to Edie, when she finished talking, that this was the most vulnerable she'd ever been on a date. If it could be called that now.

Leah touched her hand again and Edie wanted to cry at how grateful she was for what felt like forgiveness. "He'll likely get charged with involuntary manslaughter. It's not murder, but it's something."

Edie felt like she was falling off a cliff.

"They're going to call you in, too. You know that, right?"

She shook her head. She wanted to disappear. "Please don't tell them I know." They were facing each other on the stools, their legs woven together, Leah's right leg between both of Edie's, thigh against thigh. "I had nothing to do with this."

Leah looked more surprised than she had all night. "They already know. I was mostly kidding about snooping on your data. The cops have his phone records. He texted you first thing the next day."

She tried to remember what he had said. It was nothing. It was dinner.

"You know Ron, right?" Her voice was gentle.

It was all so devastating.

"It's okay." She put her hands on Edie's thighs. "It's weird, I don't know what's wrong with me." She paused, watching Edie wait. They were close again, their faces inches apart. "But I kind of appreciate how much you care."

Her lips were soft, barely pressing at all. Edie was so tired, it felt good when she let her eyes close. She felt as if she'd walked a million miles and had finally found the perfect bed to rest in. She could stay in this moment forever.

LEAH LIVED IN a house that smelled like fresh air and Meyer's soap, with a long hallway that led to her room. She had two roommates but their doors were closed. Leah's room was large with bay windows looking out onto Fillmore Street and concert posters framed on the walls.

She was drunk and she was young and she was grieving, and of course—*of course*—Edie wasn't about to take advantage of her. But she lived right around the block from the bar and Leah wanted someone with her that night and sleeping in the same bed was definitely not the same as having sex.

It felt wild to let herself worship a woman, not just privately, but physically, touching her sharp shoulder, her smooth, round stomach under her T-shirt. She did so cautiously, almost apologetically after Leah cuddled into her. There was always an element of threat, something close to hate that tinged her time with men; she had grown to like it, or at least associate it with pleasure. But this felt gentle, and terrifying.

After a few perfect, harmless kisses, Leah seemed to fall asleep easily. But Edie hadn't slept closely beside someone in three years, and the sound of her own breath, or rather panic that her breath was making a sound, kept her up, along with worry for Peter, fear for herself. Her thoughts were endless and circular.

Edie must have fallen asleep somehow because she was woken up by a kiss on the cheek.

"I'm headed to work," Leah whispered. "Just close the door behind you. It locks automatically."

"I'm so sorry again," she said, sitting up in bed, remembering the night anew. "And I shouldn't have come over." She moaned at herself. "I'm so sorry."

"I asked you to come over, Edie. That part is fine."

Leah was on her way out and squeezed Edie's foot under the cover. "I'm glad we talked. We'll figure this out." When she left the room, Edie could hear cabinets close, dishes clink, then footsteps down the stairs and the closing of a door.

She picked up her clothes slowly. She felt as if she were being watched, for no other reason than she probably should have been watched. She couldn't help but poke around what she now realized, in the light of day, was a very cluttered room. She peered at the pile of papers that lined Leah's desk, looking for what she wasn't sure, but she wouldn't have been disappointed to find a copy of Anaya's new manuscript. There were a few tax forms and a printed Datsta PowerPoint. When she heard footsteps down the hall she jumped toward the door, deeply ashamed, like deceit had somehow infected every part of her; she wanted it out. She grabbed her jacket from the back of an armchair. Beside the chair was a tall bookcase and her eyes scanned the spines innocently enough. Mostly sci-fi, but there was a section toward the top with Anaya's books, all in a row. It made Edie smile, to see Leah keep her sister's work on a literal pedestal. Something was sticking out of the most recent book, wider and thicker than a bookmark. It was a little booklet, just barely visible. She took out the book carefully, making sure to remember where it was in the stack, and her breath caught in her throat.

Helping a Loved One in Trouble: A Guide for Family and Friends

A small resource guide, with warning signs and safety plans and crisis center phone numbers for people whose loved ones were having suicidal thoughts. Her heart broke for Leah, who seemed so sure it was an accident, wondering, deep down, how she could have helped. She imagined her going to a center, picking up this guide, scouring resources for what she could have done. She felt as if she'd invaded something immensely personal and closed the pamphlet, but as she went to insert it back into Anaya's book, she saw a single sheet of paper stapled to the last page, a flyer. *Meeting for friends and family at the Downtown location, April 1, 7 p.m. 2016.*

It was a year ago, almost exactly. Leah had not just picked this up, this was old. Edie wasn't the only one who hadn't been totally honest. Leah had worried about Anaya's suicidal tendencies before, for as long as a year, maybe longer. Clearly, Anaya had been struggling, and enough for Leah to seek help. Edie took a picture of every page and carefully placed it back on the shelf.

Chapter Twenty

SHE BUZZED PETER'S door at eleven on the dot. He'd texted that morning in need of a run. It was prime time for the San Francisco sun, and she'd already worked up a sweat jogging from her house. She'd emailed her team that she was sick. Elizabeth had replied telling her to feel better.

Peter opened the door wearing a yellow tank top that worked on a micro level—his shoulders and biceps did not need to be hidden—but on a macro level made him look desperate and old. She'd told him as much a million times before.

But as soon as the door opened, he turned away. "Thanks for coming," he said distractedly as a woman with smooth amber hair and a middle part emerged from the apartment in a cropped sweatshirt and tight black jeans. Her head was down and she was at least six inches shorter than Edie so it was impossible to make eye contact. Edie watched her walk down his Victorian steps without any sort of goodbye. Only when the woman reached the bottom did she look back, her eyes red and face puffy, before looking away.

"Peter, who was—"

"Don't want to talk about it," he said, hopping down the steps.

Edie followed. "Did something happen? She seemed pretty out of it."

"Boundaries, Edie! Aren't you working on those?" His voice was light, but his jaw was tight. "I said I don't want to talk about it."

As she turned on her mileage tracker, she was distracted by two missed calls from Alex and a text asking that Edie call her back. Peter was jogging in place, staring at her to hurry up. She strapped her phone into its running pouch, tight against her arm. She would call Alex later.

"How are you feeling about everything?" she asked as they settled into a reasonable clip. Their best conversations were often while jogging. Emotion was channeled into motion, leaving the mind with logic alone. The perfect setting to interrogate each other.

"God, what a nightmare." He laughed and the sound of his chuckle made Edie feel sick. He seemed strangely energized, his eyes looked bright and rested.

"How are you not freaking out right now?" she asked between heavy breaths. Even if Anaya had had prior suicide attempts, Edie was pretty sure he had given her drugs that night and the cops were hovering.

"Primals gave me a very good lawyer. I'll be fine, it's just an annoyance." She caught a slight roll of his eyes, the kind of expression he might make at someone having trouble with a checkout kiosk at Safeway—amused, pitying.

"Have the police said anything else?"

"They've threatened charges, but my lawyer and I are strategizing." She flinched but he was staring at the sidewalk ahead and couldn't see. "They have nothing on me. I said 'no comment' to everything. I think I learned it from an old mystery movie or something."

"That's literally the guiltiest thing I've ever heard."

He laughed. "I'm not guilty!" There was a silence that Edie didn't feel like filling. "You know that, right?"

She closed her eyes. She was grateful they were jogging side by side. "You gave her the drugs, didn't you?"

"We did a little bit of K, I told you."

"Peter, I saw that she paid you that night. What was that for?"

His stride slowed. "Why are you looking at my transactions?"

"Maybe don't leave your account public like a sociopath. Did you give her coke?"

"She asked for it! Jesus." They turned toward the Panhandle. "She had to finish work and she said it helped her focus. She knew what she was doing. Everyone does fucking coke."

"Peter, if you sold her the drugs that killed her, you could get charged." She had been researching this and was shocked he wasn't more aware of his own predicament. More and more cases had been surfacing where not just dealers, but friends and family who had given someone drugs, were charged with murder. Each was more complicated than the next.

"They have no way of knowing I gave her the drugs. She could have been paying me for anything."

She had no idea if he was right, she just knew that if she were him, she'd assume that the experts would figure it out.

The air in the Panhandle was fresh. Elm trees lined their path like a cave, eucalyptus filled the air. On days like today, the sun out, nature waving its wings in full bloom, she couldn't imagine living anywhere else. The ground flattened and she caught her breath. Her legs, now without the burden of incline, felt as if they were flying. It was the kind of energy that came with the feeling of progress, that made running an essential part of her day. She felt capable.

He put a hand on her back midstride, turning his head toward her. "E, it'll be fine. My lawyer's not worried." They had reached the big intersection where Golden Gate Park started in earnest. The light was green and they sped forward. They were running fast now. It was unclear who was setting the pace, if one moved quicker the other moved quicker still and so on. "It's not a big deal."

It wasn't a conscious decision, the words just exploded out as she leaped over a crack in the path, words that had been trapped, circling her mind for days. "Peter, you had sex with her. Rough, violent sex with a woman who's now dead. You gave her the drugs that killed her and then you broke up with her. It's a big fucking deal." It felt so good to say out loud, her stride picked up, faster still. "You're honestly saying you did nothing wrong?" She needed him to say it.

When she turned to look at him there was no one beside her. She stopped. A group of tourists on Segways glided past her slowly like a row of geese, watching. She turned to look behind her. He was glaring at her from yards away. She smiled timidly to the tourists and walked back toward him.

"How do you know that?" he said when she reached him. His voice was quiet and controlled.

She stared at him, challenging him to continue the lie. "I asked you that night if you had sex with her and you said—god, I remember it so clearly—you said, *nothing bad happened while I was there.* You shook your head at me, Peter, you made me feel ridiculous for even asking. You lied to me."

"I didn't fucking lie to you. I would never lie to you. I just didn't want to talk about it that night. I didn't mean to, like, *trick* you or something. I wasn't thinking straight."

She wanted to believe him.

"Where are you getting all of this anyway? You sound like the fucking detectives."

"I know Anaya's sister. She told me everything."

He shook his head, eyes narrowed into slits, then turned around and began jogging away.

She raced after him, pulled his arm. "Peter, stop. Talk to me."

"Why didn't you tell me?" He stared at her, eyes hurt like she'd never seen him before. "How do you know her?"

She could have lied; work would have been an easy enough explanation. "I reached out to her after the death."

"You're sick." His eyes were swords, every muscle in his face clenched.

"I was trying to look out for you." As the words left her mouth the weight of their falseness hit her.

"She's probably just using you for information about me. Don't tell her anything. I swear to god, Edie." He turned and began walking away from her.

She reached for his bare shoulder, wet with sweat, and he turned. To her surprise his eyes had lost their rage. They looked empty, as if they'd already moved on to something else.

"I'm sorry," she said. "I just want to know what happened. I thought you would, too."

He shook his head. "It's sad. You need to get your own life. Leave my shit alone."

She was prepared for anger, she could have fought against anger. But his pity, the reflection of how pathetic she really was, it broke her.

PETER RAN AWAY and she crawled toward home.

A gust of wind blew against her damp skin and with it the smell of weed filled the air. A group of kids to her left were sitting on a blanket, sipping on cans of artisanal beer and munching green olives and hard cheese from the market down the street. A few feet ahead two men sat on a bench. They looked dirty and homeless. Their hair matted and their clothes ripped. She didn't see where the smell was coming from, could easily have been either group. The whole park was probably high.

Her phone had been buzzing all morning with emails from work but this was persistent—an actual call. Ron's name scrolled across her screen.

"Edie, hi. I hope you're doing okay." It felt good to hear his voice. "We need you to come down to the office."

———

THE INTERVIEW ROOM was the opposite of his office—tiny and empty, like a jail cell. Plastic tables best suited to display junk at a garage sale and an old coffeepot in the corner. The young guy who escorted her in had given her a glass of water and then left as soon as she'd taken her seat. She sat back in the plastic chair, trying to avoid the reflective window where she assumed Ron was watching.

A woman entered. Edie liked that she had spiraling curls that clearly required product, a tacit understanding of her own ongoing chore. Her eyes were alert, aware, her smile warm. When Ron entered behind her, Edie's eyes shot to the floor.

"Good to see you, Edie."

She looked up, searching his face. "You too, Ron."

"What's wrong?" He smirked. "Aren't you glad we can finally have the conversation we've been dancing around for weeks?" His laugh, loud and echoing off the bare walls of the small room, made her eyes water. She blinked quickly, mortified, trying to hold it together.

"You knew I knew Peter."

He looked up, a flash of surprise in his eyes followed by sadness for her. "Of course I knew." He pulled out an ugly folding chair and took a seat. "There was no way I could've given you all that information for nothing. Anyone that interested in an everyday overdose, who literally runs to the scene of the crime the next morning"— she hated the amusement in his voice—"usually has something to hide."

She wanted to crawl under the flimsy plastic table and live there forever.

"Plus, you were easy to identify." She wondered if he was getting back at her, making excuses for his interest, or if it really was all an act. "You literally handed me your card."

He must have seen the look on her face. "Hey, I *was* looking for a friend. That part was real." A deep kindness flashed across his eyes, a slice of the Ron she had warmed to, before they returned to the papers before him. "I'm sorry if I gave you the wrong impression."

"Okay you two," the woman said, "let's stick to the facts." She shot a quick smile at Edie. "I'm Ron's partner, Kassie. Good to meet you, Edie, we're glad you could be here."

Edie could barely take her eyes off Ron, who now seemed like a stranger, but she glanced over at Kassie. Her neatly pressed shirt, her well-manicured curls, a refined calmness in her face. She looked like a well-adjusted person who cooked full meals for herself, liked her job, maybe had a pet. They couldn't be more than a few years apart, but she looked like an adult.

"Good to meet you, too." As the words formed, she noticed she was on the verge of tears and stopped speaking to prevent them from spilling over.

"I hope you don't mind if we ask you a few questions," Kassie continued. Between the plastic table, the stale air, and the performance of friendliness, nothing felt real.

"I'll tell you anything you want to know," Edie said, trying so hard to sound truthful it sounded fake.

"Tell us about Peter Masterson," Ron said. Edie waited for clarification, anything would have helped, but they both just sat silently, staring.

"We've known each other since college. He's my best friend. He's never hurt a woman. Never. Not that I know of at least."

"And you know him pretty well?" Kassie asked.

"Very well." Even now, she felt pride associating herself with him.

Ron got up, walked casually around the room, landing behind her. "Tell us about his relationship to drugs." He was all business, like the first morning they'd met. Anything between them, even if it was all just a game, had flattened beneath the weight of what actually mattered.

"He does them. But he's never overdosed and no one he's . . ." She stopped, considering the right way to phrase his drug dealing. "No one he's done them with ever has, either."

"That you know of," Ron said.

"Right."

"Tell us about his relationship with Anaya." Ron caught her eye as he said her name.

"Take your time," Kassie added, nice as can be. "The more details the better. We have nowhere to be but here."

"They dated briefly. I met her once, after their first date. I liked her a lot." She glanced up at Ron but he gave her nothing.

"Peter must have thought she was great, too, huh?" Kassie asked.

"Yeah, he liked her. Had nothing but good things to say about her."

"How long did they know one another?"

"A few weeks, like four dates or something, not too long."

"You can make a pretty strong connection in a short time." Kassie's smile cut right through her and Edie worried for Peter that this woman was on the case.

"I agree." Edie nodded. "I told him not to lead her on. He wasn't trying to hurt her. He really did like her."

"So what happened that night?" Ron asked.

"Honestly he didn't tell me much. He didn't even tell me he had sex with her."

"What did he tell you?" Kassie again. They never overlapped questions and Edie wondered how they planned it. It wasn't a strict taking turns, one then the other and back again, it was more organic, a sophisticated passing of the baton, skillfully executed.

"He went over, they . . ." She stopped herself, rerouted. "He said they only did ketamine together, nothing else." She could see the pity behind Ron's eyes, she knew he was judging her for believing this version of events. But Kassie's face was relaxed, her head tilted slightly, taking in what Edie told her. "Then he broke up with her. Then he left."

The air in the room seemed to stiffen. Ron and Kassie sat still as rocks.

Kassie spoke first. "Why did he end it?"

Edie tried to swallow, but her whole throat had closed up. She grabbed the glass of water beside her on the table and felt incredibly grateful for the boy who had placed it there. She reminded herself that breaking up with someone was not a crime and took a long sip.

She didn't have the energy to explain his relationship with Nicole, his foray into dating, his new, mounting disrespect toward women. "He wasn't ready for a relationship." She caught Kassie's eye as she said it, she wanted her to know her sympathy for Peter only went so far. Kassie's mouth, thin and pink, grew tight around the edges.

There was a silence, then Kassie spoke up. "It'll be easier if you tell us everything, hun."

Edie could never get away with saying a word like *hun*. She'd tried it once with Alex and instantly felt like a creep. But when Kassie said it, it felt like a hug.

"Nothing will happen to him if he has nothing to hide. It's the hiding that will get you both into trouble."

Both was the key word. She had slipped it in innocently enough, but Edie knew it wasn't an accident. She didn't have many friends as a child, mostly she stayed in her room reading and watching mysteries. It was why she'd wanted to be a spy when she was younger. She knew detectives were always ten steps ahead, that every word was a move.

"Where'd he get the drugs?" Ron asked, his voice quick and piercing like an arrow.

"He didn't tell me where he got them."

Again, a silence. It was as if the air itself was frozen in place. Kassie seemed to notice her noticing this. She turned to check the clock and leaned back in her chair with a new ease, as if she were bored. "What drugs did he tell you about, hun?"

Edie wished there was an undo button she could hit—I have no idea where *they came from*, she'd meant! "I don't know." Kassie stared at her, her eyes beacons signaling everything would be fine. "Ketamine, you know, the usual." They waited. "Coke." The room was starting to blur. She hadn't slept a full night in weeks.

"So you can confirm he gave Anaya drugs that night?"

"I really have no idea where the drugs came from." There was a world where everything Peter told her could have been false. She hadn't seen anything firsthand.

Ron moved toward her. "We drug tested your buddy, a hair test, did he tell you that?"

She shook her head. He had not.

"He had the same drugs in him as Anaya, and around the same time as her death."

"Someone gave someone those drugs," Kassie continued. "Do you think Anaya gave Peter those drugs, Edie?"

Her stomach churned. "I have no idea." She wished he was here with her. She wished he hadn't been such a dick. She wished he could have loved her.

"Edie." Kassie leaned forward, her voice soft and patient. "We have a warrant, that's how we knew you were involved, because we have all his phone records and internet usage from his ISP. We know he buys from Silk Road." She paused. "We also have Anaya's, and we know she does not."

"Then why do you need me to tell you? If you have all this evidence?"

"Hun." Kassie was staring at her with those warm, comforting eyes. Edie hadn't seen another woman in the building since she'd entered. Kassie looked young for a detective. She wondered how she got into this job, if she too felt drained in a profession surrounded by men. "Your testimony won't determine Peter's fate. We just need to know what you know. It's standard procedure. It's in your best interest to cooperate."

Edie nodded, but said nothing. Should she call a lawyer? How the fuck did people find lawyers? She refused to pay money for Peter's idiotic mistakes, money that should be going toward her mother's little blue house.

Ron was behind her again. "Enough, Edie," his voice boomed. "Where does he get his goddamn drugs?"

She felt a chill, as familiar as the smell of crayons, the shiver of a man's shout. "It changes."

"What's the last place he bought from?"

"Sure, yes, he's tried the dark web, Silk Road or whatever. But she asked him for them. She said she needed them to focus." Her voice was like broken glass, she could barely get the words out. She turned to Ron, remembering his former partner. "Ron, she struggled with suicide. Ask her sister, she'd been going to meetings and support groups. If she took all that in one night, it wasn't Peter's fault." He had to understand it was more complicated.

He cocked his head and searched her eyes for something, she wasn't sure what, but he seemed disappointed. "You really think Leah—we know you two hit it off—is going to say this was a *suicide*?" When he started speaking his voice was flat, as if she were no longer worth the effort. "There's no way she would testify to that. She wants to hold someone accountable. And"—his eyes held her in place, making sure she knew that he knew she was trying to reference the suicide of his partner—"I don't blame her one bit in this case." He looked at Kassie, their faces exchanging information.

"Peter wasn't there when she took the coke," Edie pleaded.

"He was, Edie. It was in his system, and according to the drug test, it was around the same time." Kassie was gentle but firm, like someone ripping off a stubborn Band-Aid. "Unless he just happened to take it that night when he got home, which, I think we both know is highly unlikely." She paused. "Drug tests don't lie, Edie. But Peter does. And I'd bet he's lied to you about a lot of things."

Her head was pounding, a ferocious pain in her forehead, like a drumming from the inside. Her water glass was empty. It was hard to swallow.

Ron stared at her, no longer angry, but sad, almost gentle. "Has he admitted to buying drugs on Silk Road in the past two months?"

She had run this scenario in her mind so many times. She could ask for a lawyer. She didn't have to talk to them. How could Peter have done this? How could he be so stupid? Why was she the one dealing with it?

"This is not a game, Edie. Answer the question."

How ridiculous she was to think Ron had been pursuing her, that she was somehow using him and he was after nothing but . . . what? Her company? Her beauty? Her *youth*? How stupid she'd been. She wished they'd lock her up right there—a small room with books, bread, water. It would be fine. A relief.

"I think so."

Kassie and Ron turned to one another and Edie wondered if they were sleeping together. Edie wished she could let someone care about her enough, know her enough, to be so in sync.

"I can't be sure," she added, desperate.

"You might be called in as a witness," Ron said, picking up the folder and shuffling the papers into place.

The already blank room went dark. Time stopped and the moment expanded like the feeling right as you start to fall, the long, drawn-out instant before the crash when you know something's gone terribly wrong. "A witness?" she whispered.

"If it goes to trial. You'll be fine," Kassie said coldly, the warmth drained from her face. Her eyes now darting and impatient. "You'll know in the next few days."

Edie didn't know where to look, there was no soft place to land. She rubbed her eyes hard with her fists for a long time until Ron broke the silence.

"We'll be in touch," he said, and held the door open for Kassie, then followed behind her.

Chapter Twenty-One

LEAH KNOCKED LIGHTLY on Edie's door. There was a brightness in her face as she entered.

"I talked to the detectives," Edie said, taking Leah's coat. Edie had asked her over in the name of debriefing, but she'd also felt mounting guilt and wanted to talk to her again without alcohol.

"Kassie told me."

Edie felt another irrational stab of jealousy.

Leah looked around Edie's room, eyes lingering on her bookcase, Anaya's titles and her father's cassettes. "Thank you for doing that." She moved a polka-dotted pillow and sat down on the bed, patting the spot next to her. Edie took a seat beside her. Leah stared at her for a few moments before speaking. Up close, looking only at her face, her big dark eyes, she felt as if Anaya was in the room with her. "They're charging him with involuntary manslaughter."

The words felt like an intruder. She wanted to chase them away.

"You did the right thing," Leah said softly, taking her hand.

"Did I do this to him?" she asked. "Is it because of me?" The air in her apartment was stuffy and gross. She rarely noticed it because she lived in it but now the stench of her own cramped existence overwhelmed her.

"No. Of course not." Leah's voice was firm. "It's because of him."

Edie let the words sink in, roll around in her head and settle.
They were silent for a long time, sitting beside one another on the
bed, Leah's arm around her. Her head rested on Leah's shoulder. She
noticed the absence of any scent in her hair. At any given moment
Edie was wearing a concoction of at least three different hair products, in addition to the expensive treatments she used in the shower.
She wondered if Leah, who looked, in Edie's opinion, perfect, had
very literally woken up like that.

"Someone needs be held accountable," Leah continued, and Edie
was thrown back into the devastating present. There was anger in
her voice.

Edie stood up, needing to physically distance herself in order to
do so mentally. "He had no way of knowing this would happen." It
didn't feel right, the thought of him in prison.

Leah turned to her, her eyes large and glossy. "She wouldn't
have done it without Pet—" She stopped after the first syllable of his
name, choking on the word, and turned to face the window, which
held nothing but the apartment next door. "Clearly, she was not okay
that night, and he left her alone after giving her a ton of drugs."

Outside Edie could hear the Muni squeak to a stop across the
street. The brakes crying like a beat-up truck. The swoosh of the
doors opening, then closing before it clunked off to its next destination.

"She didn't deserve to die," Leah said, still staring out the window, her back to Edie. When, finally, she turned around, tears ran
recklessly down her cheeks, into her mouth.

It was the first time Edie had seen her cry.

Edie stood up, held her tightly, rubbed her fingers through her
smooth, short hair. Why was she so resistant to blaming Peter? Of
course he played a part in this. Leah was right, Anaya hadn't taken
her life before that night, it wouldn't have happened without him.

———

ONLY WHEN SHE closed the door as Leah left, did she realize she hadn't checked her email all night. It was astonishing, how little she could care about her inbox in light of actual things to worry about, when it was so often the highlight of her little day.

She forced her eyes to focus on the subject lines. Amid political campaign pleas and daily news alerts, one name stood out. It was from the university and the subject line wasn't some generic event or donation request, it was very specific:

Thomas Manuscript Request.

She hovered her cursor over the subject line, wanting to exist only in hope, aware that this might be as close as she ever got to the possibility of more work from Anaya. *Dear Edie,* it started, and she smiled at the formality. *I regret to inform you*—of course there was no way they would share the manuscript; she had been insane to ask, she shuddered remembering her performance in the office—*that we cannot share Anaya's full manuscript. I've attached an excerpt of the book, instead, which she had recently finished and requested that we share. We are sharing the work with select researchers and students only. Please keep this confidential.*

The attachment was twenty-seven pages long.

Her heart felt as if it might stop right then and there. She forced a breath and sat up straight, back to the cold plaster wall. She felt like a small child on Christmas morning, giddy and unbelieving—she had a piece of Anaya all to herself. The pages on her screen were all that mattered. She felt closer to her than ever, as if there was a reason this manuscript was now in her hands of all the hands, that on some level, they were the same.

Her phone buzzed next to her, Alex's name shining on her screen. She had completely forgotten to call her back. But she could not possibly concentrate on anything other than the twenty-seven pages before her. It felt as if they were glowing, on fire, and she needed to absorb them immediately. She silenced the ringer. Alex would understand.

She printed the pages and brought them to bed. She read it so slowly. She could see their conversation reflected in the first few sentences.

We can't assume we know what our future selves will want, Anaya wrote. *To focus on a far-off projection is a clever way to avoid the harder task of confronting who we actually are.* Edie opened her inbox, happy to take her time knowing it was there waiting, and searched for Anaya's last email. She was right—the fourth chapter, the chapter that now, incredibly, sat on her screen, was the chapter Anaya had planned to send her.

She described the slow and arduous and, according to Anaya, always incomplete process of learning to access her desires beyond the desire to please others. For most of her life she was mired in worry that she'd regret any indulgences. She lived strictly, carefully. Until she realized that what she had always viewed as *indulgence*, was simply the sensation of her own pleasure.

People have very little imagination when it comes to their lives, she argued, sounding more judgmental than Edie had ever heard her. *It's uncomfortable when someone chooses to live differently, outside the expected patterns of adulthood. Their life becomes an affront when so many of us rely on social validation as a stand-in for pleasure.*

She explained how, until recently, her actions stemmed from an all-consuming need to prove her life mattered. *I craved validation, the shape of which morphed into whatever medium lay available—academia, relationships, beauty, writing. I chased signs that I was doing it—life—"right," and these hits of approval kept me going. I erected self-imposed obstacles to prove I could conquer them, without ever asking myself why I would want to.* The whole chapter was more melodramatic than her usual style, but Edie didn't mind. If everyone admitted they were chasing after the same meaningless markers as boldly as this, maybe we could all agree none of it mattered and have a shot at happiness.

The moment it became clear to me that I did not want children was the moment I realized that motherhood—to me—was another vector of validation, an attempt to give my life meaning. And how cruel to bring a child into this world—where exploitation, of ourselves and others, is increasingly revealed as the engine of progress—for such selfish reasons. The challenge of finding my own way to matter, without children, without chasing pre-defined goals, felt far more thrilling. I craved space to understand what I wanted beyond the desire for other people's approval. In a way I wanted to be the child. I wanted to give all the hope and time and effort and love I saw women my age pouring into their children into my middle-aged self. I wanted freedom. How literally childish, how very uncomfortable.

She went on to describe the torment of her ambivalence. *There's grief in most decisions, if we consider them thoughtfully; that doesn't mean we're making the wrong choice. Was I happy with my life? Yes and no. Did I wish things were different? Absolutely. Most things are not binary. Most things are a mess.* She related her initial search for an answer to her history with anorexia, this thirst for a clear "right" and "wrong" to guide her, the need to measure and assess. *But all we can do is sit in that disarray, as much as is suitable to us, at least, and strive to see ourselves clearly.*

Edie's body buzzed with the ache of feeling understood. That this would never be published suddenly felt like the greatest offense. Anaya had clearly wanted to share it, was about to share it with Edie just days before her death. Had worked on it for *fifteen* years, for god's sake. Her room was dark, the glow of her screen was the only sign of life. There were ten pages left and she didn't want them to end.

A new section began and the first sentence made her think it was the wrong thing, like someone had mistakenly placed someone else's work in the document. *My mother died in a fire,* it read. She averted her eyes from the screen as if there was literally a fire on the page. Anaya rarely wrote about her family. Edie glanced back at the words, tiptoed from one to the next. Her mother was her hero, a writer in her own right, though never published. She had no time for it while raising her children, but had planned to take it up again when they were grown. Anaya, with two Princeton degrees, had learned every-thing worth anything from her mother. Her father had left when she was five, surely the reason for her issues with men, she explained. But her mother's death was the reason for everything she had ever been proud of. It left a hole in her so cavernous, she'd been trying to fill it since.

The writing was raw and unlike her other work, which was witty and intentional. She was throwing herself on the page; the words were chosen with precision, but the vulnerability was as-tounding. *My sister and I were my mother's pride and joy. Though she'd dropped out of college to raise us, she always insisted that we were the best things that ever happened to her. But the moments when she lit up, when I saw her utterly swept up with life, vibrant and all-consumed, not exhausted and anxious, were the moments when she was alone writing. We had a dollar-store calendar hanging on the kitchen wall—a different bright-eyed puppy at the turn of each month—counting down the days until her retirement, when she could finally enjoy herself.*

Every day, my mother reminded me to turn off the coffeepot and even unplug it when we left the house. Sometimes, when I was feeling playful, I would make a show of flipping the switch, like Vanna White, flipping a tile on Wheel of Fortune, *to tease her. "Don't laugh,"* my mother would say with love, *"you never know!"*

But on the morning of March 14, my sister, Leah, called me in tears. Anaya was living with Leah and her mother, while commuting to Manhattan, to help out until Leah graduated the following year. Easter had fallen early, Anaya wrote, and it was the Friday before spring break. Leah had left the house wearing her favorite baby blue shirt and the new bow tie Anaya had gotten her in SoHo the week before, and was attacked on her way to school.

It was a small town and anyone who wasn't normal, and by normal, I mean straight and white, was never entirely safe. Leah told me over the phone, sweetly, apologetically, that she was bleeding, that she could barely see, that she needed help. I yelled to my mother, who was still home in bed having worked the night shift, that I would take care of it. I rushed to Leah's school and took her to the hospital where we waited for hours. I remember the blood had dried against the baby blue of her shirt. Finally, Leah's face was stitched and we were sent home.

It wasn't until the car ride back, Leah safely beside me, tears all wiped away, that I got the call. There had been a fire. No one knew my mother was still inside.

Anaya explained that she refused to participate in news coverage, which was only local and easy to avoid. It was a small, poor town, and no one cared besides a few people living in it. She quit her finance job. She took what she had saved to start a new life for her and her sister. They moved to San Francisco. As far away as possible.

Fifteen years later, I thought I'd have forgiven myself. I thought the pain, even if it didn't go away, would at least fade. But it never did. I tried to busy myself with the problems of the world, bury myself in the issues of women. Soon, interests became obsessions, and it was clear, even as I submerged myself fully in their pursuit, that they were nothing more than a distraction. I noticed other people see me in higher and higher esteem the more desperate I felt. When I starved myself for control, I was beautiful. When I escaped into work, I was committed. When I wrote about my struggles, I was brave. What a twisted world it is, when the most revered people are the ones so desperately hiding their pain.

Edie's hands were ice but she sat still in the dark, afraid to move, for a very long time. She wondered why Leah never mentioned this, but the reason was clear. The journalists would cling to these details as they'd clung to every other crack of weakness in Anaya, it would become the whole story. And maybe it was. Maybe this was the piece she'd been missing. Anaya was tired of spending her life running from guilt and shame and the twisted value system that led so many to self-destruct. It had nothing to do with Peter. But why *that night?* What had he said to her?

Her phone buzzed against the hardwood floor. She reached for it quickly, hoping to see Leah's name flash across her screen. But there was no name at all. Only Tinder's bright red flame.

Another buzz, a new message. Another. She threw the phone across the room and it crashed into her wall, knocking the framed photo of her and Alex to the ground. The glass shattered across the small, tiled corner that was her kitchen.

She crawled up from the floor and flicked on the light. The glass was everywhere. She stepped around it. She grabbed her highlighter and notebook from her desk and picked up the loose papers that had fallen to the floor.

SHE HAD JUST taken her first sip of coffee when she heard a buzz at her door. She had barely slept and hit the button thoughtlessly, letting in whoever it was—a deliveryman or a neighbor without keys—it happened all the time. Her mind was still churning through the pages, trying to parse each word for meaning, as if, perhaps, Anaya had left her version of a note buried in them.

The air was crisp, a blue, cartoonish sky, and she had nowhere to be. The voices of NPR were telling her about the clouds that were expected come evening. She was about to open her Nutri-Grain bar and get back to rereading the pages for clues, signs, anything, when she heard the pounding. She reached for her phone instinctively but it was still lying, lifeless, in the corner of her room in a sea of glass. When she grabbed it there were twelve texts and two missed calls.

Peter exploded into her apartment, his body and limbs flailing in her tiny studio.

"What the fuck did you tell them?" He threw his hoodie and messenger bag onto her bed. He was out of breath and covered in sweat; he must have run over.

She wrangled the papers and her notebook quickly, shoved them in her bookcase. She had fallen asleep in her clothes and tried to pretend as if she'd been up all along; that she was dressed for the new day rather than the previous one.

"Nothing, Peter. I didn't say anything!"

"Fuck, Edie." He was pacing across her room, her home. "I was arrested this morning."

"What?"

"I bailed myself out. But they charged me with involuntary manslaughter. Apparently, they have me on the drugs. All after you went in."

"They said they had proof of the drugs already. That you had a drug test." His face turned a scarlet red, a vein in his forehead pulsed, and she wondered how often this kind of rage was lurking in him. She could smell the Chinese restaurant downstairs getting ready for the day, usually a comfort. But right now, the smell of soy and ginger was making her sick. "Peter, you said it yourself, you didn't do anything wrong! You didn't make her take the drugs. I didn't think it would matter. I was so nervous. Peter, I'm sorry."

"I told them *nothing*, Edie. Don't you remember me telling you I told them nothing?"

She decided not to mention that he'd also told her this was all dumb and everything would be fine.

"Don't you think that implies *you* shouldn't have told them anything, either?" He wasn't usually so patronizing, but it didn't feel totally off. He'd learned to quiet his confidence over the years, she'd watched him grow more patient, let others speak first. But when he allowed himself to talk freely, there was always an air of arrogance. "That stupid drug test proves nothing."

"They said they had your ISP history, proof that you bought the drugs on the dark web."

His look was fierce. She knew it well. She'd seen it often from colleagues, when she asked a question or made a comment that revealed a gap in her knowledge they deemed inexcusable; a look of disbelief at how dumb she was, how clearly she didn't belong. "They were lying to you. They can't track that. Did you listen at all when I explained how it worked? Jesus, Edie. Aren't you supposed to work in fucking tech?"

She had grown out of letting men make her feel unworthy, she was practiced at tossing their looks and comments aside, but Peter had always treated her like an equal. "Grow up, Peter. You're putting this on me when you're the one who gave her drugs. Take some goddamn responsibility. If you didn't want me to say anything, you should have fucking told me."

He shook his head, unwilling, it seemed, to waste his breath on a reply.

"Do you know how scared I was?" she asked. "Being pulled into a fucking police station to talk about *murder*? A murder I had absolutely nothing to do with."

"Neither did I!" he shouted. "It wasn't a fucking murder!"

"This is on you, Peter." She held her voice as steady as she could, as if walking a tightrope. "Don't blame this on me. This is not my fault. This is *your* fault." She repeated Leah's words to herself like a mantra. "I never wanted to be involved in this."

His laugh was a cackle. "That's a lie!" His hands were waving manically. "You've been wedging yourself into this ever since it started."

She felt ridiculous. He stood up while she curled further into herself on the bed, her knees up against her chest, her arms wrapped tightly around them. "I didn't think what I said would matter."

"That's your fucking problem!" When she looked up his eyes had twisted into a psychotic plea. "What you say matters, Edie." He was nearly screaming. "You matter, goddamnit." It was the nicest thing he'd ever said to her.

He paced across the small room, a few steps one way before he turned and went the other.

"What the fuck is this?" he said when he saw the glass. He was looking down at the broken frame, still on the ground where it had fallen. "You could cut yourself."

He turned to her, his eyes searching her face the way she had searched his for so long looking for signs of the old Peter. She wondered what he was searching for now, what version of her he wanted to find—the woman who would do anything for him, the woman who would indulge his insecurities, relieve his self-doubt, the woman who would always be there for him?

He turned away. "You need to figure your shit out, Edie."

It was the whisper of his voice that hurt most. It wasn't mean, the anger was gone. For the first time it almost sounded kind, as if he really wanted to help.

He walked to the tiny closet in the corner of her room and pulled out her broom and dustpan. He knew where every object in her life was kept. He swept away the pieces while she watched from her bed, every last shard, checking under the rug and behind the couch just to be safe.

When he was done, he sat beside her. She could smell his pine deodorant mixed up with the musty sweat from his run. She wanted him to hold her, and yet when she imagined his arm around her, she felt queasy. But the longing was fierce, a profound emptiness, like her insides were hollowed. What she wanted, she realized, more than anything else, was to want him again. If she could just love him, everything would be simple. It was so easy when he was her splint, when his approval was all she'd needed. Life was so clear when he was right and all she had to do was follow. Now she was on her own, and she was messing it all up.

"There's an arraignment tomorrow." When he spoke, his voice was calm. "I'll plead not guilty, but my lawyer says it'll likely go to trial. I'm pushing for it to be scheduled soon. I don't want this dragged out any longer."

She shook her head. "I'm so sorry it's gotten to this."

He turned to her, his olive eyes kind and warm, the way she remembered them. "My lawyer has a plan." He put his hand on her leg, squeezed the spot that made her smile, then stood and walked to his messenger bag.

"There's something called a 'but for' clause." He took out a few papers.

Edie stared at him, waiting for more.

"Apparently, her blood alcohol level was way above average, and since I didn't give her the alcohol, we can argue it's impossible to prove it was the drugs alone that killed her." He handed her the printed paper. "Defense Strategy" was bolded at the top, with the letterhead of what sounded like a fancy firm. "I just need help looking good on the stand."

She didn't have the energy to read the foreign words and what she could make out seemed like a version of what he was saying, so she handed it back to him. "My lawyer will send you details and call you to go through everything."

"I have to testify?" It was more of a realization than a question.

He sat beside her again, took her hand in his. His hands felt coarse and giant compared to Leah's. "This wasn't me, Edie. I've never asked anything of you. But I really need you right now." He squeezed her hand tighter. "You're my best friend."

She nodded. He was beyond her best friend. He had been, in a sense, her world.

IT WAS A long week of waiting until a curt email from his lawyer arrived in her inbox, inviting her to meet.

She had been researching this "but for" clause, two dozen tabs open all week as she tried to decipher pages of legalese, footnotes and references interrupting each sentence. Apparently, there was a Supreme Court case a few years back that didn't go in Peter's favor—at first. A man died following an eclectic binge, and his heroin dealer was accused of distributing drugs that caused his death. A medical expert had testified that the victim may have died even if he did not take the heroin—therefore the heroin was not the "but for" cause of death. But the Court instructed the jury to convict even if it was a contributing factor, so he was sentenced to twenty years. That would all be very bad for Peter, except the decision had been reversed years later. It was determined that the drugs in question could not simply be a contributing factor, they had to be the primary cause. There had been many other similar cases and controversies since then, and all she could conclude from her nights of research was that it was all very case-by-case.

The lawyer's office was large and windowed. There was nothing about the lawyer's face that was exceptionally handsome. His nose was too small and his eyes were hardly compelling. But his suit was expensive, his stance was upright, his body was sculpted in a way that took time. He was attractive.

His manner was curt, and, like every doctor's appointment she'd ever been to, the primary goal of the meeting seemed to be to get rid of her. The trial had been scheduled in twelve days. The tall, suited lawyer explained that she was a crucial character witness and all she had to do was tell the truth. Then, he handed her a folder of papers to help prepare her testimony.

It wasn't a script exactly, it was phrased cleverly to avoid that interpretation, but even on first glance, her directions were clear. He went through each section with her, then sent her on her way, exuding kindness in the last two minutes of their meeting as if he hadn't been rushing through the previous twenty.

At home, she read the document over and over, to herself, then out loud. It was titled "Preparation Doc" and it wasn't suggested wording, per se, it was "The applicability of law to events in issue." It outlined potential questions from the prosecution and planned questions from the defense, then explained, in-line, what they would have to demonstrate in order to prove Peter's innocence. On each page, after essentially telling her how to respond, big, bolded letters reminded her to, above all, be honest.

On the second and third read, and especially on the fifth, she decided the suggested strategy wasn't a lie so much as omissions. *If you cannot be completely sure about Peter's drug use and the way he spent his time with Anaya, it is not necessary to guess at gaps in your memory. You are not obligated to state that of which you're unsure.*

Then there was the issue of his character. The word was highlighted on the second page. His lawyer would spend the bulk of the time establishing him as credible. The defense's line of questioning: whether or not he treated women with respect, surrounded himself with female friends, was a loving boyfriend for seven years to Nicole, a loyal friend to Edie for twice as long. She put the papers next to her in bed, pulled the covers to her chin.

She had seen the word so many times in Matt's court documents: *character.* Less about him than the women who accused him. Every time she saw the word on the reports, she knew it was nothing but a tactic. None of the details ever had a thread of relevancy to the case.

She noticed the corner of her notebook, shoved at the bottom of her bookshelf, the printed pages of Anaya's chapter poking out. There was so much more to her death than Peter. And yet, Anaya had lived her whole adult life with her mother's death inside of her, he must have done *something* if it happened the night he was there. She crawled out of bed, grabbed her notebook, and read the excerpt again, searching.

Her mom was calling. She'd been calling all day but Edie couldn't bring herself to answer. Seconds later, a text. Her mom had recently learned to text and was getting into photos, a little too into them, if you asked Edie. She scrolled through five pictures of Lolly, which truthfully were the highlight of her day. Then came a picture of a maple Danish. **Yumm!!** her mom wrote.

It hit her like a punch, the way she felt in college after solving a particularly gnarly proof, or finding a bug in a monstrous pile of code and watching it finally, gloriously, run. She scrolled through photos from her mom, past a dozen still lifes of Lolly, until she reached it, the slice of apple pie her mom had sent her on Pi Day. The night Anaya died. She grabbed the paper with the article about Anaya's death. *The night of March 14,* it said, clear as day. She scrolled to the first paragraph of Anaya's last chapter, the day of her mother's death glaring at her from under the yellow highlight. The night she died was the fifteenth anniversary of her mother's death.

She opened her phone, fingers shaking. The pamphlet from Leah's book. She zoomed in on the cover. In small text in the top right corner: March 15, last year. She had sought help the day after the anniversary of her mother's death.

There was something electrifying about the clarity, like a weight lifted. She felt relief and understanding, and though disgusted to admit it, she felt joy that Anaya's death had been planned after all. That her decision had been her choice, not a careless mistake, not Peter's fault. The relief coated her like a hot bath. Anaya dying the very night of her mother's death, a death she clearly blamed herself for, could not have been a coincidence.

She tabbed to the beginning of the manuscript excerpt, relishing her ability to read the first section again with fresh eyes.

An email from Tixster popped into the corner of her screen. Elizabeth informing her that the new feature had passed QA testing and was ready to push, but Derek hadn't replied with approval. Edie responded quickly. Go ahead with the release, she said. Quickly, please.

Her fingers moved swiftly, driven by something deep in her gut, a need to be seen, to prove that this feeling that overwhelmed her with such force was real. It was strange to post on Tixster, something she had only really done in the QA environment. She had hardly any followers but she uploaded the first half of the manuscript excerpt to her Page. Not the typical cultural event, but that's what the new feature was for, and didn't Tixster pride itself on *creativity* and *innovation*? Reading Anaya's pages was her version of a cultural experience and it felt criminal that Anaya had worked this hard for it never to be read. It was the first time Edie had ever wanted to share.

Chapter Twenty-Two

DEREK WANTED TO meet her outside, so she waited for him in the wind. The sun was out but it was early and the air was still cold. Derek came out a few minutes late for their one-on-one. He asked if she was feeling better and she remembered she'd told everyone she was sick. "A little," she said.

They walked toward the water. Usually, they just circled the block a few times, but Derek wanted to make this a long one. He hadn't rolled back the Content Warning feature, and—she'd refreshed the dashboards all morning—it was getting higher than average use and positive feedback in the forums. She assumed he wanted to congratulate her, and she appreciated that he was finally taking their one-on-ones seriously. She planned to stay late today, take her mind off the case.

By the time they were done with small talk—Edie asked about Derek's kid and he complained, rather proudly, about the challenges of cloth diapers—they had cleared the busy part of SoMa and the sky opened into a clear, vast blue.

"So Edie," Derek started. "That was an interesting post this morning."

Though her follower count on Tixster was nearly zero, Derek was one of them.

"I thought it was a great piece of writing. It felt like the kind of thing that should be shared. I flagged it with the new feature, I thought you'd appreciate that release."

"You should have waited for my approval on that." She hated Derek. "But the new feature is fine." She made a mental note to tell Elizabeth she'd done a great job. "The problem is, we can't share actual art without approval, you know that. Our security team got a call this morning from the university. There are copyright issues." His voice was resigned and lacking energy.

"If we can't share art, I'm not sure what we're doing," she said softly, and then quickly, "but I know. I'm sorry."

"Where do you see yourself in five years?" Derek asked, his tone suddenly intentional.

She was glad they were walking side by side so he couldn't see the confusion on her face. She had no idea how to answer. If she was being honest, she saw herself back at Safe Home Society, hopefully—if Tixster management played their cards right and finally took the thing public—a little bit richer with her mom safely moved nearby.

"I'd like to sit on the Tixster Leadership Board."

Derek turned to her. He was wearing a Patagonia jacket, thin but puffy, the kind visitors might think were handed to new San Francisco residents upon arrival. It wasn't zipped, the cold didn't seem to bother him. "Is that really what you want? You can be honest with me. This is a total thought experiment, it was part of our management training, to see what really excites people. Like if you could do absolutely anything."

She didn't believe that Derek actually cared about her, but she was touched by the exercise. This small slice of interest, to know her in a real, personal way. "Well . . ." Her brain was still jumbled from not sleeping. "You know I worked at that nonprofit before Tixster."

Derek nodded, encouraging.

"I loved that. I love Tixster, too," she added quickly. "It's really interesting to build products people want. I love my job."

"Sure, sure," he said, moving her along.

"But yeah. I would love to one day go back to work that really matters." She caught herself. "Or, you know what I mean. Work that's helping people who are in real danger. Not right away. I'm thinking way down the line. I like being in the center of tech right now."

"That's great. I thought that about you. I can see that you have so much to offer when you really get excited about something. Like the Red Flag Project, you were obsessed with that."

The Red Flag Project was the first project they assigned her. They'd described it in her interview, and it helped her rationalize her decision to join Tixster. The product allowed users to flag when harmful things happened at an event—robberies at concerts, date rape at raves—it was more common than you thought. She'd worked tirelessly on it and she was prouder of that feature than anything else she'd ever done at Tixster.

"Yeah, I loved that," she admitted. "I'd love to work on more stuff like that." As soon as it went live, Tixster deprioritized it. It didn't get the publicity they were expecting. There was no bump in users, no Twitter talk about the feature. Red Flags still lived on, but there was no engineer assigned to the project and the bugs stacked up. It was barely functional.

"The thing is," Derek started, and she could hear a turn in his voice, "we just can't afford to prioritize that stuff right now. And I feel like you would really thrive if you could be somewhere that did."

She wasn't sure what was happening. She wanted to turn around, walk back to Tixster and reverse everything she'd already said but Derek stepped steadily ahead. They were a block from the water now, the farthest they'd ever walked together. "I love Tixster," she repeated as the light turned green and they sped across the street. "I'm definitely energized by the work. I thought we were talking about work besides Tixster when you asked me that. Like if I could do anything else. Or I would have said Tixster, obviously."

She could feel him smiling next to her. It had been nearly impossible for her to say it with a straight face and apparently it was impossible to hear it with one, too. The blue of the bay spread out before them. It was the kind of moment that made living in San Francisco worth it. Its colossal beauty snuck up so quickly it could knock you off your feet no matter how long you'd lived there.

Derek stopped walking, took a seat on a bench looking out at the view. She sat beside him. "We have to let you go, Edie," he said with a deep, apologetic breath. "We're making cuts, and I just don't think you understand the product. It doesn't feel like you believe in what we're doing."

Her heart stopped. She couldn't breathe. "I do, Derek, I do."

Derek was silent.

"You can't do this. Please don't do this."

He stared down at his shoes. Hands folded in his lap.

Her whole body turned to face him. "What did I do? Please, you can't do this to me. I need this job."

"You didn't do anything, Edie." When he looked up, his face was twisted and his eyes red. "We have to make cuts. I don't want to do this to anyone. But I can tell your heart's not in it. I think this will be the best thing for you. You shouldn't be wasting your time here."

She wondered for the first time in her tenure at Tixster if Derek was telling the truth. If he actually cared. The truth was so slippery these days, she wondered if it even existed at all. The truth couldn't shift from one person to the next without distortion; the mere fact that humans delivered it meant that it was painted with an element of deception.

"This isn't fair," she said at last. She considered the possibility that Derek was sexist. But all of Derek's direct reports were women. This didn't make him *not* sexist—if anything, it proved that he was; he loved mentoring women, he just didn't respect them as peers. But it did mean this particular act had nothing to do with Edie being a woman. She knew—he didn't even have to say it—that Elizabeth would slip into her spot. She knew she'd been eyeing the position since she'd started. The Ping-Pong tournaments she organized had been Derek's idea, she took over for him when he had the baby. She was always popping by his desk to ask how his wife was doing. He'd be happy to give it to her. In a way, Edie was proud of her.

Derek seemed to have pulled himself together but Edie had not. If anything, she was falling further apart.

"We're doing something really important at Tixster," he began, "and we need everyone on board."

She laughed. She couldn't help it. All these people running around the city thinking they were changing the world. She would work hard, she was happy to do what she was told, but she couldn't believe she was actually making a difference. Laughter felt good, great, even. She laughed so hard, harder than she had in a very long time.

SHE CHECKED HER Tixster page when she got back to her computer. It was empty again, as if the post had never existed. A text from Alex was waiting for her when she checked her phone: Chloe broke up with me. I've been trying to call you all week. It can be very hard to be your friend. She ran into a conference room and tried calling her but there was no answer. She sent an apology text but as soon as she did it felt worse than saying nothing at all—lazy and insufficient.

Elizabeth came by as Edie placed the photo of her mother in her backpack, abandoning the scattered pens and hard candy that littered her desk.

"The feature's getting good use already!" Elizabeth exclaimed.

Edie smiled at how excited she looked. "I saw that. You did a great job with everything." She zipped her bag. "I'm leaving Tixster."

"What?" Elizabeth's bright, made-up face crinkled painfully. "Why?"

She couldn't bring herself to tell the truth. A version of it would have to do. "It's not the right fit. I'm going to recommend you take my place, although I'm sure it goes without saying. Derek would be crazy not to promote you. You're already doing the job. You should get the credit." A new-hire zipped by on a scooter. "I should have advocated more for you earlier, Elizabeth. I've been a terrible boss. I'm really sorry."

Elizabeth's head twitched back. "Edie, you're why I joined Tixster. You've been an amazing boss." She looked almost hurt.

Edie remembered her interview, fighting for Elizabeth in the hiring meeting when Derek and Jim said she was uptight and nervous. Of course she was, Edie had pleaded. If they hadn't judged her for it and actually appreciated how much she wanted the job, they would have gotten to know her like Edie had. She remembered how anxious Elizabeth was pushing her first line of code, how Edie had made a point to explain every step twice, afraid that she, like Edie, might have been too afraid to ask questions. How she had encouraged Elizabeth to run the standups, assuring her she could do it because she saw, even in that first week, how smart and capable and excited she was and, more than anything, she had promised herself in those early days that she would not let that fade.

"I can't imagine being on this team without you."

Her first thought was that Anaya would be proud. She had forgotten that she did actually care about something at Tixster. "I'm still here," Edie smiled. "Just because I don't work here doesn't mean we have to lose touch. We can grab a drink sometime. Finally do something out of the office."

Elizabeth's face lit up. "Yes, please! Anything but those Ping-Pong tournaments."

THE RUSH OF air blew the tears back. It felt safe crying down Market Street in the middle of the day; she might as well have been in an empty field. The street was quiet, only a few cars and barely any bikes. Climbing up the hill was a small slice of joy, the pain in her thighs, in her chest, a distraction from the pain of everything else.

It was almost funny how poorly she had played her life, all her bad decisions now revealing themselves like a giant knot, impossible to untangle. If she didn't think about her mother, not having to see Tixster ever again made her feel as if she were on top of the world. Regarding the case, she allowed, for a moment, that Peter's mess was Peter's mess. Even though she had finally proved it wasn't his fault, not really, she repeated Leah's words in her mind—*it's because of him.* She batted each worry down like a game of whack-a-mole, but new ones kept popping up. Like Alex's disappointment in her.

Fiona Apple screamed in her ears. *I don't even like you anymore at all.* The album spun from one track to the next and back around again. In times of sadness, the only thing that felt right was to cover herself in it. To try to escape only made the sadness sharper. When she reached the top of the Market Street hill, the idea stopped her short. She didn't turn right and head toward The Wiggle, as usual; she crossed the street and sped back down. She had passed this lot nearly every day on her ride to and from the office, though it was always locked up. But now it was smack in the middle of the day and the gate was open. She locked her bike outside.

The junkyard was enormous and Edie wondered how much longer it would last before the owners were bought out and developers turned it into a high-end coffee bar or a beer garden, or, more likely, a luxury apartment building. She stepped through the tents that sat out front, trying not to disturb the people in them. Inside she wandered through old car parts, lines of storage units, piles of old furniture. Finally, she saw someone locking a gate in the back.

"Can I help you?" He was old, too old, Edie thought, to still be working at a place like this. He looked at her with disinterest.

"I was wondering if you have any window frames?" she asked.

———

IT WAS A pile of junk but they were in there. She waded through it, peeling each frame back. Her hands were full of splinters by the time she was done, her back tied in knots. Finally, she'd piled up the nicest-looking ones, which weren't necessarily the cleanest or in the best shape, but the most Alex-esque, shabby but not deteriorated, into the Lyft XXL then shoved her bike in behind them. She carried them all up the stairs, two at a time, there were a dozen in total, and rang the bell.

"WHAT ARE YOU doing here?" Alex's voice sprung her awake. She was staring at the pile of frames that surrounded Edie like a nest. A nest of wooden trash.

When their eyes met, they burst into wild, uncontrollable laughter. "What the fuck did you do?" Alex said, gasping for air, barely getting the words out.

She slumped on the step beside Edie.

"I got your frames."

Alex shook her head. Edie knew it wouldn't be this easy.

"I'm so sorry," Edie started. "I'm so sorry I wasn't there for you." She put her hand on Alex's arm and paused until she met her eye. "I know I can be selfish. I've been so obsessed with my own dumb stuff and I'm so sorry. I care about you, Alex, more than anything."

When Alex looked up she was smiling and, briefly, nothing else mattered. "Thank you for that. I appreciate it."

"I'm sorry I make it hard to be my friend."

The right side of Alex's mouth twitched up slightly. She rolled her eyes. "Just *sometimes*."

Edie took Alex's hand in both of hers.

"Like when you leave all this goddamn trash on my doorstep!" she shouted, and stood up.

Edie's laugh felt as if she'd released a valve on the highest pressure. "You don't like them? I tried to get the best ones!"

"They're perfect. You're insane. Let's bring them in."

They stacked the frames in the corner of Alex's studio with the rest of her project. "So," Edie started. "What happened with Chloe? Tell me everything."

Alex spoke for a long time. She and Chloe, who Edie, to her embarrassment, remembered almost nothing about, had apparently been dating for months and had even said they loved each other. But Chloe had wanted to move in together, start talking about a family, "settling down," Alex explained, curling her fingers in quotation marks, and she wasn't ready for that. She still needed time and space for her art. She was pretty sure she didn't want kids. "It really sucks to break up with someone you actually love."

Edie could see the pain in Alex's face. "I can't imagine. Finding that and not being in the same place. I'm sorry, Al." She let the silence rest. "I can't believe you were in love. I can't believe you were in love and I never met her."

Alex smiled. "You've never been all that interested in my relationships."

Edie's head cocked. How many times had she helped Alex draft a text, cyber-stalk a potential girlfriend, plot a breakup strategy?

"I mean when things are good," Alex clarified. "It's like you're only interested in solving my problems. I appreciate it, honestly, but it's kind of more about you than me. You're not actually there to celebrate when things go well. I don't know. To, like, be there for my joy."

Edie could feel her face flush. "Alex, I'm sorry." How childish she'd been, how childish she *was*. "I think . . ." It was so embarrassing to say out loud. "I think I was jealous of your happiness. Like, I withheld celebrating out of spite or something. It's idiotic, I know it's not a competition." Why was she such an asshole? She wanted to blame her dad, Matt, all the men in her life for how desperately she compared herself, how needy she was for any shred of confidence.

"It's really not."

"And it's no excuse. I'm just trying to explain. It's like I can't process joy without making myself feel bad. It's so selfish and immature." She looked up. "I'm really sorry, Al."

"Thank you, I know you are."

"I'm here for your joy!"

"Um, my heart is fucking broken so save it for next time."

"Well, I'll never talk about my shit again, promise." She was so sick of her shit.

Alex took the pillow and hit her over the head with it. "Shut up. You *finally* went on a date with a woman and you think I don't want to talk about your shit?" Alex leaned back on the green velvet couch. She looked tired and beautiful.

There was so much Edie wanted to tell her. That she and Leah had kissed, again, and sober this time. That she was really starting to fall for her—a woman. That she had gotten a copy of Anaya's manuscript and finally—*finally!*—figured out why it had happened *that* night. That it was the anniversary of her mother's death, a death for which she'd blamed herself for fifteen years, since she'd started writing her last book, which she'd finished and submitted the night she took her life. That she was supposed to testify for Peter and really didn't think it had anything to do with him, it all made sense now, but she felt a need to side with Leah and wanted more than anything to talk this through with her best friend.

But she had to start somewhere and really it was the least she could do. "Not today."

Alex gave her a disapproving, don't-try-to-be-a-hero look.

"No, really. I want to know—what the fuck does it feel like to be in love?"

IT WAS A rare dreary day from the little she could see outside her window and she was grateful. Sun would have been unbearable. She hadn't heard from Leah despite many attempts at contact. Edie hadn't told her she was testifying for Peter at the trial, but she assumed she knew by now; it was scheduled for this Friday, just three days away. She needed to see her, to explain.

The bike ride down to SoMa felt nostalgic although it'd only been a few days since her last ride to the office. She felt free, a thrill in the pit of her stomach knowing she didn't have to go to Tixster, smell its plastic, industrial air and pretend to smile until it got dark. But that freedom, as freedom often is, was tinged with a distinct sadness. She didn't have to be at Tixster, which meant she didn't have to be anywhere. No one needed her, no one cared.

She locked her bike in front of the salad spot where she knew Leah got lunch, the place she had first seen her, and took a seat in the corner, against the window. It was only just noon; the crowd was still light.

An email from Peter. He could get her consulting work at Primals if she wanted, give her some income until she found another job. He told her Derek was a moron, and he'd be happy to recommend her for a full-time role, he assured her he'd figure it out. It disgusted her, how easy it was to get work if you knew the right people, if you had access to the game and were willing to play. She could barely finish reading it but she was grateful, deeply so.

An hour later the place was packed. She'd already eaten her salad and now sipped on a tea and nibbled on some kind of bar made of nuts. She had brought a book, not Anaya's but an author Anaya liked. She felt out of place, reading quietly in the bustling lunch joint, everyone with a different logo on their back. She considered leaving, it was twenty past one and the shame she felt watching others move through their days, getting paid too much money, high on self-importance, was nearly too much to bear. She told herself she would read one more chapter. She was holding the book up straight so she could keep one eye on the window as she read, and at one thirty on the dot, she saw Leah's unicorn hoodie walk through the swinging glass doors.

She was with a few other Datsta employees, young guys in soft
T-shirts. Edie stood up, took a deep breath, and walked toward the
line that now wrapped around the store. Leah didn't look surprised
to see her. Edie hadn't told her about getting fired from Tixster so
running into her still had the potential to seem normal.

"Hi," Edie said, trying to smile. "I need to talk to you."

"I'm sorry I haven't returned your emails," Leah said, rote and
lifeless. "I've been busy." Leah's eyes shifted to the line, which was
moving quickly, then to her co-workers who were staring up at the
menu glowing on a big digital screen. "I need to order."

Edie followed her as she stepped into place behind her friends.
"I know about your mom," Edie blurted. "I know it happened on the
anniversary of her death."

Leah turned to her.

"What do you mean?" Her eyes were on fire.

"I read part of Anaya's new manuscript. Leah, I'm so sorry that
happened to you."

Her look was menacing as she stepped away from the line, her
face nearly touching Edie's. "You think that explains this?" she said in
a whisper that somehow sounded like a shout. "You have it all figured
out now?" There was pain in her voice but her face was pure rage. "Is
that why you're testifying for Peter? You don't know her, Edie. You
never knew her."

"I'm sorry I'm testifying for him. I don't want to." She looked
down at her sneakers, grubby and tearing on the edge. "But he's my
oldest friend. I have to tell the truth."

Leah laughed, glanced up at the bright wall of menus. "The
truth." She turned back to Edie, her dark eyes cutting into her. "Anaya would never have done this if Peter wasn't there." Her stare was
firm and unwavering, as if she were speaking another language from
Edie, whose words were so fragile and cautious, shaking like frail
leaves on a tree.

"You can't be sure," Edie managed to get out, just barely. "Leah." She paused, mustering the strength to continue. "I know this wasn't her first attempt—on that same day."

Leah shook her head, long and slow. "What is it you think you know?"

"I know she struggled with thoughts of suicide." She paused, then jumped. "I know she tried to take her life on the anniversary of your mom's death last year."

Leah blinked, too much, too quickly, and she knew she was right. "We told each other everything." The anger in her voice had drained, what was left was nothing short of certainty. "It's hard for most people to understand our closeness." She sat down on an empty plastic chair and Edie followed. "We were everything to one another." She stared up at Edie with her dark eyes, Anaya's eyes. "Her life was my life. I made her promise to tell me if it ever got this bad again. And she would never, *ever* have broken that promise." Her eyes shifted to a calm resolve. "I'm not saying she wasn't in a bad place that night, I'm sure she was. But I know that more than I know anything in my life."

It was impossible for Edie to respond.

"I know Peter didn't mean for this to happen. But it did. He gave her drugs that killed her. And then he left."

It was hard for Edie to move, but she managed to nod her head.

"It's the worst people who can avoid consequences. Everyone else pays the price. I thought you understood that."

It was true and Edie knew it. Nowhere proved it more than the Bay Area, where rich, VC-backed start-ups claimed to be saving the world while perpetuating an unbearable monoculture at the general public's expense. She hated that anyone who dared to maintain a shred of integrity, like Alex, inevitably did so at the cost of power and money. But that didn't mean Peter should go to prison.

"I thought you wanted to help." She took a long breath.

"Leah, I do." She felt an aching need to hold her but Leah flinched at her words.

Her co-workers had been inching up the line as they spoke and now it was their turn at the register. "I guess I'll see you Friday," she said, and walked to the cashier.

Chapter Twenty-Three

THE SKY WAS black in the park. The sun had set hours ago and Edie had finally pulled herself out of bed, safe and at ease in the dark of the night. She needed a run more than she ever had in her life. With her music at top volume, she felt like she was in another world, a void, unable to see the surroundings or even her feet in the pitch dark. Her mother hated that she ran at night, it wasn't safe, she'd say, and Edie suspected she was right. The joy of night runs was always offset with a nagging fear.

But it was the night before the trial and not running was impossible. She felt better with each step, a soothing reminder that she, or at least her body, had a purpose, if only to put one foot in front of the other. Tomorrow this would all be over and she could go on living her life. What that looked like exactly, she would deal with later.

She passed the museum. The streetlights were getting fewer and farther between. A man walked slowly in the opposite direction on the other side of the street. On another night, in another world, she might have been worried, but tonight she couldn't bring herself to care. An old song from her college years came on, a song she and Peter had sung together in his old Ford Escort many times with the windows open and the wind blowing. She'd whispered the lyrics, mortified by the sound of her own voice, let alone someone else hearing it, but he'd sung so loudly she felt safe letting loose under his veil. As the chorus rang in her ears now, she thought she might run to the ocean and back, the energy inside her felt boundless, until the song was interrupted by a ring. An unknown number flashed on her screen. She considered ignoring it, normally she would have, but these were not normal times.

"Hello?"

"Edie." The sound of her father's voice sent chills down her spine. She stopped midstride and stood alone in the dark, the mist thicker than she'd thought. He never called her. He had a prepaid phone for emergencies but, she remembered now, she had never even saved the number. His breath was heavy. She stood, barely able to see in front of her, terrified of what was waiting on the other end of the line. "Your mother's in the hospital." There was a long pause. "She had another fall."

It was impossible to speak. What finally came out was a scream that echoed through the dark, empty park. "What did you do?" The sound sliced the silence. She had never confronted her father for not helping more, never blamed him for the messes he left everywhere, like land mines for her near-blind, disabled mother, the way he shoved past her, hurrying to the fridge, and now her anger released like a broken damn. "What did you do?" she repeated over and over again.

She wore herself out until she could no longer speak. The tears were relentless. Silence hung on the other end of the line. Finally, her father cleared his throat. "You should come home as soon as you can, sweetie."

At first her feet wouldn't work. She sat on the curb for a long time. The cement was cold and the wind blew hard against her moist skin. She shivered but didn't move. There was something soothing about the physical pain, the chill that cut to her bone, the soreness of her muscles. Comfort felt unearned. Inescapable pain felt right. She began walking toward home until her legs worked enough to move faster and when they did, she raced.

———

PETER WASN'T ANSWERING his phone so she had to tell him by text. She was sorry, she said, but she needed to take the next flight out. She would miss the trial. She had no space to feel relief, every cell in her body was tight and anxious. Seconds after she hit send, he called.

"Edie, you can't do this. I need you to stay. It's just a few more hours. You owe me this, I'm begging you." The desperation in his voice was thick and pleading.

"I need to go home, Peter. My dad wouldn't call me if wasn't serious. I could hear it in his voice." There had been something chilling about the steadiness of his request. Her presence wasn't an option.

"Look, the trial starts at nine. You'll be out of there by ten, eleven the latest. I promise. You can leave if it takes any longer. I'll buy your ticket home. Here, I'm buying it right now."

He sounded frantic. And she barely had the money to buy a last-minute ticket as it was. He knew this. "Fine," she said at last. "But I'm leaving at ten. Tell your lawyer I have to go first."

"Of course. E, I'm so sorry. We'll get you to your mom. She'll be okay."

She hung up the phone and an email from Peter popped onto her screen. A plane ticket in her name, departing at 12:05 p.m. She stared at it, her body aching, wishing she could close her eyes and wake up in New York. It wasn't until she began packing her clothes, in the calming distraction of the mindless task, that the tears came again, heavier now. Her sadness seemed to fill her whole body, anywhere her mind went, whatever thought or image she touched, even grazed, it exploded out of her. As she closed her suitcase, full of god knew what, she realized how desperately she wanted someone to talk to.

ALEX WAS STILL out of breath when Edie let her in, and threw her arms around her. "E, come here." Alex held her so tight. Her hair smelled like an elementary school classroom, a mix of clay and paint and dust. Her hands pressed into Edie's back, comforting her like she hadn't been in she couldn't remember how long.

The two curled up in bed and the words poured out. Edie told her about her father—how she'd idolized him as a child, the night his alcoholism came roaring back, how she had watched her mom put up with his shouts, and probably far more, for years. How impossible it was for her to confront him about any of it, so deep was her need for his approval. She'd never said it to anyone out loud, not all of it. Everyone her age had issues with their fathers, it had always felt dumb and boring to detail.

It took a long time to get it all out. Each time she tried, tears came, as if her body had wired a trap to prevent the memories from ever being spoken. But she kept trying, or rather, Alex kept encouraging her to try for as long as she was comfortable, assuring Edie that she wanted to listen, until finally the words broke through.

Alex held her when she was done.

"I don't want to go to the trial."

"He's a selfish monster." It wasn't the first time she'd said it, but it was the first time Edie agreed.

"He doesn't deserve to go to prison."

Alex sat up, turned and looked directly at Edie. "You shouldn't have to put your life on hold to save him from his own mess. You didn't say anything to the cops that wasn't true. They can use the statement you've already given. What does he want you to say at the trial anyway? Why does he need you so badly?"

Edie had been trying not to think about it. To say it out loud to Alex felt impossible. She got up and took the pages out of her bag and handed them to her.

Alex took the folder, eyes wide, and began reading. It took her a long time to flip the page and Edie realized she wasn't just skimming; she was reading every word. Her mouth had stiffened, her lips barely visible as she bit down into them. When she handed the pages back to Edie, she looked pale and almost sick. She got up and walked to the bathroom without saying a word.

"Are you okay?" Edie called to the closed door. Alex came out composed, face a little less white, and took a seat on the bed. "What's wrong?" Edie asked.

"That whole thing is a very carefully worded lie."

"It's more like omissions" was what Edie had told herself. "Technically I don't know for sure that the drugs Anaya took were the drugs Peter gave her." Edie had been doing these kinds of mental gymnastics for the past forty-eight hours. She had successfully convinced herself, if she didn't think too hard, that every word she planned to say was, in one way or another, true. Because although she hated that it was mostly rich, white men who got off scot-free, in this case Anaya's death was an intentional act, so Edie couldn't quite convince herself that Peter deserved to be in jail. And anyway, wasn't it Alex who'd said not to blame the dealer?

"I'm not talking about the Anaya part, E." Water was slowly welling up in Alex's eyes now, too, and Edie wondered if the depth of her own distress was somehow contagious, like a sneeze.

"What are you talking about?"

"That you have to be his fucking character witness?"

"He's been very good to me. I owe a lot to him."

"Fuck *that*, Edie. Why do you think I hate Peter so much?"

There were a million reasons to choose from. "Because he's selfish and spoiled?"

Alex laughed, grateful, it seemed, for the chance to smile.

"Three years ago, at my birthday party, the one at that big loft space down in Bernal?"

"I loved that party. Those leather pants. You looked great."

"Yeah." Alex paused.

Edie sat up, back against her wall.

"I had gone to smoke in the back and Peter came out behind me. He was very drunk, for whatever that's worth—not much, in my opinion—but still. He asked if I'd ever had sex with men. I told him yes. He asked if I ever liked it. I told him no." Alex's voice shook just the tiniest bit. "Then he asked if he could try to make me cum."

Edie shot forward. "What? Why didn't you tell me this?" She recognized gross pricks of envy pushing on her chest. She wasn't angry at Peter, she was jealous of Alex.

Alex stared at her, disbelieving.

"God, I'm so sorry." She grabbed Alex's hand. "I'm so sorry that happened to you. Jesus." She took a breath. "Were you okay? What did you do?"

With one merciful look, Alex let it go. "I said no," she continued. Her voice was no longer shaky but firm, set on getting it out. "I didn't tell you because I know you worship him, and I just wanted to forget about it. But we were in this alley and he had me against the wall."

Edie—psychotically, she knew—wondered if they'd kissed. Her jealousy of Alex was reflexive, like breathing, so ingrained in her psyche it felt impossible to stop. The best she could do was ignore it, focus on the part of her that wanted, more than anything, to turn back time and pull Alex away from him, hold her, save her, make sure nothing bad ever happened to her again.

"I remember it was cold and brick, the wall, the coarseness scraped my back and my arms, I had marks for days."

Edie remembered the marks; they'd joked she had caught a rash from the bar. Her heart sank as she pictured Alex, fighting against Peter, a million times her size.

"He started touching me."

Edie's body trembled. Anger rose up inside her, filled her until she could feel it in her throat. All she could think about was how many times she'd defended him. How many hours she'd spent idolizing him while Alex listened, patiently, quietly.

"Over the pants," she clarified. "Thank god that leather was basically painted on."

Edie attempted the smallest smile.

"He looked at me as he did it, Edie. He was into it, like he thought he was turning me on. Like we were sharing some kind of secret."

Edie felt nauseous and dizzy, her throat was so thick she could barely swallow.

"I still remember that look. It's why I can't be around him. Just the sight of him is awful."

"What did you do?"

"I couldn't move. I just stared back at him, so furious I didn't blink, and told him as serious as I'd ever been in my life that if he didn't get his hands off me I would fucking kill him." There was a desperate thread of pride in her voice. "He stopped after that but"—she paused, took a long breath—"before he did, he pushed harder, I'm sure he'd deny it, but I remember, it made me wince." Whether she meant to or not, she winced now, her eyes closing for a moment.

"Alex, I'm so sorry," she said, and took her in her arms.

They stayed like that for a long time. Finally, Alex lifted her head up. "He was mortified, of course, begged me to forgive him. He said he was drunk, wasted and high. He said he didn't remember the details, just that something had happened. He said he was just playing around, he was an asshole and an idiot. But he never apologized. He never considered how mortified *I* was. To be treated like that, to know that someone in the world—a *friend*, Jesus—thought they could treat me like a fucking game."

Edie could barely believe the words. But she did. She believed every one of them.

Chapter Twenty-Four

ALEX HAD CRAWLED out early, before the sun came up. Edie pretended she was still asleep though she hadn't slept at all. Outside, the morning looked sunny and crisp, a perfect day. May was one of the few months when the weather in San Francisco fit. It was always either spring or fall in the city.

Alex had left a note on the nightstand wishing her luck and assuring her that her mom would be okay. There was no update from her father. She made herself coffee because it was something to do. Her body was already wired and jittery, her nerves frayed. She would have tried to run if it weren't for her stomach, so twisted she could barely move. She showered and dressed, threw on some slacks and a decent enough blazer. She had no idea how to "do" makeup but tried to apply all the standard elements—foundation, some blush, a hefty dose of mascara. She wanted to look credible and for a woman that meant looking attractive enough, but just enough. She did everything quickly so as not to leave space for her mind to wander. She didn't want to think about the trial. She just wanted it to be over.

It was too early to leave but she couldn't stay inside. She had planned to treat herself to a car but decided to walk down to the courthouse instead, rolling her suitcase behind her. Market Street was deserted this early. A few men in suits sped by on bikes, cars rolled by unrushed. It was, in fact, a beautiful day. The sky was a bright blue and the wind hadn't yet gotten started. She couldn't be bothered with NPR, words in any form felt like an affront, a scrambled mess of noise. Her mind was too busy to make sense of them. She shuffled to a girl band she used to like—dreamy and desperate—nothing to process, only feel. Walking was a welcome distraction. Like mail she didn't want to open, the trial was inevitable, she would get to it; but for as long as she could she wanted to sit in the empty space of unaccountability.

The night had felt like a war with herself. Why did she care so much about Peter? Why did his well-being surpass everyone else's? She didn't want him as a friend, not after what he'd done. Why was she still so desperate for his approval? Stick to the truth, was what she'd decided. Peter had never given Edie drugs—though he'd offered a million times—and she'd known him for fifteen years. He had helped her escape Matt, in the moment and for years after. All of that was true.

Her stomach was a wreck. What happened to Alex years ago had nothing to do with this case, she reminded herself. She would confront him about that later, with Alex's permission she would demand a real apology, some retribution, but she wasn't being asked about that now. And yet, could she really be a *character* witness? Tell the truth, she repeated to herself over and over again. She'd stayed up practicing lines, playing out scenarios, words and phrases endlessly swirling. Tell the truth.

The further she walked toward the Civic Center, the more tents lined the sidewalk. By the time she reached the courthouse they were everywhere. A few blocks east, multimillion-dollar office buildings were churning out unimaginable profits, bright-eyed men claiming to disrupt the world one neon call-to-action button at a time. For a brief second, she allowed herself to appreciate that she no longer had to participate in that world, if only temporarily—she no longer had to pretend. There was real joy in that.

The courthouse was huge and authoritative-looking, like a relic

from another century or at least a different part of the world. A
large fountain sat in front of it, glistening in the San Francisco sun.
Against the tents and trash, the sparkling fountain looked like the
most beautiful thing she'd ever seen. Her nerves were wild. She
could feel sweat pool in every corner of her body, her blouse already
drenched under her blazer.

Her pocket buzzed. For the first time in her life, she was glad to
see her father calling. She wanted nothing more than to talk to her
mother, to tell her she would be there soon. To hear her voice. To tell
her she loved her.

"Is she awake?" Edie asked without a hello.

"She . . ." Her father's voice was stiff. "She fractured her hip." He
paused. She waited. "And hit her head. There are complications."
Edie froze, breathing no longer occurred to her. "They're doing the
best they can. It'll be good to have you here. Just get here soon. We
love you."

Her knees seemed to disappear. She fell to the ground. People
flocked around her. She waved them away, staring at nothing but the
dirty gray gravel. She thought she had no tears left but they came in
droves, a flood. She saw smudges of black and pink on the back of her
hand as she wiped them away.

She sat on the cold sidewalk for a long time. She had left early,
there was no rush. The people walking by were a blur. She stared
at the fountain, its never-ending flow taunting and relentless, until
finally the buzzing of her phone was impossible to ignore.

Where are you?? Peter was asking.

Her phone read 9:35. With every last bit of energy, she forced
herself up and walked toward the courthouse.

THE ROOM WAS small, wooden, and eerily quiet. The closing of the
tall, thick door and the tap of her shoes announced her entry to the
room. Peter sat at the front and turned to look at her. She took a

seat in the back. People began saying words but she heard nothing but a hum. It was no longer her stomach that hurt, it was something deeper, heavier in her chest. She felt as if she were trapped under a giant slab of stone, she could barely breathe.

When she heard her name, it was as if someone was waking her from a dream—a nightmare. She walked quickly to the stand, her heels clinking clumsily against the tiled floor. She had practiced in the mirror the night before, in her head on her run, she had whispered the words to herself over and over so she wouldn't forget. But as she hit the hard wooden chair, the words seemed to evaporate.

When she looked up, she saw Peter, wearing his favorite suit, the suit he'd gotten handmade in Thailand, that he'd worn to every holiday party she'd ever accompanied him to. The suit that used to make her heart catch in her throat because of the way it hugged his tall, lean frame. But now the fit seemed maddeningly precise. That so much time and effort could be spent perfecting a suit seemed like the most unjust thing in the world. She wanted to jump out of her seat and tear it off him, rip it to shreds. If only she could move.

The sides of his mouth tilted downward, his brow furrowed and focused. His face was wan and tired, as if someone had let the air out of him. She felt, on an almost cellular level, sad at the idea that he had to deal with any of this. The Peter she knew was bigger than the room, bigger than anything. His life was better than this. She wanted to sweep him up and take him away from here.

Edie was asked to confirm her name and relationship to Peter— easy enough—but when she tried to speak her voice wasn't there. It came out wobbly and hoarse. She coughed and everything hurt, then blinked quickly so as not to cry on the stand. Without thinking she wiped her eye with her sleeve and saw dark tracks of black mascara smeared across her light gray cuff. It had to be all over her face, like a lunatic. She took a breath but the air was nothing but added weight on her chest.

"Are you okay, Ms. Walker?" A voice asked. Peter's lawyer, tall and clean, was standing at the front of the room with urgent eyes.

"I'm fine," she said.

She looked at Peter, searching for help, or at least a reminder of what she was doing there. She caught his big bright eyes and didn't let go. She let herself be consumed by his stare, hoping their years of shared language would kick in and tell her what she needed to know—whatever that was. His body, erect in his suit, made him look like a tired king. She needed him to realize how much she cared, how much she was willing to do for him. She needed him, even with just a look, to love her.

The corner of his lips twitched into a small, nearly imperceptible smile. He gave her a fierce nod. She felt the familiar rush of knowing Peter Masterson's language, the only one who really knew it, the only one who ever had the patience to learn. The rush of feeling like his equal. A rush that had sustained her for so long.

Peter's lawyer stepped to the front of the room and her eyes darted from Peter's to the crowd. From the head of the room she could see all the faces before her and she watched them as the stenographer typed and Peter's lawyer said words that floated past her like sirens. Peter's mother and father, a couple that looked like royalty, must have flown out from Boulder. They gripped each other's hands as if they were the last people in the world. But most of the other faces were unfamiliar. It wasn't until Peter's lawyer stepped closer to her that she recognized someone else behind where his head had been. Glowing and young, out of place in a sea of worn, jaded stares, her long blond hair framing her unwrinkled face. The girl from the party—Maggie, Edie remembered—stared up at her.

Edie was high above the courtroom looking down on herself. Isn't this ridiculous? she thought with a wild grin. She saw the version of her here in the chair collapse, like a popped balloon, and the self from above invade her body, trying on her skin like an old coat, moving her limbs as if she were a puppet. Now, in the costume of her body, she caught Peter's smile and crushed it. The puppeteer tugged at something deep in her chest, a part of her that hadn't been touched for a very long time, or maybe ever. She pried it open and let it free.

She turned away from Peter, staring at the suited man before her with a cold gaze.

"You've known my client for a very long time." The lawyer's voice, once echoing through the room, quivered just slightly. She nodded. "Could you please describe his character?"

She recognized the question but the answer had vanished. In the empty space of her silence someone shouted "objection" and voices cluttered the room.

Her mind drifted to her mother as the lawyer and judge argued about whether or not she could speak. She imagined her mother retreating to her bedroom, running away from the only man she'd ever loved. Silencing his shouts with the familiar blast of network television. She imagined how easy it must have been for him to push her, not intentionally, but carelessly rushing to the fridge. She imagined him thinking nothing as he did it, just letting his needs take shape, not considering the consequences.

"How long have you known Peter?" the tall man was asking.

"Fifteen years." Her answer was shorter than they'd practiced. His brow grew moist and she began to feel something like comfort, even a bit of delight.

"All right then," he continued. "Has he ever given you drugs?"

"No." The wooden chair in which she sat was blond wood, old and smooth and laminated like a teacher's desk. At the tip of the right arm was a scrape in the veneer, the wood beneath was cracked and coarse. She rested her eyes on the crack and rubbed her thumb against the shards of fraying wood as she spoke.

"Can you tell us about Matt Watson?"

"Matt was my boyfriend in college. Junior year, he tried to rape me. Held me down. Peter came in and stopped it. He helped me get away from Matt that night and supported me emotionally for years after." The lawyer continued to pry. She answered every question. Her thumb red, sore, splintered.

"You met with Peter the night after Anaya's death."

She nodded.

"If you could state your response for the court, please."

"Yes." She wondered if her mother had been conscious in the hospital. If she'd had to stare at the man who hurt her while he stood by caring for her. She'd heard the concern in her father's voice, she knew how much he loved her and her mother. She imagined her mom, stuck in that house for her entire adult life, how his inconsistency paralyzed her. How disorienting it is when the person who harms you most is the person who's always there for you.

"Tell us what happened."

In the far corner of the room, she spotted Leah. Her face pale and drawn. She caught Edie's eyes for a moment before looking away.

The words from the lawyer's document came back to her as she spoke. She had met Peter the next day, he was shaken up about Anaya's death. He'd told her he'd had nothing to do with it. He wasn't there when Anaya had passed.

She scratched out a particularly sharp piece of wood and rubbed it against one of her splinters from Alex's windows, right on the tip of her thumb.

The lawyer cut in to ask the next question but the words, new words, kept coming.

He had gone to Anaya's to break up with her, she explained, remembering Ron freeze with something like triumph, when she'd told him. They had been spending lots of time together. He thought it'd be easier to break up if they were high, so he gave her ketamine, he always had drugs on him. He'd offered Edie drugs a million times, she explained. The only reason he hadn't given her any yet was because she regularly refused. The lawyer's voice boomed louder than before, trying to interrupt but the judge wouldn't allow it. She was told to continue.

She told the room Peter had sex with Anaya, though they knew that already. She told them he'd said the women he was dating liked it rough, she couldn't help but smile as she said it, how sick it made her. None of it mattered to the case or even at all, but she knew what mattered didn't matter, it was all how people perceived it.

When she looked up the lawyer was glaring at her. He looked horrified and she thought again of her makeup, how absurd she must have looked to him—a mess.

She imagined Anaya in her apartment alone, an image she'd conjured millions of times. Every idle moment in the last few months she had been collecting clues about who this person was, and, in turn, how Edie, herself, should be. She felt Anaya's struggle and her shame like a weighted blanket, her desperation to get rid of it. Did she intentionally take her life? It was the question she'd fallen asleep and woken up to, trying to understand herself, as much as the woman she barely knew.

The room around her was fuzzy and insignificant. For the first time since she was a child, she was not performing for others, and in this vacuum of sorts, the words came clearly. Most things are not binary, Anaya had written with the same clarity Edie felt now, in her chair, realizing how simple it all was. Most things are a mess.

Of course Anaya wanted an escape. Of course she was in pain. Did she want to hurt herself in that moment?—surely. Edie knew it well, the need for a sensation more all-consuming than the ordinary, relentless torture of existing every day. But she also knew Leah was right, it couldn't possibly have been planned, because she, Edie, would never take her own life if she had promised her mother she wouldn't. More than anything, she knew that the truth, whatever that meant to Anaya, would never be fully known to Edie.

"Those are all the questions I have," a man's voice boomed.

A woman in a blue suit stood up on the other side of the room. She had a bony face, bold blue eyes, and a short bob—every strand in its place. She greeted Edie and moved closer.

"How would you describe Peter's relationship with women, generally?" she asked.

"Objection," the tall lawyer shouted.

"She's a character witness, Your Honor."

"Denied. Continue, Ms. Walker."

There was a room full of people, waiting for her to speak. She thought of Anaya spending years spinning shreds of elusive insight into tangible pages. Edie released the question of whether or not Peter had done this to Anaya, a question that couldn't possibly be answered, and moved on to the more concrete, now more important, question of whether or not he deserved to be punished.

Her thumb had gone numb and she could see the blood dripping onto the chair. The red color, stark and alive, looked beautiful against to smooth blond wood. The words came from a place deep in her chest, a place once inaccessible that was now shattered open. She spoke of the women he slept with, how proud he was of it, like it was a game, sometimes three in a day. "He hurts so many women," she said, smiling at how good it felt to say out loud.

"Has he ever assaulted a woman?" The lawyer's voice was careful, but firm.

It wasn't her story to tell, but she had no doubt what Alex would want her to do. She told the whole truth, and nothing but the truth, so help her God.

The Gap blouse under her sports coat was sodden with sweat by the time she looked up. The entire courtroom was a different shade, tense and quiet. She looked at Peter. His face was uglier than she'd ever seen it. Sweat dripped from the crown of his thick, silky hair.

"Thank you, Ms. Walker, that's very helpful," the woman said, her eyes fixed on Edie's. "Are you aware of any time Peter has given drugs to any of the women you've mentioned?"

She wanted so badly to scream: *Of course he has! He's the dealer at every party, he wants to be loved by women, he's desperate to be seen as generous and exceptional in their eyes.* She, herself, had fed that need, acted as a steady source of it for years, asking for so shamefully little in return. But the answer to the question the lawyer had posed was no, she had no idea if he had given drugs to the women he'd slept with.

She looked back at Peter, his head shaking, eyes red and un-blinking.

She didn't want him to be this way. She didn't want her father to be this way. She remembered no joy as a child greater than their afternoons recording, their mornings listening to their creations. He had taught her that this itching curiosity, an urgency toward action that woke her up every morning and made it hard to go to bed, was something to cherish. If she thought hard enough about something, he assured her, she could do anything. She didn't want to hate her father. In fact, all she'd ever wanted was to love him.

"I don't know if Peter gave those women drugs," she said at last.

All she'd ever wanted was to love him.

"Thank—"

"But he has offered me drugs at nearly every party we've ever gone to." The new words, the script she'd spent the night crafting in her head flooded forward. "Coke, ketamine, MDMA, Vicodin; he always has options. He said he recently started buying it from Silk Road. He was very impressed with the onion routing," she added to amuse herself. The lawyer nodded, and with a flash of her blue eyes, signaled Edie could talk for as long as she wanted. She had spent the night mulling on his lawyer's strategy, their stupid "but for" clause, such a weaselly out. "And I have never seen him go anywhere, especially not to a woman's house, without alcohol."

The lawyer's face had stayed steady and controlled, but with this her lips twitched upward. "So you're saying Mr. Masterson brought alcohol to Anaya's house that night?"

"Objection, leading the witness!" A pushy, desperate voice.

"Sustained."

"Do you know if Mr. Masterson brought alcohol to Anaya's house that night?"

She searched for the details of their conversation at the taqueria; how often she wished she had a control F for her memory. They had done K, he wasn't ready for a relationship, he was surprised at how fine she'd seemed. Spinning, scanning. He had stopped by unplanned. And then. Tequila. On ice. She had been drinking tequila, not wine. There was no way Peter had brought tequila.

There was a world where this was not Peter's fault, he had not, after all, given her the alcohol or forced the drugs on her. Anaya was her own woman, had made her own choices. But more pressing, more undeniable, was that this was not Anaya's fault, either. She had not asked for her suffering. Why did Peter get to insist on fairness, when everyone else had to push through what they were dealt? Anaya should not have died that night, and someone—Leah's eyes burned in her mind—deserved to be punished. "I have known Peter for fifteen years," she said for the court, "and he has never come to my house, or anywhere else we have gone together, without bringing a bottle of alcohol."

"Thank you, Ms. Walker," the woman said with a deep, appreciative nod. "We know this is hard for you and we're grateful for your honesty. If there's nothing else, you may step down."

She walked toward the door, avoiding his eyes, though she could feel them burning a hole into her. There was only one person in the room who she searched for, twisting her head to find the glowing blond girl. Edie wanted to look her in the eye and assure her that Peter really was a bad person. She wanted to look at the girl and convey that she hoped, someday, she would understand.

When she found them, Maggie's eyes were steady and alert on Edie, as if she'd been waiting. As she held Edie's gaze, her head nodded, firmly up and down. There was no question she had listened, not with judgment and disdain as Edie would have if she'd watched a messy, unhinged woman defame Peter, but with trust and even, it seemed, appreciation. And Edie noticed, for the first time, the people beside Maggie, a group of Leah's co-workers, the woman with the bob just a few rows in front of her. She was on Leah's side, against Peter. She thought of the woman leaving his house with puffy eyes, how blatant his behavior had become, how many excuses Edie had made for him. This woman understood, Edie thought as she exited the room. Maybe she had understood all along.

SHE SAT ON the stone steps waiting for her car. The sky was still a bright shade of blue but now she wished it would go away.

When she felt a hand on her back, she jumped.

Leah stood across from her, her face calm and steady. "Thank you." As she moved closer, the pressure of her body felt like a spell that melted Edie. The tension of the day bled out of her as Leah's grip tightened, her breath heavy in Edie's ear. After a long time, she let go.

"Thank you," Leah repeated when their eyes finally met.

There was nothing to say. It wasn't about Edie. It wasn't about Leah.

"Are you okay?"

Edie tried to speak but the words caught in her throat. She shook her head, swallowing.

Leah took her into her arms again, held her head against her chest.

She wanted to fall asleep against Leah's scratchy gray sports jacket. Her neck smelled like Ivory soap, not so different from Peter. She could not imagine a second after the one she was in now. Her life had crumbled, each piece falling one after the next. Even if she could gather the energy to move, what would she do?

"Are you okay?" Leah asked again, pulling back to look at her.

When the words finally came out, they were so tight they cracked. "My mother's in the hospital."

"Oh my god." Leah's face dropped. "What happened?"

"I don't want to talk about it." She knew the words wouldn't come, only tears. And she was so tired of tears. "Do you think he'll be convicted?"

Leah's eyes were brighter than she had ever seen them. "I think we have a good shot." Her expression changed. "I'm so sorry Peter did that to your friend. I had no idea."

Edie couldn't help but think there was a flash of judgment in her face. "I didn't know about it until last night. I never would have considered defending him if I'd known." She caught Leah's face twitch. "I should never have considered defending him in the first place."

"It's fine. I know it was hard." Her words were quick, steeped in the energy of the morning. "I never thought Anaya would do this again."

Edie glanced up at her from the gum-speckled ground. The right corner of Leah's lip curved slightly: a knowing smile Edie had studied in Anaya's photos. There was something close to victory in the curve, but surrender, too. Leah didn't know what had happened that night, either. She wanted vengeance for her sister, but she understood that Anaya's actions stretched far beyond Peter's influence.

Leah stepped closer to Edie, almost touching. "You did the right thing."

And ultimately, Edie had arrived at the same place, although hers had been a far longer and windier path. There was still a part of Edie, a part she worried might never actually go away, that felt terrible for making Peter's life difficult. But a new part of her, a part seeded the day she'd met Anaya, was growing. She felt remarkably—thrillingly—in control. In a way, she felt, for the first time in her adult life, like she was finally thinking for herself. It was harder, messier, but the choice on that stand had been hers.

She leaned forward and kissed Leah. Her lips were soft and patient. In the brief flash of closed eyes, she imagined life with this woman, the same dark eyes as Anaya's meeting hers each morning.

No longer enduring the monologues of men, but lying next to this gentle person, legs entangled on the bed. She was younger and full of an energy Edie had lost, but she could make herself go out if she had to, listen to electronic music every now and then, the occasional festival wouldn't kill her.

"I really like you," Edie said when they released each other. The court must have emptied, people streamed by. Edie could see, through the corner of her eye, people watching them.

"I like you, too." Their noses were touching.

"I don't want to see my dad," Edie said. "I can't see him." She imagined confronting her father. She couldn't even picture it. It was as if her world ended with the thought.

"You'll be okay. And your mom will be okay," Leah said, squeezing Edie's hand. Their connection was layered with an understanding, a shared love for someone gone. "We'll hang out when you're back. You can introduce me to that sushi burrito." She smiled.

"I would love that." She held on to the feeling, something she'd felt in Anaya's pages, but was utterly new in her everyday life, of accessing what she wanted.

It would be five days after Edie had flown home, but many days before her mother would leave the hospital, that she would find out that her testimony was wiped. Because of her mother's condition they considered it invalid, altered based on her emotional state. It would be two weeks until she found out that Peter was, in fact, convicted of involuntary manslaughter but he'd appealed. It would be four months until she found out, after a long, drawn-out retrial, that he had gotten off free of charge. It would be a very long time before Peter and Edie ever spoke again, though for years, she would fight the urge to text him after a date. And when they did speak, years later, passing one another in SFO, they would say no more than a quick, cold hello.

But for now, she sat gloriously in the idea that she had power.

"Come with me to New York," Edie said. It rolled out of her mouth, propelled by the unfamiliar sensation that what she did and said mattered. She hadn't yet understood, although she would, many obsessions and even more disappointments later, that the last thing she needed was another person to worship.

Under the sunny San Francisco sky, Edie trembled as she noticed Leah arch her back, her hand, resting in Edie's, jerk. "I can't do that." Leah stepped back, putting distance between them so she could look at Edie directly. Her face was so earnest, so kind. She reached for Edie's hair, frizzier now, she imaged, than Leah had ever seen it. "I'm so sorry." Leah's voice was gentle and unrushed. "I think you're amazing. And I love spending time with you. But I have so much going on right now." Edie didn't need her to continue, didn't want her to continue. "I need space," Leah continued. "I feel so overwhelmed." Edie shook her head, desperate to make it stop. "I'm not ready for anything serious."

THE 101 TO SFO was a certain kind of trance. Edie texted Alex to let her know that Peter would hopefully be sentenced, that she had tried her best. She thanked her for everything she'd told her the night before and apologized again for not being there for her when it happened. Alex wrote back promptly: **Proud of you,** she said, with many crossed-finger emojis and a heart.

Leah's rejection had felt like a blade to her throat. But for the first time in her life, she realized as she relaxed into the pleather seats of her Lyft, she was not wallowing in her rejection. Even with women, as she'd expected, she had failed in romance. But she was so tired of that version of her story, the version that made her the victim. She and Leah had never been right for one another, she knew that, and it was unacceptable for her to have pursued her while she was grieving her sister. Fuck, Leah had probably used *her* for all she knew, played her to get justice for Anaya. She felt ashamed, mortified, the more she thought about it, that she had even considered it. But there she went again, feeling bad for herself, as natural as blinking. A romantic relationship was never the point.

She rolled down the window, as she'd done that night with Peter in the cab, and took a long, deep breath. She had found her version of the truth, even if it took longer than most to get there. She was finally—she could feel it—learning to trust herself.

"You're trying," she said into the sharp Bay Area breeze. And she was. She would. *Embrace the freedom of it*, she remembered Anaya saying that first night. She took out her phone. It started, she knew, with deleting the dating apps.

As her eyes closed for what felt like the first time in weeks, she wished she were curled up, Lolly in her lap, mom by her side, under a faux fur blanket reading her books. It wasn't the adulthood she'd imagined, that she'd strived for, but, when everything else was quiet, it was all she wanted.

Acknowledgments

To MY AGENT, Aurora Fernandez, who took a chance on me and this manuscript before anyone, I am forever grateful. To my editor, Tessa James, who always understood what I was trying to do with this book and worked hand in hand with me to get it there. It has been such an honor to work with you both to put this story into the world.

I started writing in my thirties, with no literary background or creative writing experience. It has taken the support of everyone close to me to get here, to identify dreams I didn't even know I had, let alone pursue them in earnest.

Thank you to the writer-friends I've met along the way, without whom I would never have kept going. To Sara Petersen, who has read my roughest drafts and indulges my wildest obsessions, thank you for your generosity, thoughtfulness, and wit; it's impossible to imagine writing without you. Maya Rock, the first person who read this manuscript, thank you for the invaluable feedback and encouragement throughout the process. Your rigorous introspection—in life and in writing—always pushes me to think harder. Thank you to Mia Rovegno, Sarah Kasbeer, Serene Khader, and Nikki Summer for being ongoing creative inspirations and beacons of support.

To Chloe Caldwell, Courtney Preiss, and Jillian Eugenios—my

writing family. The fact that women as talented as you let me into your company when I was just starting out was what made me feel like I could maybe, one day, call myself a writer. Our weekends together have kept me going for nearly a decade; I'm the best version of myself around you. Chloe, thank you for making my first ever writing class transformative, for introducing me to a world of remarkable, creative women, and for taking my work seriously before I did. You changed my life.

To the friends who read this manuscript and support me, always. Rumana Hussain and Ryan Thomas—you both read early drafts multiple times and have supported me at every step of my winding journey, long before writing was on the radar. Rumana, your intelligence, curiosity, and sense of adventure is a regular inspiration. Ryan, you have been the best kind of mentor from day one—a teacher and a friend. Our conversations shaped this book and my life. To my friends in arms during our grueling online dating journeys and since: Alison Corwin, Katherine Marino, Cindy Chen, Annie Lo, Grace Yang, Zee Clark, and the entire San Francisco crew.

To all the men who see themselves in these pages, thank you for the material. To Mike and the gang at 710 for our years in Ithaca jumping on couches to whatever angsty male pop CD was in rotation, you will always feel like family. To Janak Ramakrishnan, I'm infinitely grateful to have you—and our debates and our jump-dancing—in my life. Thank you for a friendship like no other, for consistently being there for me, and for your unflinching support of this book.

Ben, thank you for your love, commitment, and patience. For wanting, with certainty, something serious, accepting me fully, and inviting me to be part of Charlie's world. Charlie, the most imaginative kid I know, who can always make me laugh. I love you both so much.

To my aunt Deedee and uncle Mike, who have always cheered me on and believed in me. To Cynthia and Joan, whose lives and love are a regular inspiration, thank you for all the cozy days I spent writing in your farmhouse. To my grandparents, who embodied wisdom, creativity, and love. I didn't realize my grandma wrote feverishly for her own interest until after she was gone, though I should have known—her ability to craft stories from the smallest happenings was a gift.

To my dad, who unwittingly taught me how to write through our long email exchanges while I was miserable studying computer engineering and beyond. Your notes—consistently packed with encouragement—were the highlights of my day, and taught me what "voice" was long before I'd ever heard the term. Matching your wit and brilliance has always been my motivator.

To my mom, who worked harder than I could possibly imagine to give her children opportunity. Your love is the foundation from which anything I have done is built. Thank you for teaching me the value of kindness, the importance of friendship, how to notice and appreciate beauty, be grateful for all that I have, and for showing me—as you did for so long—how to stay the course. You've shaped every part of me; I am so lucky to have you as my teacher.

Finally, to my sister, Annie Smith, whose support and influence in my life is impossible to put into words. There is no one who makes me think or laugh harder. Thank you for reading my drafts long before I had "writer" friends, when I was terrified to show a soul, and for being the one to urge me to write in the first place. Your thoughtful, gentle nudges sit behind anything I can possibly call growth. I would be a shell of myself without you.

About the Author

EMILY J. SMITH is a writer and tech professional based in Brooklyn. She has led teams at top tech companies and founded the dating app Chorus. She holds a BS in Electrical and Computer Engineering from Cornell, and an MBA from UC Berkeley's Haas School of Business. Her writing has appeared in *Catapult*, the *Rumpus*, *Slate*, *Vice*, *Washington Post*, and others. This is her first novel.